MW01002733

# COLD BONES

*Also by Jane A. Adams from Severn House*

*The Naomi Blake mysteries*

MOURNING THE LITTLE DEAD
TOUCHING THE DARK
HEATWAVE
KILLING A STRANGER
LEGACY OF LIES
SECRETS
GREGORY'S GAME
PAYING THE FERRYMAN
A MURDEROUS MIND
FAKES AND LIES

*The Rina Martin mysteries*

A REASON TO KILL
FRAGILE LIVES
THE POWER OF ONE
RESOLUTIONS
THE DEAD OF WINTER
CAUSE OF DEATH
FORGOTTEN VOICES

*The Henry Johnstone mysteries*

THE MURDER BOOK
DEATH SCENE
KITH AND KIN
THE CLOCKMAKER
THE GOOD WIFE
OLD SINS
BRIGHT YOUNG THINGS
THE GIRL IN THE YELLOW DRESS
THE ROOM WITH EIGHT WINDOWS

# COLD BONES

Jane A. Adams

SEVERN
HOUSE

First world edition published in Great Britain and the USA in 2024
by Severn House, an imprint of Canongate Books Ltd,
14 High Street, Edinburgh EH1 1TE.

severnhouse.com



*British Library Cataloguing-in-Publication Data*
A CIP catalogue record for this title is available from the British Library.

ISBN-13: 978-1-4483-1437-9 (cased)
ISBN-13: 978-1-4483-1544-4 (e-book)



*All Severn House titles are printed on acid-free paper*

Typeset by Palimpsest Book Production Ltd.,
Falkirk, Stirlingshire, Scotland.
Printed and bound in Great Britain by TJ Books,
Padstow, Cornwall.

# Praise for the Henry Johnstone mysteries

"Puzzles aplenty for coppers young and old"
*Kirkus Reviews* on *The Room with Eight Windows*

"A good pick for fans of British historical mysteries"
*Booklist* on *The Girl in the Yellow Dress*

"Lovers of tweedy English murder mysteries will find much to like"
*Publishers Weekly* on *The Girl in the Yellow Dress*

"Excellent . . . Fans of golden age mysteries will be delighted"
*Publishers Weekly* Starred Review of *Old Sins*

"Vivid . . . well-constructed . . . will appeal to the *Downton Abbey* crowd"
*Booklist* on *The Good Wife*

# About the author

**Jane A. Adams** was born in Leicestershire and still lives there – even though it is too far from the sea. In addition to writing, she has taught creative writing and writing skills for various arts organizations and universities and enjoyed a number of years as a Royal Literary Fund Fellow. Her first book, *The Greenway*, was shortlisted for the CWA John Creasey Award and for the Author's Club Best First Novel Award. When not writing she can often be found drawing racing dodos, armoured hares and the occasional octopus. As well as the Henry Johnstone series, she is the author of the highly acclaimed Naomi Blake and Rina Martin mystery series.

# ONE

*Late August, 1931. Thoresway, Lincolnshire.*

Frank Church had fallen. It could have been argued that he had fallen from grace long since, that he had fallen irrevocably that day three years past, when he had let another take the blame for Frank killing a man. But now he was falling for real, and his screams were loud enough to wake the dead.

Frank had been atop the threshing machine, freeing up a jam that had halted the behemoth. He'd been impatient, pulling on the wedge of straw and twine that had been dragged into the feed. They were already behind schedule for that morning's work, and he had no wish for more delay while they waited for the machine to be shut down and then fired up again. While Frank tugged one way, the machine strained to do its own bit in hauling the offending blockage through. As Frank pulled one way and the machine pulled another, the contest was bound to be an unequal one, many horsepower against that of a single, strong but wiry man.

Those on the ground who stood watching had been urging him to come down or at least to use the billhook to hack at the blockage rather than, as Frank was doing, grabbing on to the offending bundle and pulling hard, but when Frank was in one of his obstinate moods, there was no telling him, and Frank's state of obstinacy seemed to have become permanent this last year or so.

And now he was screaming as he fell. The wad of straw and twine had suddenly succumbed to the thresher's insistence and as Frank jerked back in a last-ditch effort to keep his hands clear of the works, the thresher jumped into frantic action. The loose belt driving the mechanism from a stationary engine momentarily flipped against the roller, the thresher groaned and creaked, shuddering along its length, and shook the now inconsequential man free from his perch.

Frank was tumbling. He tried to regain his balance but the machine had thrown him backwards and then forwards and his footing was gone. He was tossed against the belt, then against the thresher, then spat out on to the ground. He lay there, screaming in shock and pain as someone finally ran to cut the engine. In the sudden silence that followed, Frank's cries seemed uncannily loud. Someone ran to fetch Elijah Hanson. Another had the presence of mind to tear off his own shirt and press it against the blood flowing from the man's chest.

'Christ,' he whispered as he stared down at Frank's ruined hand. The thresher had taken flesh and left bone.

Elijah Hanson arrived and Frank was carried in a blanket, gripped by a half-dozen men. He was not a heavy man, but pain had him thrashing and writhing so that it was like carrying a serpent that did not want to be restrained. The Home Farm was closest and so they took him there, and Ted, Elijah's oldest son, telephoned the doctor, hoping he would be home from his rounds. It was a little after midday. Miss Elizabeth, Hanson's daughter, who had at fifteen taken over the running of the household when her mother passed that spring, ran down into the village to fetch Frank's wife.

No one expected him to survive. Frank did not expect to survive.

'I need to tell you things. I got to confess.'

This was later when, his wife Helen by his side and Dr Fielding having administered morphine, Frank had ceased to toss and writhe with the pain though, in Fielding's view, that was the only improvement. He'd lost enough blood to soak the sheets and mattress of the bed on which he'd been laid, to soak through the bandages Fielding had applied. Pink froth bubbled at his lips with each breath. The doctor knew that all he could do to help was to take away as much of the pain as was in his power to do, even if that meant treading the very fine line between keeping his patient eased and keeping him alive until his injuries finished him – or the pain grew so bad that Fielding's medication slipped gently across that line. Fielding's conscience would not trouble him, should that prove to be the case.

But first, it seemed, he had to listen, so this man could die in peace.

'Should I get the minister?' Fielding asked gently. It was clear from Frank's face that whatever he had to tell was now weighing on his soul.

'Whatever it is can wait until you're stronger,' Helen told him. She looked at Fielding for reassurance that this might actually be the case, but he shook his head gently. Helen closed her eyes and took hold of Frank's undamaged hand. She was, Fielding knew, just twenty years old, with a child of two, currently in Elizabeth's care, and another due that autumn. He also knew that, though she and Frank had made the best fist of things they could, their marriage was one of convenience rather than of passion. Worse, Fielding had a dreadful feeling he knew what Frank was about to say, and that would kill any regard this pretty young woman still had for her husband.

'I have to tell you about Robert,' Frank said, his voice a whisper, breath coming in gasps, the pain-easing morphine also suppressing his breathing. It would not be long now, Fielding thought.

'About Robert?' Helen sounded puzzled. She looked at Fielding again, questions in that look that he did not feel qualified to answer. No, Frank must have his say.

'What really happened that day?' Dr Fielding asked.

And Frank told them. Slowly, hesitantly, but with grim determination, and though Helen still gripped his hand, compassionate enough by nature to give the dying man what solace she could, Fielding watched as her face grew red with anger and then pale with shock. Then the tears began to flow and, as Frank Church died, Helen sobbed as though her heart, already broken, would now never heal.

And so it was, a few days later, that Dr Fielding – after much debate with himself – wrote a letter. He wrote to a man he had met three years previously, a murder detective, come up from London to Louth to investigate the triple murder of a young woman, her child, and a cousin who had died trying to defend them from their assailant. He had then been dragged into the investigation of Robert Hanson's murder. The evidence against Ethan Samuels had seemed watertight; no fault of the detective that he, like everyone else, had read that wrong. Ethan had run, leaving Helen behind, and Helen had married Frank. Fielding, along with the rest of the village, had counted the months but, as was customary, no one spoke harshly, at least in public, when her child was born a scant seven months after. The families had settled the matter, the young people would make the best of it – and so they had, Fielding thought. Frank Church had provided for his family and proved a good father to the son that was undoubtedly not his.

Fielding had been inclined to like Inspector Henry Johnstone and his sergeant, Mickey Hitchens. Or, perhaps it was more accurate to say he had admired the intellect of one and the general good humour of the other. Henry's attitude and general demeanour did not always earn him friends. They had kept in touch the way acquaintances often do, with an exchange of Christmas cards. In the last one Henry had told him that he had left the police force as a result of ill-health and also left his London apartment. He had given his sister's address as a means of contacting him while he settled himself elsewhere. So, Fielding wrote care of Cynthia Garrett Smyth and, feeling that he had now done his duty, put the matter from his mind.

*Late August 1931, London*

The trouble Dan Trotter had was that he could never delegate or, if he did, that he either didn't trust the person he had delegated to, or that he always seemed to pick the wrong person for the job. So it was that he was lurking behind a broken wall, close by the old Tobacco Dock, waiting for a fire to start.

He had been there since close on midnight and was now impatient. Kimberlin, his father's old manager, had told him that all was in hand and that he should trust him to get the job done and done at the money Dan had been prepared to pay – he recalled the scorn in the man's voice when he had said this, as though Dan had been some kind of cheapskate – but Dan was still uneasy.

The pub a little way down the road had long since closed, though Dan was uncomfortably aware that not all the drinkers had exited before the landlord ushered most of the customers out and locked the door. Chinks of light escaping from the shuttered windows suggested that the merriment was still continuing, albeit in a less crowded atmosphere.

Dan had never drunk there; not his kind of public house nor his kind of clientele, he told himself. The truth was Dan was not the sort of drinker the landlord of The Maid wanted either. Dan admitted to himself that he wasn't good at holding his liquor and, yes, he did when drunk have a tendency to pick fights. They were usually brief. Dan was no more a fighter than he was a businessman. Unlike his father who had been both.

Right then, Dan was bored; his vigil had been long and he was almost on the point of going home.

From time to time people came and went from the area. Late workers returning home, a couple of drunks who had enjoyed themselves far too much and were singing raucously about Nelly Dean. A woman carrying a small child walked quickly and nervously past his hiding place and turned into a side road. He heard her knocking on a door, the brief burst of conversation, anxious and irritable, and then the sound of tears before she went inside. Then all was quiet again.

Occasionally the rear door of the pub would open when someone went out to use the privy. Twice, a woman appeared with a man in tow, and the pair disappeared into one of the narrow alleyways between tall buildings. There were houses here, remnants of what had once been streets of workers' cottages between the docks and the warehouses, but by and large the landscape was dominated by tall, red-brick structures that housed merchants and sorting offices and distributors. And warehouses like the one he was now watching closely.

It was a rundown place, out of use and out of purpose – apart, that was, for the purpose Dan had in mind for it. He asked himself again why he hadn't just taken care of business for himself, and in the next thought he congratulated himself on having commissioned the work to experts who had already set a number of successful fires. He could not afford to risk this enterprise going wrong. True, the insurance companies were assessing the three last – a fact Dan had used to get himself a better price on the job – but general opinion was that they'd found nothing they could actually prove, and that it was only a matter of form that they should insist on an investigation.

Dan had negotiated the payment through Kimberlin; of course, the arsonists would not deal directly with someone they knew nothing about. Kimberlin had told him that he'd, in turn, been put in touch with an intermediary by someone he knew slightly but not well. And there was the rub. It was, in part, because of the doubts that had crept in at the shakiness of such a chain of contacts that Dan had decided to come and watch for himself, ensure the job was done right. And it was also partly down to a driving curiosity. Who were these arsonists? Could he find out and then use that knowledge to his advantage?

Anyone who knew Dan well would have shaken their heads in despair at this scheme and Dan knew it. Daniel Trotter was a man who, no matter how he tried, could never seem to make his proper mark on the world, and now that general failure and the more particular one of being unable to keep his late father's business afloat, threatened to pull him well and truly under. The only way out, so far as Dan could see, was this one.

It was almost two before Dan noticed any significant activity around the warehouse, and he could scarcely believe what he was seeing. Three boys came walking down the street as though they had not a care in the world. Laughing and joking and pushing one another as teenage boys are wont to do, passing a flask of something between them. The smallest of the three carried a painted petrol can. Any doubt Dan had that these three were his potential arsonists faded, and with it the last of Dan's hopes.

'What the blazes?' Dan muttered to himself. Surely this was just some bad joke? It was beyond belief that these three gangly, ill-dressed youths could be what he had paid for. What had Kimberlin been playing at? There had to be some mistake.

It slowly dawned on Dan Trotter that the great deal he had

been given had not been so great after all. He had been well and truly dealt a duff hand. Most likely his father's old business manager knew it and was laughing up his sleeve.

Dan sank down behind the wall and put his head in his hands. 'He took you for a fool, Dan Trotter, because in truth you are a fool.' He would wait until the boys had gone and then do the job himself, as he always should have done.

He watched and he waited, hearing faint noises from inside the building. The shifting of timber, perhaps, the sound of breaking wood. Once, a loud sneeze and a laugh and a voice telling them to hush. Then the smell of smoke.

Dan perked up. Maybe, just maybe, the three youths had managed to set the fire after all. After all, how hard could it be to set a blaze in a place like that? Furthermore, it didn't really matter if the insurance company for *that* building decided that arson had been the cause; it was the next-door building that mattered to Dan. The one that had belonged to his father and was now his – or his for as long as his creditors did not foreclose. So long as that one burned, and the insurance company paid up, he could clear his debts and he'd be home free.

Peering around the end of the broken wall, Dan saw the boys depart. They were in a hurry now, eager to be clear of their handiwork before it really got a hold. He noticed, absently, that they had left the petrol can behind.

Dan scrambled to his feet and crossed the yard, entered through the loading-bay door and took stock of the situation. Wood and old sacking had been piled up in one corner and was well ablaze. The smell of petrol was overpowering, and he worried for a moment that the boys might have sprinkled it all around, if he was in any danger where he stood. But no, the blaze was just in that one corner but it was spreading fast. The petrol can had been set down in the middle of the vast space, presumably when the boys left, and it occurred to Dan that perhaps he should throw that into the flames. That would help things along.

He had the can in his hand when a small sound made him turn. A man stood in the open doorway of the loading bay, his hands flapping in consternation. The light coming in from the streetlamps exposed an expression of worried agitation on the round face.

'Oh, I say. What on earth is happening here? We should call the fire brigade.'

Dan stared at this apparition, unable to comprehend that this man was real. This was all just some appalling kind of joke.

He had expected this stranger to go running off and raise a hue and cry, maybe hammer on some doors asking for help, but instead he bustled into the warehouse, hurrying over to Dan, the look on his face, illuminated this time by the encroaching blaze, now one of concern.

'My dear fellow, you can't hope to deal with this blaze alone. We must get out of here, summon the experts. Come now, please.'

He thinks I came in here to put it out, Dan thought in astonishment. Then: but now he's seen my face.

The man turned, clearly expecting Dan to follow. Dan never thought about what he did next. He later told himself that some instinct for self-preservation had conducted his actions. He swung the petrol can at the stranger's head, felling him with the blow. The man went down hard but then, to Dan's astonishment and consternation, began to rise again. He was stunned, he was bleeding. But he was not staying down. He stumbled to his feet and turned to face Dan, a look of astonishment on his round, bland features.

Dan dropped the petrol can and felt for the pocketknife he kept in his jacket, fumbling for it in among the jumble of handkerchief and keys and pocket change. He wasn't even thinking now, his one impulse just to stop this man from raising the alarm. As the man stumbled to his feet, Dan opened the knife and struck, a single blow aimed into where he thought the heart might be. The man fell heavily to the floor and this time, to Dan's relief, he did not move.

What to do, what to do? The blaze was lively now, still confined to the corner, but Dan was certain it would spread. He could feel the increasing heat from where he stood, and the flames now illuminated the space, red and orange light dancing around the room, brightening the face of the fallen man.

He must make sure the body was destroyed, Dan thought. Could he drag the man into the flames?

From somewhere at the front of the building Dan heard a commotion. The sound of someone hammering on a door, and of voices raised in panic. Oh, God, no time. He must go.

He picked up the can again and shook it. Still, some of the fuel left inside. Would there be enough?

Getting as close to the blaze as he dared, Dan dripped a little of the fuel on to the floor, on to the broken timber and old rags and general debris that had collected in five years of neglect. He backtracked to where the body lay, shaking the dregs on to the floor, hoping there would be enough, leading the flames back to where the stranger lay. The final residue he shook on to the man's head and chest. And then he ran, still clutching the petrol can, back across the yard, skirting the wall, keeping in the shadow of the next building until finally he was forced to dash out on to the street.

A woman's voice, loud and coarse, shouted after him. He glanced back, recognizing the prostitute he had spotted earlier.

Dan cursed, ran faster, cutting down a side road and running on. The sound of the woman shouting faded into the distance and he glanced back again. No one was giving chase. No one had followed him.

Dan took stock of where he was and made his way home by a circuitous route. He was both horrified and exultant. He had done it. He had arranged for a fire and the fire had happened. He had reacted in an instant when that man had threatened him. The fire would spread and his father's old business would burn down. It might take a little time for the insurance to be paid but after that Dan would be free of it all. He could go anywhere, do anything. He could walk away.

Dan Trotter went up to his room, sat down on his bed, put his head in his hands and wept.

# TWO

Ex-Detective Inspector Johnstone was not currently a particularly happy man. He had been badly injured late in the previous year, injuries he could ill afford to suffer. They had come hot on the heels of surgery that had only partly eased the pain of a shoulder wound sustained the year before. This had effectively ended his career as a police officer. The beating he had received back in December of 1930 had then put him further out of action for several weeks. It had only been at the end of February that he had felt able to begin the new phase of his life and he had taken up residence in this little office, with the flat above. His sister had rented the office for him, and his brother-in-law had undertaken to have the legend *Johnstone's Detective Agency* written in gold on the glass pane of the office door.

Henry had enthused, gratefully, but frankly he found it a little ostentatious and the idea of this office housing an actual agency almost laughable, seeing as he didn't even employ a secretary, never mind agents.

Now, more than six months on from the start of his new business, and he was not content. It wasn't a lack of work that had led to his present mood. In fact, he had been genuinely touched by the efforts of his friends and his previous colleagues to ensure that he was kept busy. He had declared, right from the beginning, that he was prepared to take on just about anything – apart from divorces. There were genuine agencies aplenty that specialized in establishing proof or providing evidence for couples wishing to end their marriages and, although he believed they provided a necessary service, Henry had sufficient dealings with them in his previous work to not want the bother now. Besides, he was hardly fit enough to be minded to fling open a hotel room door, take the relevant photographs and be off smartish. The idea made him smile grimly; even knowing that most of these evidence-gathering escapades were staged, the young women involved frequently being female detectives employed by private agencies just for this purpose, he doubted they'd take kindly to his telling them to give him five minutes while he limped away.

It was Friday, and Henry poked irritably at the sheaf of paper on his desk. It had arrived, courtesy of his old sergeant and dear friend, Mickey Hitchens, the day before. Over the past few months, the powers that be at Scotland Yard had occasionally sanctioned Henry's review of old cases, as fragments of what might be new evidence emerged. This was a case of fraud and blackmail that may have led to murder. It was therefore tedious to review, the evidence being technical and legal rather than based on interview and observation, but that was not really the cause of Henry's unrest. His intellect naturally bent towards the meticulous, and ordinarily he would have buried himself readily in the minutiae. Today, however, he could not seem to settle to his task.

Henry sighed. He would walk, he thought, clear his head, and come back to his desk in a better frame of mind.

Stiffly, Henry rose from his chair and took his jacket from the rack. He fed his left arm into the sleeve before wrestling with the right. His left shoulder could barely be moved these days. Last year's surgery to remove fragments of bone that had been causing pain and infection had helped, but the beating he had endured last winter, and that had nearly killed him, had undone his recovery and set him back. He still could not walk without a stick, the injuries to his ribs and back having proved to have a longer-term impact than he had initially hoped, and though he forced himself to keep his left arm and hand as much in use as possible, there was little range to that movement and little strength.

He found himself wishing, and not for the first time, that his office was on the ground floor and not down a flight of stairs.

Henry walked slowly down the side road and on to the promenade, pausing to lean on the railing and look out to sea. It was a bright, late August day, the holiday season bringing a bustle and noise to the Bournemouth seaside as holiday-makers and, at the weekends, day-trippers swelled the population. For a few minutes Henry watched the families on the beach, women in bright summer dresses and children running into the water, squealing at the sudden cold. Men walked along the strand with their jackets off, shirtsleeves rolled back. Others were in bathing suits, encouraging their offspring into the cold swell while mothers watched, standing ankle deep in the waves. It interested Henry that it seemed acceptable to be on the beach, only scant yards from the promenade, in a state of relative undress. Women with bare legs (Cynthia had confided that it was best to roll and garter your stockings at your knees before leaving home to make it easier to remove them on the sand), men sans ties and summer jackets or in short-sleeved, short-legged bathing wear that in another context might be classed as underclothes. The beach was a liminal space where the normal societal rules did not apply, he thought. Before any of these happy holiday-makers ventured back on to the promenade, stockings would be rolled back into place, sleeves pulled down and jackets donned and the bathing suits removed in the hired huts further along the beach, social propriety restored.

He turned and walked along the promenade, his attention now on the throng of walkers but no longer on the lively families in their summer dress. The holiday season brought another kind of tourist, those who would take advantage of the crowds who dropped their guard and relaxed in the sunshine and who made themselves targets for the pickpockets and the thieves who followed them, much as the gulls followed the fishing boats, ready to seize anything left unattended or insufficiently guarded. Henry had an encyclopaedic knowledge of their methods (one to jostle and distract while the other dipped), their faces, and their habit of following the holiday-makers south from London during the season. On several occasions this summer he had been able to notify the local constabulary of the presence of such predators. Thanks to his contacts at Scotland Yard, and his newer acquaintances like Inspector Fox along the coast at Shoreham, Henry still received the various bulletins of the *Police Gazette* and kept an eye open for the latest miscreants who came to try their luck on his bit of coast.

He had also used his detective skills to investigate the backgrounds of witnesses and suspects in various ongoing investigations, and to suggest possible avenues of enquiry to Fox and other officers. He had even got used to the idea that he should charge a modest fee for their use of him. This, alongside his investigations for members of the public, ranging from tracking down lost heirs and establishing their bona fides, to finding a stolen racehorse (he had so far avoided lost dogs) had kept Henry busy, if not exactly interested.

Nothing, he thought, as he paused again to lean against the promenade railing, had stimulated him intellectually the way his old job had done.

Henry was bored; worse than that, Henry felt that he was failing to be properly useful . . . to anyone. Yes, his information had helped the local police to make a few arrests. His case reviews had also turned up new lines of enquiry that, so far as Henry knew, had been acted upon. He was rarely informed of the outcomes, though, unless Mickey or someone else he knew personally took the trouble to tell him. And that was the problem. He had been a man at the centre of things; a respected murder detective, whose careful preparation and thoroughgoing establishment of the evidence had caused more than a dozen men to hang for their crimes and many more to be imprisoned. Whereas these days he had to stand by and watch his dear friend, now Inspector Hitchens, apply himself with the same vigour and attention Henry had applied to cases that Henry could have no part in. That hurt far more than Henry had ever anticipated it would.

No wonder he had the occasional glum day.

Tired now, his body aching but his mind a little more settled, Henry turned and began to make his slow way back to his office. He was a little surprised to find Malina seated on the bentwood chair set on the small landing outside his office door.

'This is a pleasant surprise.'

She smiled at him, stretched up to kiss him on the cheek. She had a picnic basket in her hand. 'I've brought us both some lunch,' she told him.

Henry smiled back, a genuine smile, and unlocked his office

door. 'I needed a walk,' he told her, 'but I think I may have gone a little too far.'

'Don't you always? Sit down; I can see to things.'

He sat, watching her with pleasure as she unpacked the picnic basket and set a game pie and some fresh tomatoes and a jar of pickle on his desk. She filled the kettle, producing the small, screw-topped medicine bottle she used for milk for their tea from the depths of the basket, and then pulled out a letter. 'This came for you today, care of Cynthia,' she said.

Henry took it curiously.

'Open it later,' she told him. 'It will give you something to look forward to this afternoon, when I've gone.'

Her tone was light, teasing, but he knew better than to oppose the suggestion. With only the smallest hesitation, he set the letter aside. Malina Beaney was technically his sister's secretary, but she was far more than that. She had become Cynthia's friend, and increasingly was involved in the business Albert had inherited. Cynthia, Henry knew all too well, had steered their business affairs away from near disaster following the Wall Street Crash and the crash of the London stock market and some very ill-advised investments her husband had made. Albert was still the public face, but increasingly his wife had become the strength and power behind that face, assisting and suggesting and even transacting on Albert's behalf. Increasingly too, Malina had become a trusted part of that team.

She and Henry had been close friends for quite some time, but over the past year that friendship had slowly and carefully blossomed into something more. Malina now wore Henry's engagement ring.

'So, what did you see on your walk?'

What might have been a casual enquiry from anyone else was, Henry knew, asked with unalloyed interest. They had grown accustomed to sharing their observations and thoughts, even regarding the most casual events. It was something Henry had come to value.

He told her about his walk and the notion of the beach being a liminal zone, separated from the everyday.

Malina nodded, slicing her pie thoughtfully. 'I feel much the same about fairgrounds,' she said. 'They are also places where the rules don't apply. All manner and classes of people ride the carousel, shoot metal ducks in the gallery, venture on to rides that threaten their modesty and think nothing of it. It becomes a separate world somehow.'

Henry nodded. Unusually, considering where she had ended up, Malina knew that travelling community well, being herself of Romani stock and her family often sharing winter quarters with some of the showmen. 'Theatres too, and music halls,' he said.

'Perhaps, though there's segregation in some. The toffs in their boxes and the poorer folk in the cheap seats. Less so in the cinemas though. In the dark it's harder to see who's who.'

She paused and he was conscious of the twitch of laughter starting at the corner of her mouth. 'Go on,' she said, 'open your letter. I know you're itching to.'

He smiled back at her and seized the letter and paperknife from his desk. The envelope was of good quality, laid paper, with a postmark of a Lincolnshire market town that he recognized. He glanced again at the handwriting on the envelope, recognizing it now that the postmark had prompted him. 'It must be from Doctor Fielding,' he said.

'You've mentioned him. You and he exchange Christmas cards. I've not known him to write to you before though.'

'No, he's not.' Henry unfolded the letter, skimmed the contents and then began to read aloud.

'"*My Dear Fellow,*

*It must seem strange to be hearing from me, but an incident happened a day or so ago that has a bearing on that messy business you and your sergeant looked into back in '28. I doubt you've forgotten the incident that led to the death of Robert Hanson and that the accused, young Ethan Samuels, took to his heels and fled the scene. Well, I'm sure you, like the rest of us, assumed that was the matter closed.*"

'In fact, I did not,' Henry said. 'I viewed it always as unfinished business. A young man had his life taken from him and no one was brought to justice.'

Malina peered at him over the rim of her teacup. He continued with Fielding's letter.

'"*However, it seems that we were all in receipt of only half the story. That the Samuels boy fled believing that he had killed Robert Hanson but that, reprehensible as his actions were, he was not in fact responsible for Robert's death.*

*I imagine you also recall Frank Church, who claimed to have witnessed the entire incident? Well, two days ago that unlucky man was involved in an accident which led to his death. I won't bore you with the details, but the fool of a man attempted to free a blockage in a thresher, while the machine was still under power. As a result of this he was mortally injured, and all I could do when I arrived was ease the pain of his passing.*

*It seemed, however, that Frank Church wished to clear his conscience before he went to meet his maker, and he confessed to both myself and the young woman you knew as Helen Lee (Helen Church she is now, having married Frank, in accordance with her family's wishes, shortly after Ethan Samuels so precipitously fled). The marriage produced a prematurely born son and she is currently expecting her second. She had, of course, been summoned to her husband's side, and I suppose it is something to his credit that in his final moments he wished her to know the truth of the matter.*"

'So, she married Frank Church after all,' Henry said wonderingly. 'Her refusal of him and her affection for this Ethan Samuels was what led to this disaster in the first place.'

'I imagine she had no option in the end,' Malina said. 'She wouldn't have wanted her child to be born out of wedlock. Though if what I suspect is next in the letter, it seems to me that offering her and her child the protection of his name was the least this Frank Church could do.'

Henry nodded. 'Indeed,' he said.

'"*Frank Church confessed that Robert Hanson, blind drunk as he had been, had offered little resistance to Samuels' beating and that he had fallen from his horse, fallen hard and likely hit his head. You and I both saw the bruising and broken skin consistent with both events. Indeed, I blame myself for not looking more deeply. I made the assumption that the appearance of bruising and discolouration were formed post-mortem, and the cause of death seemed so obvious that I did not excise tissue from any of the wounds in my subsequent examination of the body. Such samples, examined beneath my microscope, would have told me that the discolouration was in fact bruising.*"'

Henry paused, glanced over at Malina.

'Suggesting that this Robert Hanson continued to breathe for quite some time after he fell from his horse,' she said.

'Indeed.' Henry scowled at the letter. 'At the time, the cause of Hanson's death seemed so obvious and the witness so persuasive . . . Fielding is correct; we should both have looked further.'

'What does he say next?' Malina asked.

'"*On his deathbed, Frank Church told us this: that when Ethan Samuels ran – and it seems this was at Frank's urging, Church reminding Samuels that he was destined to hang because he had killed his boss's son – the Hanson boy was still alive. That he was senseless but still breathing and could perhaps have survived the fall. Frank Church confessed that he watched Robert Hanson as he lay there in that field, waiting to see if he would breathe his last. He did not know how long he kept vigil, but he told me that the sun moved and the shadows deepened, such that would suggest it had been an hour or more at the very least. Then, when Robert Hanson showed no sign of dying, Frank kicked the lad in the head, three, four times, that he remembered, until the breathing stopped. Only then did he shift to raise the alarm.*"'

'That's horrifying,' Malina said. 'Why would he do that? Was it just to rid himself of a rival? Ethan Samuels had run; he couldn't defend himself.'

'And crucially, he seems not to have examined the body. Had he done so, he would have known that Robert Hanson still lived. He would have been charged with assault, served time in prison, but he would not have hanged, and I believe Helen Lee would have waited for him.'

He recalled the young woman clearly. Dark hair shining, eyes blazing with anger. She had despised Henry for his coldness. The investigation had been everything to him; he had had, he realized now, little time for compassion back then, either for Helen and her loss or even for the families involved. This had merely been a problem to be solved.

He had changed since then, Henry thought, and in large part that was due to this woman sitting across the desk from him.

'"*So, it seems we both got this wrong, Henry old chap, and I must say I am sorry for that. The Samuels boy still has guilt to carry, but he did not deprive Robert Hanson of his life. From what I hear, the Hanson lad was forever goading Church about losing his woman to another. You might remember that there had been an understanding between the families that Helen and Frank would wed, and both seemed content with that until young Samuels came back to the village and proved the more attractive option.*

*I don't know if this information is of interest to you after this time or if there is anything you'd consider that you could do, since you are no longer a detective with Scotland Yard. I do however suspect that your concern for completeness would indicate that you would wish to know. I felt therefore that I should relate this strange second act to our little play.*

*I remain, etc., Walter Fielding.*"'

'Well, that changes the complexion of the day,' Malina said.

'It does.' Carefully, Henry folded the letter and placed it back in the envelope.

'So, what do you plan to do?'

Henry considered for a moment. He glanced around his little office, poked a finger at the papers stacked on the corner of his desk. He could review this old case from anywhere and telegraph any thoughts he might have to Mickey. Then he slumped back in his chair, defeated even before he began.

'What is it?' she asked him.

'I can't drive all the way up there.'

'You can't drive at all – not easily, anyway,' Malina reminded him.

'And the train will take me only so far, then I will need a vehicle to take me out to the village.' Truthfully, he wasn't sure that he could cope with the train journey. It was a long way from the south coast to the middle of the Lincolnshire Wolds. The thought filled him with dread.

'We'd have to break our journey,' Malina said. 'At least one night and perhaps two. I can get Albert to advise as to decent hotels en route. He can call ahead and book our rooms for us, and we both know that Cynthia will let us borrow her car.'

Henry stared at her. 'I can't ask you to do that for me.'

'And why not?' She held up her left hand where the small sapphire danced and sparkled. 'We are partners in this as in everything else, Henry. We may not yet be married, but this ring is a statement of that intent, and you know the depth of my commitment as I know yours. You need help, and I will help you.'

An hour later it was settled. Albert would organize the overnight accommodation and Dr Fielding, surprised but seemingly very pleased at Henry's telephone call, assured them that he had two spare rooms in his house and a live-in housekeeper, 'So your fiancée can be reassured all will be seen as respectable.'

'Are you going to try and find this Ethan Samuels?' Henry's sister Cynthia asked him as they sat together after supper.

'If I can. I should have pursued him with more vigour before, but the trail was cold.'

'Colder still now. Besides, it's as well you didn't chase him down before. Likely he'd have been hanged by now if you had. But Henry, if you find him, he'll still be sentenced to prison time.'

'As he deserves,' Henry said.

'You don't think perhaps he's suffered enough – losing the woman he loves and any claim he had on family and friends. He's been quite alone all this time.'

'He beat a man senseless.'

'No, he beat a man who was so drunk he fell from his horse. The ground knocked him senseless. He was a young man acting out of a sense of anger and injustice.' She paused. 'Henry, I know how you are when you get the bit between your teeth, but please think about the consequences before you act.'

'You think he should go unpunished?'

'I think he's received his punishment.'

'You think I should just let this be. You don't think I should go.'

'I'm not saying that. Yes, you need to go and speak to the

families again, to his love, Helen. Mark my words, Henry, she will have received some word from him. But also think. Talk to them, his friends and family, and listen to what they say. Don't find him just to satisfy your own craving—'

'My craving?' he snapped.

'For a puzzle to solve, a mystery to clear up to *your* satisfaction. *Just* for your satisfaction.'

'I'm not that shallow or craven, Cyn, you should know that.'

'And that isn't what I'm saying . . .'

He could tell by her tone that he'd really annoyed her now.

'What I'm saying is that this last year and more you've been cast adrift from everything you knew and valued, from everything that defined you. Henry. I've seen how much you've suffered because of that; we all have. All I am saying is, don't leap to the chase just because you've picked up a good scent. Stand back and consider what might be for the greater good.'

Henry frowned. He grasped what she was saying, he even recognized that there might be some sense in her words but . . . He really did not want to argue with his sister. 'I'll have Malina with me,' he said. 'So, I'll have a woman of good sense who'll no doubt keep you apprised of our adventures and be ready to convey your opinions.' He had tried to sound justifiably aggrieved but – even to his own ears – he simply sounded petulant. He was unsurprised when Cynthia laughed at him.

'You'll do what's right,' she said. 'But you should let Mickey know what's happening. He'll be interested too and, if you do need to track your man down, Mickey might be able to smooth the way for you.'

'Now I'm no longer a detective,' he said bitterly.

Cynthia leaned over to kiss him on the cheek. 'You'll always be a detective,' she said. 'The difference now is that you don't have any bosses to report to, that's all.'

He supposed, in that regard, she was absolutely right.

# THREE

It was a bright Saturday morning and Inspector Mickey Hitchens, who not so very long ago had been Henry's sergeant, surveyed the scene laid out before him with some distaste. Burnt timber and broken glass crunched beneath his boots and soot, wet from the water used to douse the flames, crusted the turn-ups of his trousers. It would be a devil of a job to brush that away later.

The police surgeon crouched beside the body that lay a few feet away from where Mickey stood. The limbs had contracted, the body curled in on itself in what Mickey had heard described as a pugilist pose; he thought it unlikely the description derived from anyone who actually boxed.

'Until the post-mortem is performed,' the police surgeon said, 'it is impossible for me to say for certain that the fire killed him. However, I can certainly confirm that the poor fellow is dead.'

Mickey thanked him. At least he and his men could get on with their work.

'Would you like him taken away directly, or do you need to examine him in situ?' the doctor asked.

'I can arrange for his removal,' Mickey told him, sensing that the man was keen to be on his way. Perhaps he had an evening appointment that had nothing to do with death and criminal activity, Mickey thought, but he did not know this Dr Keen well enough to ask. He was standing in as locum for the usual man.

'Right you are then,' Keen said, and was on his way.

Beside Mickey, a younger man bounced impatiently on the balls of his feet, as though preparing for a race. Mickey had grown used to Sergeant Tibbs' idiosyncrasies, but he noticed the amusement on the faces of the watching constables. 'Right then, lads,' he told them. 'Take a look at what's left of the offices but watch your step. The fire brigade can't guarantee the walls won't fall down.'

This last was greeted with somewhat derisive laughter from the younger of the two constables, and a look of some anxiety from the older, more experienced man. The ground beneath Mickey's feet, despite the dampness of the rubble and burnt timber, was still uncomfortably warm. Personally, he'd be more than glad to be out of this place. He stepped over to the body and, once there, took in the scene.

The man lay a few yards from what had been a wide rear door that opened at the top of a flight of steps with a yard beyond. The steps had been built in the days when goods were loaded and offloaded from carts and wagons, and Mickey suspected that the setup was not so convenient for the trucks and vans now more commonly in use for transportation. That, he thought, was most likely the reason this property had stood empty for the past year, and in the five before had been designated as a facility for longer-term storage, rather than the bustling short-term warehouse it would have been when it had been built some fifty years before. The side of the yard, behind the building, had moorings for barges to load and unload. The goods would then have been sorted, packed and sent on their way. Long benches, charred but not destroyed in the blaze, still stood against one wall. To the front of the building, office space had been constructed and rented out, though Mickey knew that the enterprise had not been successful. For one thing, the spaces would have been difficult to heat, with ceilings still at the full height of the warehouse – they'd have been better building in a mezzanine floor – and the building itself being in a location more suited to storage and industry than to anything that required a shop front or secretarial help. For the past year it had stood empty, used only by the down-and-outs who looked for easily accessed shelter. Mickey had entered that evening through the offices at the front of the building. Relatively untouched by the blaze, they stank of unwashed humanity, of poverty and of despair, old blankets tossed aside as the vagrants had run from the building as the fire spread. It was they who had raised the alarm, hammering on the door of a pub, closed at that time of the night, but frequented by the bargemen and stevedores who frequented the docklands by day. They had fled the scene before it had been possible to question them, and Mickey was not surprised at that. There was little trust or willing contact between vagrants and police.

It was, however, probably down to this raising of the alarm that the fire brigade had been summoned quickly enough to douse the fire before it spread, pumping water from the dock to soak the roof before the flames broke through and into the next-door building. Water now mixed with soot to create black slurry on the cement floor.

This place might have been out of use for a while, but Mickey now knew that it was still insured. There had been three similar fires in close proximity to this backwater dock in as many months. All empty, all insured for good amounts, and that alone would have guaranteed investigation. Mickey knew that the insurance companies had used their own people for this but that the police had also assisted. It would have been down to the local division to liaise in this instance too, if it hadn't been for the dead man lying at Mickey's feet. A suspicious death meant that the case was shunted up the ladder of importance and dropped in the lap of the murder detectives at Scotland Yard.

'Photographs first,' Mickey said, and Tibbs moved to obey. Mickey watched for a moment as Tibbs methodically took the contextual images he knew Mickey would require. Mickey had taught him well and Tibbs had been eager to learn, though even now Mickey was amused to note the careful way he handled the cameras, as though he was still a little in awe of the technology – or, more likely, the cost of its replacement. Mickey thought always of Henry at moments like this. His old inspector had purchased these bits of equipment himself, taught Mickey their use and, when he had been forced to resign, had given them over into Mickey's care.

Perhaps, Mickey thought, Tibbs was not so wrong to be just a little in awe.

He shifted out of the way so his sergeant could photograph the body as it lay and then crouched down to take a closer look. He swore softly.

'What is it?' Tibbs asked. He had crouched beside Mickey, his long limbs tucked, mantis-like, beside his body.

'You tell me, lad.' Mickey pointed at the dead man's chest. The hands were clenched tightly and the arms raised against the body, like a boxer blocking a punch, but to Mickey's practised eye the wound was still obvious. How had the police surgeon missed it? It irked Mickey that the same police surgeon would, as custom dictated, also be the one to perform the post-mortem examination. Mickey would be sure to attend and to point out his lack of observation.

'You see it, Sergeant Tibbs?'

Tibbs twisted his long neck so he could get a better look. He reached out, almost touched the dead man's chest, then drew back. 'The skin could have split with the heat,' he said, 'but the edges of the wound look too cleanly parted, and I think I can see where the weapon notched the ribs.' He looked up at Mickey for confirmation.

'As you say, the heat could have split the skin and the muscle could have torn from the ribs as the heat got to it, but frankly, I'm doubtful that's the end of it. Look, you can see here where the skin is blackened and charred but there is still redness beneath. The fire did not burn through the full depth of muscle and fat and yes, there is splitting of the tissue, but here, just between the ribs, the wound is more uniform. It looks to me as though a blade brought an end to this poor sod, not the smoke or the fire.'

'So, if that's the case,' Tibbs said, 'was the fire set to conceal the murder, in which case why not start the fire closer to the body, or even set it on the body itself?' He pointed to a corner of the room. 'There's old sacking there that would burn fast enough and could be piled on top. Yet the flames would seem to have started over by that back wall, where old benches have been torn into pieces and stacked up.'

Mickey nodded. The fire officer had pointed out where he believed the blaze to have started and then how it had spread and, even to Mickey's unpractised eye, there was a clear trail from where the timber and sacking had been stacked to where the body had been found. That and a strong smell of petrol still in the air, an oily scum floating on the puddled water. Whoever had started the fire had intended it should spread but, unlike those other three fires, the reports of which Mickey had seen, and which had burned hot and swift and been all-consuming, this looked to be the work of an amateur hand. He had said as much to the fire officer, who had broadly agreed with his assessment.

'Perhaps there was a falling out among confederates,' he said. 'Perhaps the killing was not planned. One thing is certain, whoever set this fire did not make a particularly good fist of it. A child could see where they've made a bonfire in that corner, and you'd not need to be a genius to catch the smell of petrol in the air even now the fire brigade has done its work.'

Tibbs had stood up and was now looking down on the body. 'Do you think he was a tramp?' he asked. 'His boots look too good for him to have been a vagrant.'

Mickey looked at the man's boots. The man's trousers had been burnt and the flesh blackened, blistered and striated from the heat and flame. There arose from the body the scent of overcooked meat, scorched cloth and overheated leather. The boots had been damaged by the fire, but it was still possible to discern that they had been made of thick hide, and it was even possible to discern that they had been well polished. Those parts that had been protected from the blaze by the position in which the man was lying were relatively untouched. It was a fascination for Mickey, the way a body in a fire didn't burn evenly. In some cases, if the clothing had been tight against the body, where it was belted or corseted, for example, the flesh beneath the restriction might be relatively untouched, even if that around it had been blackened and burnt to the full depth.

The soles of the boots were robust, welted and of a double thickness, no doubt designed as work boots or for someone who did a good deal of walking and, as Mickey looked more closely, he could see minimal wear on the heels. Tibbs was right about them seeming better than a vagrant might wear. 'So they do,' he said. 'Well, we must get our man delivered to the mortuary and see what else can be discovered about him. We'll see what has become of our constables, get the matter of our victim's removal in hand and then get ourselves a nice cup of tea while we attend to the report. My throat is parched.'

Tibbs nodded his agreement.

The constables were still in the offices, poking through belongings hastily left behind by the men who had fled the scene, and the remnants of previous tenants who had used the office space. There were three offices set along a very narrow corridor, created by the construction of a crudely made partition. No wonder, Mickey thought, there had been few takers when it came to renting them. The public would have entered the building via a small lobby furnished only with a run of numbered pigeonholes. They found the constables in the furthest of the three rooms. A filing cabinet stood against a wall, the drawers opened and the cavities empty. A cheap wooden desk, scuffed and ink-stained, sat beside it. Mickey asked if they had checked the drawers on arrival and was told that they were empty. There was evidence that these rooms had been used by 'vagrants and vagabonds', as the younger constable told Mickey.

'And you know that the men who slept here are vagabonds?' Mickey asked him.

The constable looked offended. 'Why yes, sir. I'm certain of it. They didn't hang around, did they, once the police and fire brigade had been summoned.'

'But they did raise the alarm,' Mickey reminded him, 'and in that they did the owners of the neighbouring buildings a great service.'

The younger constable looked at him as though he was a little mad. 'Do you know why the vagrancy act was constructed?' Mickey asked him. He saw the older man smile and wondered if he'd heard the lecture already. Mickey had delivered it often enough.

'I . . .'

'Evidently you don't. It was brought in because those soldiers who had fought the war against Napoleon had returned in such large numbers there was nowhere for them to go. They returned after such a length of time that they found their homes occupied by others and their jobs long gone. Indeed, so many of them took to the streets, reduced to begging, that the government of the day, who had been glad enough to fete these same men when they'd taken the king's shilling and gone off to fight, decided they must do something to get them off the streets. Instead of making provision for those men, those old soldiers, many of whom were wounded and maimed and in dire straits, they decided that the only thing to be done was to deprive them of the right to beg and ensure they could settle nowhere so-called respectable folk might be inconvenienced.'

The younger constable looked troubled for an instant, but then came back with, 'Yes, sir, but that was long ago. These men were hardly likely to be old soldiers from that war, now were they?'

He was clearly pleased with his reasoning, and looked at Mickey so hopefully that he almost wanted to laugh. 'You've forgotten the war we fought not so long ago, I suppose. I imagine Constable Higgs here is of an age to have served in that conflict, as am I. And we both know that many a man has returned and found himself without a place to be or a family or work or help. Some of them end up sleeping where they can. Others fall by the wayside for other reasons and yes, some choose a life of villainy, but by no means all. It is the policeman's job to make judgements only when the facts are known. Now, there's a body in there needs to be moved to the mortuary. To St Thomas's, for preference. I'll leave that in your capable hands, Higgs. You,' he indicated the young constable, 'will go door to door and see what can be discovered about the men who slept here and any other comings and goings in the past weeks. Constable Higgs may join you when he's organized disposal of the body.'

'Yes, Inspector,' the constable said as Mickey turned to go. His tone indicated what he felt about that idea. Mickey wheeled, and suddenly the young man found himself lifted off his feet, Mickey's fist wrapped tight around the high uniform collar.

'I'm giving you the benefit of instruction here, before someone less tolerant than I am comes along and knocks your block off, is that understood? I'll put up with a certain amount of backchat and insolence because youth has to learn. But hear me. Smarten up, know when to shut up, learn how to do your job or you'll soon find yourself out of one.'

The constable's face was beetroot now. Mickey let him go and he dropped to the floor. Mickey nodded amicably to Constable Higgs – who had made no move to intervene or to protest. He wished Mickey and Tibbs good day and announced his intention to walk to the nearest police box, so that an ambulance could be summoned to remove the body.

'Now for some tea,' Mickey said as he and Tibbs walked away.

'He'll not forgive you for that,' Tibbs said mildly.

'I don't imagine he will, but can you imagine if he'd tried that attitude with some others of our esteemed colleagues? If he's wise, he'll consider it a lesson well learned.'

'You know he won't though.'

'You disapprove?' Mickey asked, his tone implying genuine interest. A year ago Tibbs would have been horrified.

'Not particularly. My one concern, I suppose, is that he will not understand why you were so angry with him. Constable Higgs will no doubt try to interpret your disdain, but it won't stick. And, of course, he might report you, in which case Higgs and I will both have to lie and say that we saw nothing untoward. It's that which troubles me.'

Mickey nodded. 'I can see the problem there,' he agreed. 'You are an appallingly bad liar.'

Dan Trotter had woken with a sense of relief and well-being he'd not felt since the day his father died. He bathed and dressed, was momentarily distressed to discover that the clothing he had dropped on the bedroom floor still smelt of smoke from the night before, comforted himself that he could easily dispose of it. He was glad he'd chosen to wear his oldest garments for the job, though he'd be sorry to lose the old jacket he kept for pottering in the garden. Perhaps he could hang that back in the potting shed and blame any residual smell of smoke on the bonfires he made to burn the garden prunings.

Feeling better for having sorted that particular problem, he went down to breakfast, eating alone as he had done for more years than he could count.

Breakfast over, he went back to his room, transported the

jacket to the potting shed and dumped his other clothing in the brazier ready for burning later. He paused in the garden to admire his rose bed. The truth was making things grow was one of the few gifts Dan felt he had. He should have been born a gardener, not the unconsidered son of a businessman. He would have been happy then. But Dan was going to put the past behind him now, and he felt almost jaunty as he left the house.

That joyful feeling lasted precisely twenty-seven minutes and thirteen seconds. Dan knew this because he was in the habit of timing his regular walks – shaving a few seconds off the time taken each time filled him with a sense of great accomplishment. He glanced at his watch before he turned the corner and looked towards where the warehouses should have been. To where the warehouses still stood. Red-brick and glass towering against the blue sky.

'No, no, no!' They couldn't still be there. There had been a fire.

Rooted to the spot by his sense of disbelief, Dan took in the scene. Police constables stood chatting to the driver of the mortuary ambulance. Passers-by strained to see what might be going on inside. A man carrying a doctor's bag walked towards a waiting car. A doctor? But why? He had killed the stranger who had bounced so precipitously into Dan's life. Surely, he could not have survived?

It occurred to him belatedly that it was usual for a doctor to be called to confirm a death.

He wanted desperately to wander over to the constables and enquire, with casual interest, what was going on, but Dan knew he did not possess such sangfroid. He would stammer and talk too much and make too much of the fact that he was just a passer-by asking a question, not because he was in any way involved but because he just wanted to know, as you do. And then he would laugh, that awkward laugh that begged the listener to ignore everything he'd said, and it would be a disaster, just like it always was.

Well, you blew it good and proper this time, Dan told himself as he turned and walked swiftly back the way he had come.

# FOUR

It was unthinkable that Henry could embark on his mission without speaking to Mickey Hitchens. Mickey had been his sergeant for many years when Henry had still been an inspector in the Central Office of Scotland Yard. As murder detectives, the two had travelled widely, investigating death and the causes of death from the south coast to the wilds of the Scottish borders. It had been a professional relationship, brought to an end initially when Mickey finally became an inspector, a rank he should have achieved years before, and made even more final when Henry was forced to give up his career due to injury and ill-health.

He had telephoned his friend at work after Malina had left him that Monday afternoon. When he was finally put through to him in the Central Office, they arranged to meet the following lunchtime at a Lyon's Corner House close to Scotland Yard. For Henry it was somehow unthinkable that he should go and meet Mickey in his old place of work. He was horribly aware of how much he had changed in the past year; or, should he say, in the past two years. Truthfully, he had not been the same since being attacked while rescuing his young niece, Melissa, from kidnappers. He had been on the mend from those injuries and had even managed to return to work for a time, but his return had been premature, had led to further complications and eventually surgery. Then, while trying to recuperate he had walked into more trouble; trouble that this time had come close to killing him.

No, he could still not bear to be greeted by his old colleagues, perhaps to catch the pity in their eyes, or even the satisfaction that Johnstone had been knocked off his perch.

He knew he was probably being unfair in this last assumption, but somehow he had not been able to risk the possibility, not yet. He really had been knocked off his perch, Henry thought, though he'd probably not realized until it was far too late just how unsure his grasp on that perch had been for quite some while. The job had been wearing him down. There had been so many nights when he had been unable to sleep.

He thought about this now as he sat waiting for Mickey to arrive. The train to London had got in an hour before. Henry had got a cab to the rendezvous. He was early, as always.

Thankfully, so was Mickey Hitchens.

Henry watched with pleasure as the solid, square shoulders filled the doorframe and his friend then made his way between tables to where Henry sat. Mickey was built like a heavyweight prize fighter, and though his hair was now greying and his face had gained a few wrinkles, his sheer physicality was the same as it had been when he and Henry had met on the battlefields of the Great War. They ordered sandwiches and more tea and then Mickey turned his full attention towards his old boss. Henry was very aware of Mickey's close scrutiny. He waited patiently until the assessment was complete and then said, 'I'm told I'm looking less like a dead man than when you last saw me.'

'Somewhat less,' Mickey agreed. 'But it would not take much to improve on that. How the devil are you, Henry? Congratulations, again, for finally putting a ring on Malina's hand. It was well overdue.'

'As everyone keeps telling me. I'm well, all things considered. I'd still be lost if someone wanted me to run, but I take a daily walk along the promenade and no longer have to sleep afterwards.'

'A major improvement indeed.' Mickey laughed. He looked relieved, Henry thought, and was momentarily sobered, remembering how close a call it had been.

Their waitress arrived and set food and drink on the table. Once she had gone, Mickey said, 'So what's this about Doctor Fielding writing to you?'

Henry took the letter from his pocket and handed it to Mickey. He was suddenly acutely and painfully aware that Mickey's time would be limited. He broke off a piece of his sandwich, nibbled at it, watching contentedly as Mickey munched happily while he read. Mickey perused the letter twice, before setting it aside.

'An interesting story. Do you think it's true? Or could it be that a man who knows he's dying chooses to take the opportunity to rehabilitate his friend. After all, what did Frank Church have to lose by making the confession? In comparison to what Ethan Samuels and Helen Lee had to gain. He might, belatedly, have taken pity on them. The threat of death focuses the mind somewhat, as we both know.'

Henry nodded. When he had first received the letter, he had tended to take the information it contained at face value. The man was guilty and didn't want to go to his death without making confession. Later, it had also crossed his mind that this might be a convenient and compassionate gesture from a man who had nothing left to lose.

'I wondered,' he agreed. 'He married Helen Lee, as he had wanted to long before Ethan Samuels came back from the sea. It would have been hard on both of them though. He would have known that Helen's child was not his own. Now she's expecting a second, which is definitely Frank's, but which he's got on a woman who can't really love him, not in the way he wants. However much the two of them might have tried to make the marriage work, I can't but think there would have been resentment and pain on both sides. Perhaps he confessed because of that.'

'But you're not convinced?'

'No. A man on his deathbed, a simple man like Frank Church; he'd want to clear his conscience. That, I believe, would have been his first concern.'

'Is he a simple man though?' Mickey questioned. 'By his own admission he was a man who watched and waited for a man to die, and that takes a certain amount of intent and dedication. It takes a mind that can assess a situation and work to take full advantage. And prior to that, he'd thought swiftly enough to put the blame on another. He'd seized the chance to get what he wanted, to kill a rival. Had the Samuels boy been caught he'd have been hanged, and I can't see Frank Church confessing to save him from that.'

'He must have been certain that Ethan would not be caught, I think. Everyone I spoke to seemed sure of that. And they were right,' Henry said a little bitterly.

'As may be, but let's concentrate on the motives of Frank Church for now. Both on that day and then on the day he died. If he told the truth on his deathbed and was the one who kicked the Hanson boy to death, then his motives for doing so were two-fold. To get revenge on Robert Hanson for humiliating him, and to make doubly certain Ethan Samuels could never return home. Ethan ran because he believed he had committed murder. He would have hanged. If Ethan Samuels had stayed around, gone to fetch help, or sent Frank Church to do so, the truth might have been known then, and Robert Hanson survived. Samuels would have been banged up for a time, but he'd have still been a young man when he got out. He could have gone on to marry Helen and make a fresh start somewhere.'

'We don't know the full extent of Hanson's injuries.' Henry felt the need to play devil's advocate. 'It could be that the beating and the fall injured him for the long term. He fell from a horse, don't forget. That could even have damaged his brain.'

'In which case Samuels would have served a longer stretch, but he would still have survived the experience. No, Frank Church thought fast; likely he could see how shaken Samuels was, once the first fit of rage had passed him by. Likely he'd have taken little convincing that the other lad was dead and that he'd no choice but to run, and that sharpish. Frank Church dealt with two of his problems that day, and did so with calm and reason, albeit that reason led to the death of another man.'

Henry laughed. 'Which undermines the possibility of him confessing in order to help out his wife and her erstwhile lover. No, he confessed because he was fearful of judgement in the afterlife, not because he cared what would happen to those he left behind.'

'And yet he refused the offer of a priest,' Mickey countered. 'No, Henry, you are forgetting the effect that guilt will have over time, even upon the mind of a man who believed himself justified in his actions.'

'I've not forgotten that.' Henry paused, frowned. He had enjoyed this play of ideas with Mickey, this to-and-fro and tearing apart of possible scenarios and arguments. He had missed this most of all, he realized.

Mickey was taking advantage of the silence to demolish the rest of his sandwich and was now reaching for another. He poured them both more tea.

Henry broke his own sandwich into small pieces, wondering if he really wanted it at all.

'Eat,' Mickey said. 'How are you coping without me to tell you that?'

'Badly, I think. Though Malina does her best.' He ate a small piece of bread and tongue and then set his plate aside. 'The thing we should be remembering is that we did not and do not know any of those involved. We encountered them, briefly and at a time of crisis. Helen Lee struck me as a young woman driven by passion at first, but I soon amended that. She was seventeen, a mere child, and yet I believe she judged Ethan soundly for all that. She knew him to be imperfect; she could not see him as a willing murderer. I want to know what she makes of all this.'

'Well, you're going to get the opportunity to ask. I doubt she'll welcome you, Henry.'

Henry shrugged. That in itself didn't matter. He would find a way. 'And Doctor Fielding – from what we saw of him at the time, we know him to be a thoughtful and an educated man, more broadly knowledgeable than would be expected for a country doctor.'

'Ah, you've not lost that patronizing air,' Mickey said.

Henry ignored him. 'He knows all of those involved, knows them well, knows the community. It seems he is willing to take Frank Church's confession at face value. I think that counts for something.'

'As do I,' Mickey agreed. 'But I've enjoyed myself, examining the conundrum from other angles.' He removed his pocket watch from the red waistcoat and glanced at it. 'I'm sorry, Henry, but I must be off. I've a post-mortem to attend. We're dealing with a case of arson, probably with intent to defraud, but this time with a dead man thrown into the bundle.'

'It seems you have your hands full,' Henry said. He could not quite keep the regret out of his voice.

'Nothing changes in that regard,' Mickey said. 'Be sure to

keep me informed about the Samuels business and if I can offer assistance, you know I will. I've already apprised those who need to know that this old case has new developments.'

'Thank you,' Henry told him. 'And how is Bexley Tibbs?'

'Sergeant Tibbs is showing promise,' Mickey said. 'And as he's considered an awkward cuss by the other inspectors, he seems to have become mine for the duration, seeing as how I've a reputation for dealing with awkward cusses.'

'You had practice with me,' Henry agreed.

'Take care of yourself, my friend,' Mickey told him. 'Belle will be happy that I've seen you and that you are looking almost well. We must all visit together very soon.'

Very soon, Henry thought as he watched his friend stride back between the crowded tables and out of the glass panelled door. He missed his daily conversations with Mickey Hitchens more deeply than he could put into words.

Mickey would have liked to have stayed longer, but the post-mortem of the man they had found in the burnt-out warehouse had been arranged for that afternoon. Mickey made his way to St Thomas's Hospital and descended into the chill of the tiled basement.

Dr Keen, who had attended the warehouse, had the body ready when Mickey arrived. His assistant was present to make notes, ready for the report which Mickey was promised would be with him the following day.

'Before we begin,' Mickey said, 'I had my sergeant take photographs of the scene and I spoke to the chief fire officer who attended and who explained to me how the fire might have spread. If we could examine the body and the burning with reference to both those pieces of evidence, it would be very useful to me.'

Mickey set the photographs on a clear bit of bench, just past the scales Keen would use for weighing organs. Keen came over to take a look. Mickey had laid the pictures down so that they showed a layout of the scene and the position of the body within that.

Dr Keen grunted his interest. 'This is detailed,' he said. 'It must take a great deal of film.'

'An expense that pays back in wealth of evidence,' Mickey told him. 'Look, that's where the fire began. Petrol was likely spread around the area where the bonfire was stacked. Then, presumably after our man was down, a trail of accelerant seems to have been laid from there to the body. Now that raises several questions in my mind.'

Keen narrowed his gaze and stared at Mickey. 'You are suggesting he was dead before the fire was started? If the trail, as you call it, was laid from the bonfire to the body . . . No, that would have to be done before the first fire was lit. Or the fire would have overtaken whoever poured the petrol.'

Mickey grinned at him. 'Exactly. So my assumption is that our man was either dead before the fire reached him, or incapacitated at any rate. That whoever assaulted him then decided to light the fire in the hope of concealing the body. However, that leads us to another question. One my sergeant is particularly keen to have answered.'

Keen thought for a moment and then said, 'Why not take the body to the bonfire or start the fire around the body?'

'Exactly that. You see the scene is all wrong. It makes no sense, as it stands.'

'No, a much more complicated scenario has been played out here,' Keen agreed.

He sounded enthused by the puzzle, Mickey thought. That was all to the good. 'And there's another thing that in the dimness of the warehouse we none of us saw completely. Not until I had the chance for a proper squiz.'

He could see a slight bristling in the other's manner at the implication that he had missed a clue. 'Perhaps you could look and see if my guess is correct,' Mickey said, not wishing to alienate the man. He guessed that the curiosity Keen had exhibited regarding the photographs and the puzzle of the scene would win out. He was correct.

'Show me what you think you noted,' Keen said.

Mickey led him to the table. 'You see, just behind the raised left arm, what initially looks like a split in the skin caused by the heat? See how the muscle has been parted, so the lips of the wound are smooth and there is possibly a small nick on the rib. Of course, that can't be told for certain until you do your work.'

Keen peered into the wound. He called for a magnifier and peered again. 'By Jove,' he said. 'I think you're right. That could be a knife wound.' He set the magnifying glass down and rubbed his hands together in anticipation. 'Well, fellow, let's see how you met your end,' he said.

Mickey watched as the clothes were carefully cut from the body and set aside. What was left of them was charred from the fire and soaked through from the action of the fire hoses. They would need to be dried before they could be properly examined. The fragments of clothing were laid out on brown paper in the order in which they were removed. When Keen and his assistant lifted the man to take away the clothing from the back of the body, Mickey was interested to note the lack of charring on those parts which had been pressed against the ground. So, most likely the man had been down before the fire reached him.

Keen bent forward and sniffed at the abdomen and the vest the dead man had worn beneath his shirt, inviting Mickey to do the same.

'Petrol,' Mickey said. 'The man's abdomen was badly burned, the charring spreading from a point around the navel and up on to the chest, down to groin and upper thighs.'

'The incineration is most complete here,' Keen said. 'I will have to analyse the tissue more thoroughly, but it looks to me as though there are fourth to sixth degrees of burning in this area. So, a range from full destruction of all layers of the skin, through destruction of muscle and thence charring of the whole tissue down to the organs. I would expect to retrieve at least some of the organs intact. The fact that by their very nature they are moist or wet usually ensures that some remain, even in extreme cases. We'll analyse the blood and tissues for carbon mon- and di-oxides and take samples from both ventricles of the heart. That should afford some clue as to how long this poor fellow remained alive after he was stabbed. The amount of carbon in the lungs will give us further information.'

Mickey nodded. There was little doubt now that the man had been stabbed. Removal of the clothing and careful repositioning of the arm had allowed the doctor and Mickey to get a better look at the wound. The knife wound didn't seem to have pierced the heart. Dr Keen was of the opinion that it had entered the lung. It would have killed, but perhaps not instantaneously.

'The blistering on the legs, where the burning is not so complete. I've heard that can't form if the victim is already dead?' Mickey asked.

Dr Keen nodded. 'There is still some small dispute about that, but the consensus is that blisters cannot form and definitely cannot fill with albumen after death has occurred. That's a response only of living tissue. Sydney Smith carried out a series of experiments to try and raise blisters of this type on dead bodies, at various stages post-mortem, and was unable to recreate any to his satisfaction. My own observations and records agree with his findings.'

'So, the fire got to him before he breathed his last,' Mickey said. 'I hope he wasn't conscious when it did.'

Mickey's hope seemed likely to be fulfilled when they finally turned the body to examine the back. The wound to the head had not been obvious at first, hidden behind charred and matted hair and the sludge formed when the fire brigade had poured water on the scene. 'So, he was bashed over the head, stabbed and then set alight,' Mickey said, wonderingly. 'Someone wanted to be certain he was dead.'

'That someone was inept,' Keen added tartly, 'if it took three attempts to kill him.'

'Perhaps he's related to that Rasputin,' Mickey suggested. 'Didn't it take three or four attempts to finish him?'

Mickey stepped back and examined the man again. Yes, he was wearing workmen's boots, but they were cared for and polished and seemed little worn. He might just be someone who spent a good deal of his time on his feet, not necessarily involved in full physical labour. In his days as a constable, Mickey had spent his boot allowance on very similar boots. The location in which the victim had been found had suggested a labourer, someone involved in the boats or in loading and unloading of cargoes or something of that kind, but looking again, Mickey realized that his judgement had perhaps been clouded by that. The man was not tall. Five feet five, according to the measurements that had been taken, and somewhat soft and rounded, certainly not heavily built. That, of course, meant nothing. Mickey had met plenty of lean men also possessed of sinews like cables and muscles that looked insignificant until you were on the receiving end of a punch. But this did not look like the body of someone making his living from physical labour.

'Is there any means to look at his hands?' Mickey asked.

'You're looking for fingerprints? I think it's unlikely, though I will do my best—'

'No, I'm looking for calluses. For clues as to what manner of man this was. His occupation.'

None too gently, and with an unpleasant sound of tearing and breaking, Keen opened the man's left hand, this being the one less burnt. 'Oh, look,' he said. 'The little finger. I might be able to raise you a print from that one.'

Mickey, who had been untroubled this far, felt his breakfast rise as Keen matter-of-factly snipped the finger from the hand with what looked like a pair of garden secateurs and gave it to his assistant for processing. 'The flesh beneath is still supple,' he explained. 'It should be possible to remove the upper layers and perhaps gain a partial print from the inside, as it were. I say, old man, are you feeling all right?'

Mickey acknowledged that he was finding the room quite oppressive.

Dr Keen nodded. He continued to examine the hands of the dead man and then gave Mickey the magnifying glass so he could take his turn. 'I don't see evidence of the skin thickening into calluses either on the fingers or the palms,' he said. 'Of course, I can't be one hundred per cent certain, but . . .'

Mickey nodded. They repeated the examination for the right hand, but the burning was more severe on this side and it was hard to reach a conclusion.

'What about the feet?' Mickey asked.

The feet had been enclosed in the heavy boots, and covered also with thick wool socks and a thinner, cotton pair beneath. It was a trick Mickey was aware of for preventing too much rubbing and chafing of the feet when breaking in a pair of new boots. Looking at the boots more carefully reinforced

Mickey's opinion that these might well be a pair of well-maintained second-hand footwear. So, not so much breaking in of a new pair as the remoulding of an old to suit a different pair of feet. It was possible that the thick socks, worn in summer, meant that the boots were a little too big or even a little too small and the socks meant to help with the stretching.

He and Keen examined the dead man's feet with care. They were oddly untouched, having been protected from the worst of the burning. From the ankles down, the body seemed that of a different man.

'A rather nasty bunion,' Mickey commented. 'A corn or two. A callous on the side of the heel that is probably down to the bunion shifting his weight when he walked. The skin on the feet isn't hard, but then he was able to afford decent socks, whoever he was.'

He went over to examine the clothing more closely while Keen prepared to make the first incision. Mickey could hear him as he dictated notes to his assistant and the scratch of the man's pen on the notepad. There was a label in the shirt, but it was faded and soaked in sooty water. That would need examining. The fabric at the back, which had not been so badly damaged, looked to be good quality. He could see no immediate evidence of patches of mending. He would put in a request that the clothing be examined. Scotland Yard made use of university laboratories and some other industrial institutions for much of their forensic work. It was not, he reflected, a particularly good system; the experts involved had to juggle their academic or research work with requests from the police, and not all academics who partnered the authorities were particularly able as expert witnesses. The skills involved could be disparate. Still, he would try, and if no one was available would examine the clothing further for himself.

The socks were perhaps more interesting. The cotton socks were commercially made but the wool socks had been hand-knitted and the toes expertly linked with what Mickey recognized as a Kitchener Stitch so they would not chafe. Mickey, who had pained memories of rubbed toes and coarse fibre from his time as a soldier, was admiring of that particular skill. So, socks made for this man by a wife, a mother, a sister?

Someone would be missing him, which meant with luck they had already reported him.

He stayed to watch Dr Keen earn his two pounds and two shillings for the post-mortem and guessed he'd be earning at least his further one pound eleven shillings and sixpence, for presenting his findings to the coroner in due course. Perhaps further dues if Mickey could lay hands on the murderer and bring him to court.

There was no doubt that murder had been done here. The only question left in Mickey's mind – apart from the who and the why and the identity of the victim – was if more than one assailant had been involved. And why they had not laid the body closer to the fire.

# FIVE

Dr Fielding had felt obliged to tell Elijah Hanson that the ex-inspector, Henry Johnstone, was returning to Thoresway in light of Frank Church's confession and so he had called on him on the Monday afternoon when he had finished his rounds.

Hanson senior was not impressed. 'What in hell's name does he think he's going to achieve with that? No one wants him here, Fielding. What possessed you to write to the man?'

'Frank Church's confession changed everything,' Fielding said mildly, well used to Elijah Hanson's outbursts.

'It changed nothing. The Samuels boy is gone, God knows where. He didn't even have the courage to face up to what he'd done. I've no time for cowards. None at all.'

'He ran because Frank Church told him he'd killed your son. The truth was very different. Now, I'm not defending the boy for running, but the truth of the matter is out now and he has a right to know. Hanson, his family have suffered terribly because they believe their son to be a murderer. Don't they have the right to see justice done now?'

'And how is that going to happen? Frank Church is dead. His family are now suffering the shame of that. And the Samuelses will still have the guilt of what their boy did hanging around their necks, no matter what. No, Fielding, least said soonest mended. Better you'd left things as they were. Those that mattered would know the truth, the rest of the world would have left us alone. Now you've invited this man here and all he's likely to do is to pull the bloody scabs from half-healed wounds. How the hell is that going to improve owt for anyone?'

He probably had a point, Fielding thought. Perhaps he had been wrong. But it was too late now; Henry would soon be on his way and nothing Fielding might say was likely to change that.

'He's not even a bloody policeman now, is he?' Hanson said.

'No, unfortunately he had to retire due to injuries received in—'

'Likely for sticking his nose where it weren't welcome,' Elijah Hanson said, and Fielding was forced to speculate that there might be some truth in that.

Helen Church did not welcome the news with any more enthusiasm. It was a Monday and, as she'd done since she was big enough to fetch and carry, she was helping her mother with the laundry. Helen's family had taken in washing for as long as Fielding could remember. Sewing and mending too – and a fine job they made of it, Fielding could attest. Farm work employed many hands, many of those belonging to unmarried men, travelling where the labour took them. The larger houses in the neighbourhood, large enough to need someone to launder, not so large as to have the staff to do it, also made use of local women. They were careful and efficient and filled the gap left by the reluctance of young women to go into service for a pittance of pay. Fielding reflected that these local women probably earned only a fraction of that pittance for the heavy work they did, but that was the way of the world.

Helen finished loading sheets into the boiling copper, pushing them down into the hot water and harsh lye soap with a pair of wooden tongs. A bath of cold rinse water stood close by and she used a paddle to submerge the clean sheets before finally turning to face Fielding, one hand now resting on her swollen belly.

'God, men are fools,' Helen said.

Fielding was taken aback. 'Ethan should know he is no longer accused of murder,' he protested. 'I thought you would be pleased someone was coming to investigate.'

'Pleased that man is coming here? What good will that do? You say he's not even a policeman any more, so he's hardly coming to investigate, is he? And even if he was, Ethan's gone, and good luck to him. If you or that man were to find him, you'd have him locked away for God knows how long.

Mr Hanson would make sure it was for a long stretch, don't you think? They'd break him, cage him like some animal. You think I want that?'

Attracted, Fielding supposed, by Helen's raised voice, her mother arrived, carrying yet another basket of laundry. Trotting behind her was a little boy with dark hair and blue eyes. Helen scooped her son up into her arms and held him tightly. Looking at the child, Fielding could see Ethan's stamp all over him, in the shape of the face, those oddly pale eyes that, it was said, came into the family when one of the women had married out. Her daughter, as usually happened, married back in again. How would it have been for Frank Church, Fielding thought, to have looked daily on this child's face and not even been able to pretend to himself that the boy might be his. No wonder he'd been so eager to father one of his own. Though from what Fielding had observed and heard, he'd tried to do his best by the boy.

'He's growing well,' he commented.

'He needs a sleep,' Helen said. The child had laid his head on his mother's shoulder and his eyelids were drooping closed.

Fielding followed her as she left the laundry shed and walked back towards her mother's house. She laid the child down on a blanket covering a thin mattress, set in the alcove next to the fireplace. Covered him over, soothing him gently as he protested at being put down. Fielding watched as the child settled and his mother straightened up, resting a hand on the fireplace to help herself up.

'Tell him I'll speak to him,' she said, her expression resigned and, he thought, more world-weary than any young woman should wear. 'And you should talk to his family. If he should turn up at their door unannounced—'

'I will,' Fielding promised. He was starting to regret his impulse to contact Henry Johnstone.

# SIX

Inspector Mickey Hitchens' heart was pounding and his chest and his lungs were on fire, but he could not help but laugh as he saw the young man streak by him, legs pumping and skinny arms waving wildly. Tibbs was not exactly the most elegant runner in the world, but the lad was fast, there was no arguing with that.

He watched as his protégé hurtled down a flight of steps, limbs still flailing, head down, gaining on his quarry. The constables were also closing in, so Mickey decided to stay where he was to catch his breath. Sergeant Tibbs was now within yards of his quarry, pursuing him across the narrow walkway, deep water on either side, that led to where the barges and lighters were tied up three and four deep. Mickey watched with interest and a little trepidation. He had seen men run across the boats before, men who were used to moving platforms beneath their feet, who had a sense of balance. If the young man Tibbs was chasing decided that the best course of action was to run out across the boats and then cut back to the dockside, would his sergeant be able to follow him safely and not take a tumble into the water?

Two constables were closing on the scene, one pursuing both Tibbs and the lad he was chasing, and one making his way from the warehouse where they had been keeping watch, hoping to cut off that avenue of escape, though there was still the chance the young man could get past before he made it to the walkway. Mickey examined the landscape carefully. If the lad was canny he could still evade his less able pursuers. There was no doubt he knew the area and knew the boats better than they did and, from the look of the way he ran, and his lightness and economy of movement compared to Tibbs and the bulkier constables, there was a chance he might outpace them all.

Tibbs was now reaching for his man. He had no hope, Mickey thought, of grabbing him as yet, but he got the impression Tibbs was preparing to hurl himself at the man's legs, rugby-tackling him to the ground. He worried that they'd both end up in the dock. And if they fell between the boats, it would be hard for either of them to break the surface without being crushed. Mickey swore, regretting his impulse to stop at the top of the steps, and feeling he should have kept up his own pursuit, not left it to the younger sergeant.

Mickey watched as a slender, wiry figure stepped off a lighter. He held a boat hook in his hands and he took a swipe at the running man, knocking his legs out from beneath him. Mickey laughed in relief. In the heat of the moment, he had forgotten where Kem had stationed himself. He was not part of the police action, but the intelligence from Kem and his captain, who knew this area intimately, had been helpful in setting up the surveillance. Obviously Kem had continued to watch as the action unfolded.

Mickey jogged down the steps to where the young man lay writhing and winded on the floor. The constables dragged him to his feet, examined him briefly, decided he was fit enough to arrest and took him away.

Sergeant Tibbs had his hands on his knees and was catching his breath. Kem was laughing and patting him on the back. Mickey wasn't sure that was going to help.

'Nicely done, both of you,' he said.

'You rounded up the others?' Kem asked.

'We did indeed; he was the last of them. Stupid little fools. What did they hope to gain?'

'The pair of you got time for a brew?' Kem asked. 'I put the kettle on just in case; it should be boiled by now.'

Mickey said indeed they had and Kem turned, walked the length of the lighter and then the next and then across the third and on to the sailing barge beyond. Tibbs followed him, Mickey bringing up the rear, somewhat surprised that his sergeant was untroubled by the rocking vessels beneath his feet. This is not the first time he's done this, Mickey thought. He knew vaguely that Tibbs and Kem had become friends; had initially been surprised considering Tibbs' previous attitude towards the travelling folk, though his encounter with Malina, Kem's sister, had done a great deal to adjust that attitude.

He thought about the young man they had just arrested. A generation and more ago, the legendary Fred Wensley, then a mere constable, but until his retirement in 1929 one of the big four who ruled over the Metropolitan Police, had been involved in crushing the ongoing battle between the Bessarabians and the Odessians, vicious gangs who had sought to carve up part of the East End – and each other. They had been troublesome rather than successful, focusing for the most part on intimidating newly arrived immigrants, and also looking to infiltrate the racing gangs, dominated then by the Italians and the Irish and the Gypsies. They had found themselves in trouble with those who resented the attempted incursion, as much as with the police. Although the original members of the gang were long gone, from time to time others picked up the banner. The young men they had arrested this morning saw themselves as inheritors of this tradition, one being a direct descendant of a member of the Bessarabian gang. They had grown up with the stories of their successes rather than the ultimate failure, and it seemed wanted a cut of what they saw as their unassailable and inherited right.

Mickey had no doubt that their arrests on this fine Tuesday morning would have saved them from a worse fate. The surveillance and the ultimate success of Mickey Hitchens and his associates had come about as much from information received from the local criminal fraternities, who resented these young upstarts cutting in on their territories, as it had from intelligence that the police had gathered. In light of the most recent warehouse fire and the finding of the body, word had gone out. Three young lads were likely responsible – though any intelligence on why, or who had paid them, was yet to come Mickey's way. A woman, a prostitute but in Mickey's view a good witness, called Betty Moran, had also come forward and said she had seen three boys, one of whom she recognized, going into the warehouse with a petrol can just before the fire started. More interesting, from Mickey's point of view, was that she had seen another man go in shortly after and then run away. Could this have been the killer?

Much of this information had been relayed via John Teesdale, the master of the boat that Kem crewed. He had been waylaid outside a local pub by one of the district's hard men and instructed to pass the details on to Inspector Hitchens. Kem had then been charged with the task of conveying this intelligence to Mickey – which he had done, arriving at Mickey's home at two in the morning.

Kem's help on this occasion would cause him no harm. The wider community would have approved, but Mickey wondered briefly, as he accepted his mug of tea, if Kem was getting any grief from the fact that his future brother-in-law had previously been a detective inspector. Eyeing the younger man thoughtfully, noting his solid build (he might look slender, but it was all muscle and those muscles were powerful), he thought probably not. Kem's square hands, calloused from years of working with rope and bale and boat hook and all the other tools of the boatman's trade, would be formidable enough, when bunched into fists, to deal with any casual insult.

Besides, Inspector Johnstone had got himself an interesting reputation. He was known for his sternness but also his fair dealing, and for being a man of his word, and Mickey had been surprised, when dealing with the boatman and the gang leaders and the publicans, and indeed just the members of the general public, how many had enquired after Henry's health.

Perhaps, he thought, they were worried Henry might come back.

'Have you seen anything of my sister?' Kem asked.

'No, but I saw Henry yesterday. I know that he and Malina are headed up to Lincolnshire this morning. She is driving him there.'

'For any particular reason?' Kem asked.

'New information arising in an old case, not enough reason for the local police to be taking much action, it seems, but Henry has a bee in his bonnet about it.'

Kem laughed. 'Ah,' he said. 'So while he goes and stirs up the hornets' nest, Malina is there to apply the salve.'

Mickey grinned.

'And how is he?' Kem asked. He was, Mickey knew, genuinely fond of Henry, and though his sister's choice of husband had surprised everybody, he had come round to the idea that it was good, if only because two lonely people would no longer be lonely. Malina, for all her confidence and for all that she had been welcomed into Cynthia's family was, Mickey felt, used to feeling she was something of an outsider. She had certainly never considered marriage before.

'He's better than he was. He's bored, but then Henry is often bored. Being an inspector suited him because he always had a problem to solve, and I think the problems he has to solve these days are somewhat less engaging.'

'Missing jewels and lost dogs?' he said.

'I don't believe there have yet been any lost dogs but . . .' Mickey shrugged. 'He's lasted longer as a private investigator than any of us thought he would, but I feel that's down to bloody-mindedness rather than enjoyment.'

'Are we still meeting for the concert next Sunday evening?' Tibbs asked Kem a little later as they left the barge.

'Of course, we can eat there before it starts.'

Mickey raised an eyebrow at young Tibbs as they walked away. 'And where might the pair of you be going?'

'To the Workers' Circle on Alie Street.'

'I know it well,' Mickey said. 'It's also a good place for the gathering of intelligence,' he observed. 'All those political types who frequent it.'

He was conscious of the slightly wary look that Tibbs cast his way. He laughed. 'Lad, you are far too easy to tease,' he said. 'Henry and I have been to many a lecture there and to the concerts; it's a cheap place to grab a bite to eat. Kem is a good sort,' he added. He noted a slight flush reddening Tibbs' cheeks and wondered at it.

'He's been a good friend.'

'But not, perhaps, one you'd take home to meet your parents,' Mickey goaded gently. Tibbs' parents had some very strict ideas when it came to suitable friends. His father was a nonconformist minister who insisted his son remain teetotal and put in an appearance for services on a Sunday. Mickey had often wondered how the young man had survived his police training and, particularly, the inevitable ribaldry of the section house. It was even more of a miracle that he'd made it to detective sergeant, though on balance Mickey thought it was an accolade he well deserved.

'I've not been back to visit in a few weeks,' Tibbs said suddenly. 'We had a bit of an argument the last time. They think I should resume my education and follow in my father's footsteps.'

'What, become a minister?'

Tibbs nodded. 'They always saw my joining of the police force as a kind of rebellion. My mother persuaded my father to allow it, telling him it was obviously some wildness I had to get out of my head.' He laughed suddenly and added, 'When I was a lot younger, I evinced the desire to become a poet. She reminded my father of that and told him that things could be a lot worse.'

Mickey guffawed. 'And do you still versify?' he asked. Then added when he saw a look of dismay cross the younger man's face, 'Not that there's anything wrong with that. Belle is very fond of Mr Eliot and also Mr Yeats. I suppose with her being an actress and so a woman who makes her living from words, it's natural that she should enjoy verses.'

Noting Tibbs' continuing discomfort, he sought to change the subject. 'And so your parents think you should throw in your career and become a minister.' He could not, he realized, quite keep the disapproval out of his tone. 'What is it about your current job they so dislike?'

'They are afraid I'm coming under bad influences, that the job has brought me into contact with people they can't approve of. For one thing they don't like my visits to the club. I told them, I go to hear the concerts and sometimes the lectures. It's not as if I drink. Not really.'

Mickey stopped in his tracks and turned to look at his sergeant. 'I understood you'd signed the pledge,' he said.

'I did. But I was fourteen and it had never occurred to me that . . . well, that life would ever be any different. Inspector Hitchens, I heard about Mr Wensley and how he never really drank, but he was in the habit of buying himself a pint of beer just for the look of it. So he didn't draw notice to himself. So, I thought, what harm could that do? It's hard to sit in a public house and not at least have a glass for the look of things.'

Mickey nodded and they moved on. What Tibbs had said

about Fred Wensley was true. He'd arrived in London as a young man of around twenty, up from the West Country, never having even touched a drop of the very good cider produced there which, to Mickey's mind, was a crying shame. As a constable living and working in the East End of London, in streets then characterized by the number of public houses and what you might call a culture of drinking which most adopted at an early age, not to imbibe set him too much apart and caused him to stand out among the other clientele, something he wanted to avoid when he was there doing a spot of quiet surveillance.

'Fred Wensley taught himself to tolerate the odd pint,' Mickey agreed. 'He could make it last far longer than was ever natural,' he added. 'And you, do you actually like the beer?'

Tibbs pulled a face and shook his head. 'I can't say as I do,' he admitted. 'At the Circle, no one worries if you keep to the coffee, and there's tea always in the samovar, but I've found being at least able to stomach the beer is a useful skill if I don't want to draw attention to myself. Though,' he added, 'I don't think I'll ever learn to down a pint the way some can.'

'Like Kem?'

'No, not really. Kem drinks only in moderation. He likes to keep his head clear. I think he does it for the look of things almost as much as I do. But it's expected, isn't it, of a boatman? It's expected of a man.'

'I suspect Kem could deck any man who questioned his masculinity,' Mickey said, not certain now where this conversation was leading. He paused again. Touched the younger man's shoulder. 'Kem is a good sort,' he repeated. 'He's loyal and true and I'm glad you've found a friend. I'll offer a small bit of advice to you both. Never live your lives by what other people think makes you a man. But, at the same time, remember you don't have Kem's fists or his skill as a fighter.' He nodded as though satisfied. 'Sup your beer slowly, laugh at the jokes, show your public face where it needs to be shown.'

They walked on in silence and eventually Tibbs asked, 'So what is this old case that has taken Mr Johnstone to Lincolnshire?'

'Ah, well. Some three years ago, we were sent to look into a triple murder that we solved to everyone's satisfaction, but while we were there a young man by the name of Robert Hanson was knocked from his horse and beaten to death – or so it seemed. There was a witness to the crime, a man by the name of Frank Church, who gave evidence that his friend had knocked this Robert Hanson down and beaten him so hard he died at the scene. The accused had fled by then and so couldn't speak for himself, but it now transpires that all was not as it seemed.'

As they walked back along the Embankment towards Scotland Yard, Mickey explained the matter to Tibbs. 'And so off he's gone to inspect the case anew and see what might be found out. He's set on finding Ethan Samuels this time, even though we failed to discover his whereabouts three years since.'

'You think he will?' Tibbs asked.

Mickey shook his head. 'I doubt it, somehow. Though I find myself hoping someone will get word to him that the truth has come out and that the gallows are no longer waiting for him. I'd like to think he and his young woman might find one another again, but then, Belle tells me I'm a romantic at heart.'

Tibbs nodded. 'The travelling folk know how to disappear,' he said, and Mickey smiled, thinking of how Tibbs might have spoken about Malina and Kem and their people only a year before, when he'd worn his prejudices on both his sleeves and had some hard lessons to learn. Such views, Mickey knew, were commonplace, considered normal, and Mickey himself viewed as soft and even abnormal because he differed in his attitudes.

But then, as Henry was always telling him, he always had been a little bolshie.

He could not help but wonder how Henry was getting along and how he was coping with the long journey. He didn't like thinking of his friend in pain.

# SEVEN

Georgie Tullis was the youngest of the three boys arrested that morning. He was fifteen years old, red-headed and freckled and skinny as a rake. He was also very fleet of foot, as Mickey had witnessed, and somewhat bruised from Kem's swift action with the boat hook.

He sat with his arms folded across his chest and stared belligerently at Mickey. The other two in custody were eighteen-year-old Marcus Reynaldi and his slightly younger cousin, Mal Eagen. Those older two were familiar to Mickey – general troublemakers and petty thieves who had until now not done anything serious enough to land them in prison.

*Until now*. He had left the interviewing of those two to Tibbs and another officer with the warning that they'd get little out of either boy. 'They're old hands at this malarky,' Mickey had said. 'It'll be all hear nowt, see nowt, say nowt from that pair, but give it your best – something might shake loose with the right persuasion.'

Mickey looked straight at George. 'So, lad,' he said. 'Who paid you to set the fire?'

'I don't know nuffin about no fire.'

'You were seen,' Mickey told him. 'The three of you, on the Tobacco Dock, walking towards the old Brinton warehouse, with you carrying a petrol can.'

'I don't own no petrol can and I can walk where I like.'

'True, and as it's likely you stole both can and petrol, I may accept the argument that you own neither. However, you were seen carrying said can and disappearing, the three of you together, into the Brinton place at an hour in the early morning when you should by rights have been asleep in your bed.'

'What's it to you when I go to bed?'

'So, you're willing to admit to being out of it?'

'I never said that. I weren't there; I don't have no petrol can.'

'A little later,' Mickey went on, 'the three of you – yourself, Mal Eagen and that cousin of his Marcus Reynaldi – were seen running from the scene, unencumbered by said can. A few minutes after that, the alarm was raised that the building was on fire.'

'Nothin' to do with me. I was home in my bed.'

'Not according to your mother, you weren't, and not according to my witnesses.' Mickey paused, studying the boy carefully. He would crack in the end. Already he was getting a case of the fidgets, crossing and uncrossing his arms, wriggling in his chair like a much younger boy might. He glanced at the constable standing by the door and then looked back at Georgie. Yes, Mickey could wait him out, but frankly he wasn't inclined to continue with this game for that long.

Abruptly, Mickey leaned forward and slammed both hands down hard on the table. The sound of it made the constable flinch and the boy jump so hard he nearly fell backwards in his chair. 'So, which of you hit him over the head?' Mickey demanded, his tone no longer quietly reasonable. 'Which of you stabbed him through the chest? Which of you set him on fire?'

The boy was staring at him in shock, the colour drained from his freckled cheeks. He stared at Mickey as though he'd gone mad. 'I don't know nothing about stabbing no one! I only heard about it after.'

There was, Mickey thought, no doubting his shock. 'Nor about bashing someone's brains out or about setting him on fire?'

'We never . . . there was no one . . . it was just—'

'You're all deserving of hanging for murder,' Mickey said. 'Now, lad.' He brought his tone back to a state of steady reasonableness. 'If one of the others did the deed, then likely you can save yourself from the hangman's noose if you come clean about it? While it's true that you'll still be found guilty for having been present and not preventing the crime, or of at the least not reporting the crime to the relevant authorities, the judge will go easier on you if you admit now to what you witnessed. You're still young; it's understandable that you couldn't stand up to the older boys. That you—'

'They didn't do nothing! None of us murdered anyone. There was no one else there!'

'No one else where?' Mickey asked, his tone almost gentle now.

The boy dropped his gaze and stared sullenly at the table. 'You know where.'

'At the Brinton warehouse. Where you set the fire.'

George Tullis nodded.

'You saw no one else?'

He shook his head.

'Did you know that there were men sleeping in the offices at the front of the building?'

He looked up then, the shocked expression and the violent shake of the head convincing Mickey that he probably had not.

'Fortunately they woke and raised the alarm. Which is why the building did not burn down and take half the street with it. The man found close by where you'd set the fire was not so fortunate.'

'There was no one there, I swear on my mother's life.'

He had come to his feet, leaning over the table as though to emphasize his point, and Mickey could see the distress on his face. The constable came around the table and, hand on shoulder, pressed him back into his seat.

'But you set the fire,' Mickey said.

Reluctantly the boy nodded.

'And who told you to do it? Or was it at your own whim?'

He shrugged. 'Mal said someone paid him. I wanted to come along. I saw the Sutherland place go up a month ago, watched the fire engines and the flames and the smoke and . . .' His expression was rapt now, exultant even, and Mickey felt a shudder go through him.

'You enjoyed watching it burn.'

Georgie, seemingly realizing that this might not be the best thing to admit to, shrugged his shoulders. 'It were exciting,' he said.

'So, you wanted some of that. So, who paid Mal and to do what? To burn the building down?'

'I don't know.'

'The owner, after the insurance money?'

Georgie laughed at that. The self-assurance suddenly back. 'You don't know it all, do you copper? Old Man Brinton died three weeks ago. He's not going to collect nuffin, is he?'

Mickey, annoyingly, hadn't known that. He would have to dig deeper into who might benefit.

'So,' some of his cockiness back now, 'who ratted on us then?'

'Who do you think? Was there anyone out who might have seen you?'

He could see the cogs whirring in the boy's brain as he reran the events of that night. 'Man with a pushcart and sweeps' brushes. A woman with a sailor in tow.' He grinned suddenly as though, Mickey thought, imagining what the two would be getting up to.

'Anyone else?'

He shook his head. 'Pubs were closed; there was no one else on the street.' He sat back in his chair and folded his arms once more. 'We never killed no man.'

'What did you do with the petrol can?' Mickey asked.

The boy shrugged. 'Left it there. We didn't need it no more.'

'And where did you get it from?'

The boy shrugged again, unconcerned now, even a little bored, Mickey thought. 'Mal borrowed it, didn't he? From someone called Kim or summat like that.'

'And this Kim, they didn't want it back?'

'I dunno, nothing to do with me.'

So perhaps the killer had taken it away. Now why would he do that? Mickey wondered.

# EIGHT

Dr Fielding did not manage to see the Samuels family until Tuesday evening. He had already taken too much time from his usual rounds and, besides, Dar Samuels would have been out of the house, working. He therefore waited until he was certain that not only would Dar have returned but that the family would have eaten their evening meal. His own was waiting for him at home, his housekeeper having warned him that she would still be cooking at the usual time, but that she would keep things warm for him. Fielding knew better than to argue the matter.

It was still light, though the sky was already adopting a more golden tone as late summer prepared to give way to autumn. Fielding spotted Dar as his car struggled around the final bend. Dar Samuels was sitting on the bench outside the house, an enamelled mug clasped in his large hand.

He had probably been watching as Fielding drove his car up the rutted track, a bone-shaking experience Fielding had undertaken only because the hill was too steep for him to want to climb at this time of night. Bogle Hill, round and high and studded with sheep, only a mile from the nearest village and yet, he thought, it might as well have been in another world.

Come winter and it likely *would* be another world, cut off by snow and chilled by the winds that raced down through the valley, cut between the hills and swirled, enraged, around their summits. Hanson had moved the family here three years ago, after Robert's death. Moved them away from the village and kin and friends, the young ones now trudging down into the valley to get to school, in all weathers and all seasons, trudging back up again on the long walk Fielding himself had been at pains to avoid.

Dar rose when Fielding got out of the car and spoke through the open door of the cottage. His wife, Eliza Samuels, glanced out, and a moment later brought Dr Fielding his own tin mug of tea and saw him settled on the bench. Then she went back inside and left the men to talk.

'You're here to tell me that detective's coming back,' Dar said.

'I am, yes. Seems I could have saved myself the trouble. As he's making the journey because of me, I thought I'd best come and speak to you about it.'

Dar sipped his tea, making the moment last, Fielding thought. This little bit of peace at the end of a busy day.

'I appreciate your coming by,' he said at last. 'I'm just not sure what will be gained from that man coming here. My son is gone, who knows where.'

'Perhaps the inspector who was involved at the time, Henry Johnstone, can find him. Tell him he's innocent of murder; tell him that—'

'That he can come home and all is forgiven?'

There was no anger or accusation in Dar's voice. It might almost, Fielding thought, have been better if there had been. Instead, there was only weariness and resignation.

'I should have looked harder, questioned more deeply,' Fielding said. 'But there seemed no doubt about what had been done or who had done it. Inspector Johnstone feels the same, I know that.'

Dar shook his head. 'You both followed what seemed to be the right path,' he said quietly. 'And I never reckoned Frank Church for a killer. There, I was wrong.'

'And Ethan?' The question was out before Fielding could think about it.

'Ethan neither, but it was clear someone had done for the Hanson lad. When tempers are lost, folk can say and do things they never meant to do. Things they can never take back. I thought Ethan capable of that, not of murder. His ma never believed even that. She had Frank Church guilty from the very start. Seems she was right. But then, who'd listen to a woman?' He turned to look at Fielding and the doctor found he could not manage to hold his gaze.

'No,' he agreed, 'we would have just passed it off as a mother's fondness for her son clouding her judgement.'

'The women listen,' Dar said. 'They talk, they argue it

through, they listen to one another, offer comfort and help, and they deal with whatever needs dealing with, but she's been denied even that, being here. We go down to chapel on a Sunday but this isn't our community.'

'She must be lonely,' Fielding said.

They both looked up as the two younger Samuelses came into view. It had been a while since Fielding had seen Ned and Alice, and he was surprised at how much they had grown. Ned carried a brace of rabbits and Alice carried the stick they must have used to cudgel them. How long and how still had they waited, Fielding wondered absently, until the rabbits came into range. The Samuelses had no shotgun, so snares or a stick had to serve. They greeted Dr Fielding politely and then took the rabbits round to the back of the house to skin and paunch. Fielding remembered that you either butchered your rabbits fresh or you left them to hang a day or two until rigor had passed and they were easier to skin.

'They are looking quite grown-up,' he said.

'Ned will be fourteen come January. Alice is already twelve. Mr Hanson's making noises about Ned working for him when he leaves school in New Year. He's after me coming back, now Frank's gone and he has no one else he can appoint to look after the beasts.'

Fielding nodded. Dar Samuels had been Elijah Hanson's much valued stockman until Robert had been killed. That occupation had then passed to Frank Church, who was able enough but didn't have Dar's almost legendary skills with potions and cures or his knowledge of both beasts and the land on which they lived. Now Dar was up here, tending sheep, though Hanson had always been ready enough to call him back when problems arose that Frank Church had been unable to handle.

Fielding could not imagine that improved relations. 'He was a fool to part with you,' he said. 'I dare say you'd be glad to go back.'

He was genuinely astonished when, after a moment's hesitation, Dar shook his head. 'I think it's a bit late for that,' he said. 'We'll be giving notice, come Michaelmas, once we've been paid for the year. We'll be leaving then, before the weather gets too bad for travelling. I'm trusting you to say nowt,' he added. 'It's no one's business but ours.'

'No, it's not,' Fielding agreed, but at the same time he was glad that he was unlikely to be asked about the Samuelses' intentions anyway. It occurred to him that Dar spoke of giving notice only after they had been paid for the season, which meant, most likely, that no notice would be given at all. Dar would take what he was owed for the half-year just passed and then take his family and go. He was, of course, within his rights to do so then, but it was usual to warn the employer that you'd not be staying on. Having said that, such a warning could make the last weeks difficult, and men like Hanson were not above being short with money owed, if they'd been crossed. It was in the landowner's power to cite lower than expected profits, so lower than expected wages. It was beyond someone in Dar's position to argue with this or to prove otherwise. No, he could not fault Dar's reasoning. He felt oddly touched that he should be the recipient of Dar's confidence.

'Where will you go?' he asked.

'Liza's got family down south. There's better work there, better opportunity for the lad. He'll be always under his brother's shadow if we stay here.'

'But now we know Ethan is innocent of murder—'

'But not innocent of raising his hand to the boss's son,' Dar reminded him. 'Ethan did wrong, no matter how you look at it. There's nowt I can do to change what's past and gone, but I've still got to think of the young'uns and the future they might have.'

Fielding drank the rest of his tea and emptied the dregs on to the grass. 'Mr Johnstone might want to speak with you,' he said. 'He's no longer an inspector. Ill-health has forced him to retire from the force.'

'Then what brings him here?' Dar asked.

It was, Fielding was beginning to think, a very relevant question. Perhaps in future, he thought, he should restrain the kind of impulses that had led to him writing to Henry Johnstone. Though it was a little late to be worrying about that now.

# NINE

'Tomorrow we get constables out searching for that petrol can,' Mickey told Tibbs. 'Though I doubt we'll find it. Whoever took it will most likely have weighted it down and tossed it into the dock.'

'You think George Tullis is telling the truth?' Tibbs asked. 'They could simply have taken it with them and the witness not seen it.' He paused. 'You know if this comes to court that our witness, Betty Moran, will be seen as unreliable, due to her profession.'

'I'm aware of that,' Mickey said 'and I'm sanguine about it. We must look for other evidence to prove what young Georgie is telling us and what the others are not. But that's not my major concern for now. Who killed that chap in the warehouse is of much greater concern.'

'The boys still committed arson. You really think they had nothing to do with the murder?'

'With a fair level of certainty, yes. You got little from the others?'

Tibbs shrugged. 'Confronted with what George Tullis had confessed, Mal Eagen admitted to being there and finally to setting the fire as a prank. He denied anyone having paid them to do it and denied absolutely having anything to do with either the murder or the other fires.'

'And again, I'm inclined to believe that,' Mickey said. 'The previous arson was a professional job. So professional that the insurance investigators have found in one case that it's impossible to prove anything more than an accident, and in another that faulty wiring was the cause. Both the investigators for the insurance company and the fire brigade believe arson to have been the cause of the third but neither can prove it. The fire in all cases had a single origin, and though accelerant is suspected, the quantity used must have been small enough to have spread the fire without leaving sufficient residue to leave evidence. The third fire is still under investigation, but in the end the insurer will probably have to pay. This instance, on the other hand, was three boys playing silly buggers and no more than that. They may well have been paid to do the job, and if so then their employer is going to be far from satisfied by the outcome. They'll deserve and get a few weeks in clink and the youngest will be sent to a hearing at Toynbee Hall and might do a stretch in a remand home, or in an industrial school, which might do him more good than harm. Though it's likely he'll be released to his parents' care until the other two have had their day in court and sentencing has been carried out. What Georgie gets will depend in part on what comes up in their cases. Of course, none of this will take account of the petty thievery and the raiding of gas meters that they've entertained themselves with these past months, and which fall outside our present investigation. They are bad boys, but I hope not irredeemable. The murder – that is something else, I think.'

He clapped Tibbs on the back. 'Time to be getting home,' he said. 'The three of them are safely locked away for the night and we'll see if any of them are more prepared to talk after a night in the cells.'

'Safer here than if they were still walking the streets,' Tibbs said. 'As you say, whoever employed them for the arson attack isn't going to be happy, and the community they've been upsetting will be unhappier still.'

'If their families have any sense, they'll send them off somewhere for a while once they are released from His Majesty's custody,' Mickey agreed. 'Better still if employment can be found for them elsewhere. A stint of hard work would straighten them out.'

But he was right, Mickey thought as he headed for home, the three boys had drawn the wrong kind of attention to themselves even before this latest incident. The Reynaldi boy in particular fancied he had the makings of a hard man, which was ironic since it was the Eagen boy that had a history to support that. The Reynaldis, according to Mickey's enquiries, were a law-abiding, hard-working second-generation immigrant family, deeply upset by their son's shenanigans. Young

George Tullis had a much older brother who'd tried his hand at thieving and housebreaking and been put away for both at one time or another. It was possible that young George, now of an employable age, had decided this might be an easier option than a twelve-hour shift in a factory or attempting to make a living on the boats. He was a skinny little eel of a boy, Mickey thought, with not enough bulk on him to get a job loading cargo or in any of the other manual trades. There were rumours that the gang his brother had run with had made use of the boy when he was younger. Posting him into houses through pantry windows so he could unlock the doors for them, but his brother had denied that and George's mother had, until now, made certain her young son was never interviewed by sending him off to stay with unspecified relatives. If she'd got any sense, she'd do the same thing after this escapade.

So, if the three boys had not killed the mystery man, then who had, and how had he ended up in the warehouse? That was the crux of the matter.

And there was, Mickey thought, an ancillary set of questions. Had someone paid the boys to set the fire? If so, who had that been? And the final one, had their employer anything to do with the murdered man?

# TEN

It was six days since Malina had brought Dr Fielding's letter to Henry, and the second since they had set out from home. Malina had wanted to stop another night on the way, and had suggested Lincoln, it being close enough to make the final miles easy. They could telephone or telegraph Dr Fielding about their delay. Henry would have none of it, however. He was in a lot of pain, but he was also impatient to reach their destination and, she realized, the thought of another day's travelling was beyond bearing. So it was that they arrived at Dr Fielding's at seven on the Thursday evening.

Fielding himself was affable and seemed, she thought, genuinely glad to see Henry again. He assured them that supper would be ready as soon as they'd had time to refresh themselves after their journey. The young daily maid had taken Henry's luggage up to his room and had now returned for Malina's. She could see that the girl was eager to be off, and guessed she'd normally have left for home by now. Guests could be a nuisance when you had your routine, Malina thought.

Fielding had called for the housekeeper to come and meet his guests and to confirm that supper was imminent. Mrs Fredericks bustled through from the back of the house, chiding Biddy, the maid, for taking too long with her task. Indirectly chiding the doctor too, Malina noted, as she told Biddy that she ought to be off as soon as she'd finished with the luggage as her mother would be worried. For that, Malina silently applauded her, but some instinct also caused her to hang back as Fielding made the introductions.

'This is Mr Johnstone. I've spoken about him, I'm sure, on several occasions.'

'Indeed, sir, you have.'

'And this is Miss Beaney, Mr Johnstone's fiancée. She's been kind enough to drive him all this way.'

Malina caught the slight frown that crossed the woman's

face. Mrs Fredericks turned towards her and the frown deepened. 'Miss Beaney, is it?' she said.

'It is,' Malina agreed. She returned the woman's look steadily, noting the housekeeper's examination of her smart jacket and expensive shoes and bag – the latter being one that Cynthia had bought with great enthusiasm and then decided she could not abide. Malina had benefited from her change of mind.

'I must get back to my kitchen,' Mrs Fredericks said and bustled off.

Let's just hope she doesn't decide to spit in the soup, Malina thought. She had recognized the woman's look.

She took a few minutes to change her dress and renew her lipstick, looking at the deep bath with some regret. The drive had been long, and Henry's obvious discomfort had made it longer still. But, if by some miracle he decided he wanted to go back home right now, Malina would not have objected.

Leaving her room, she knocked gently on Henry's door, worried in case he'd slumped down on the bed and fallen asleep. He told her he was almost ready, so she stood on the broad landing and waited for him. This was not a big house; she guessed perhaps four bedrooms and a second small bathroom that she had been told by Biddy was for her use alone. She appreciated the thought. It was, however, luxurious – two bathrooms, for a start – and well-furnished, and she guessed that Fielding had money in addition to whatever he earned as a general practitioner. The pay for that job was dependent on long hours and wealthy patients of whom, she supposed, there would be plenty around here. She'd noticed a number of substantial houses and farms, but from what Henry had said, Fielding was also involved in other activities. He acted as police surgeon, carrying out post-mortems on occasion – which was how he and Henry had met – and he seemed to know the inhabitants of the local villages well enough for Malina to assume he was also involved in their care, from time to time. On the whole, Malina was inclined to like him.

She was about to knock once more on Henry's door, to see if he needed help getting his shirtsleeve over his injured arm. She knew that in the house of a relative stranger, he'd be resistant to her coming into his room. Henry had an old-fashioned concern for her reputation, but he'd accept her help if he was really struggling.

She was halted by the sound of voices from the hall below. Malina leaned over the railing of the mezzanine landing and peered down. The speakers were beneath her, out of sight and speaking in hushed but impatient tones. She recognized Fielding's voice and that of the housekeeper. Both sounded angry.

'She's a guest in my house and you'll be satisfied with that,' Fielding was saying.

'And you've no right to expect me to wait hand and foot on one of her kind.'

'I have that right, as your employer. Now, enough, woman, unless you want to be looking for another job. More of this, Mrs Fredericks, and you'll be out on your ear by morning.'

Henry's door opened and Malina heard the housekeeper walk quickly away, the kitchen door slam.

'Ready?' Henry asked her.

Malina fought to hide her discomfort. 'Ready.' She eyed him critically. 'You look exhausted.'

They made their way downstairs and were greeted by Fielding in the hall. He led them through to a small but elegant dining room. It was wood panelled and cheerfully lit, with heavy chenille curtains that looked as old as the house hanging at the large window. It was still light enough for Malina to see out into the pretty walled garden. She commented on it, noting the espaliered fruit trees against the wall.

'A little hobby of mine,' he said. 'This was my father's house; he moved here when he was widowed and seemed to find great solace in the garden. I've done my best to keep it up.'

Mrs Fredericks arrived with a steaming terrine and set it on the table. The sideboard was already loaded with covered dishes, kept warm on chafing stands. 'I've told Mrs Fredericks that we'll serve ourselves,' Fielding said, 'so Mrs Fredericks can retire for the evening. Don't worry, Mrs Fredericks, I can manage to put the leftovers in the pantry and cover them down. You can clear the rest before breakfast in the morning.'

'Very good, sir,' Mrs Fredericks said stiffly and left, closing the door firmly behind her.

Henry raised an eyebrow. 'I hope we've not put her out. I know we were a little later arriving than we intended.'

'Not at all,' Fielding reassured him. He took the lid off the tureen and lifted the ladle. The soup, Brown Windsor, by the look of it, smelt good, and Malina realized that she was hungry. There were warm rolls under a napkin and Fielding invited his guests to help themselves. At least, Malina thought, Mrs Fredericks was less likely to have despoiled her soup if she knew her employer would be eating from the same dish.

Later, lying in her very comfortable bed, Malina reflected on the evening. It had been quite some time since she had met the out-and-out prejudice Mrs Fredericks had displayed – and on first meeting. Because she now lived in Cynthia's house, had the title of Cynthia's secretary, that was what most people took account of. Her unusual name – Malina Beaney – might be commented on, but Cynthia's money and status shielded her in ways Malina had almost come to take for granted. Like Cynthia, Malina had had to make her own way in the world from the time she was little more than a child. She had resisted the convention of early marriage and security, and left her family, gone to London, found a job, taken evening classes in typing and shorthand, lived in a women's hostel until Cynthia had come so fortuitously into her life. Until Cynthia, having received an urgent call for help from her brother, had undoubtedly saved Malina's life.

Cynthia's friendship, her employment, her genuine happiness that Malina and Henry had finally become engaged were joyful things, and Malina never stopped telling herself how lucky she was. She never forgot her family or her wider kin either, and Cynthia and her daughter, Melissa – the boys being away at school – had been welcomed at family events, both at the permanent encampment where Malina had spent several years, and at the stopping places where, at certain times of the year, Malina knew she could meet up with more distant family members.

She was very close to her brother, Kem, who worked as a boatman, ferrying cargoes down the Thames and the Medway and around the Kent coast. Kem hadn't married either, though she guessed his reasons might be different to hers. Malina's mother had married out of their community, not realizing at the time that her husband was not quite what he seemed. It wasn't his habitual criminality that was the problem, more the people he later got himself mixed up with and then people he crossed.

Most painful in their wealth of shared memories was that freezing night when those men had come to their little cottage, banging on the door and then tramping over the clean floors in their heavy, muddy boots.

'We had to kill your husband,' they had told Malina's mother. 'But the boss says you're free to go, provided you get far away and never come back.'

They had been given money, taken to a station, told to board a train, but Malina's mother had other ideas. Malina and Kem both had vivid memories of the long walk that night, through the sleeping town, out into the cold and exposure of the countryside, arriving at the encampment in the wee small hours. Her mother's appeal for help.

They'd been taken in – of course they had – and life had, for a time, become more settled, though her restlessness, her desire for something more and different had eventually taken her away.

She turned on her side. The sheets were smooth linen, washed soft and well-pressed, so that here and there she could feel the ironed-in folds beneath her fingers. She felt at home in Cynthia's house; she felt needed and wanted and useful. She was content to move to Henry's more modest apartment when they were married – it was only a short walk from Cynthia's house – and they had all agreed that she would continue with her role as Cynthia's secretary and assistant. Albert's too, really. And as Henry ate dinner at Cynthia's at least three or four times a week, the only real change to her life would be where she slept and where she spent her other evenings. That's if Henry continued with his work as a private investigator, of course. If he didn't get bored and search around for some other distraction.

Being here though, in this house, with Mrs Fredericks no

doubt fretting in her quarters somewhere below, Malina felt restless, ill at ease, despite the linen sheets and the scent of the garden drifting in through the open window.

She got out of bed and stared down into the garden. 'I want to go home,' she said aloud. 'I hope to God we're soon done with this.'

# ELEVEN

Mickey Hitchens and Sergeant Tibbs returned to the warehouse that Friday morning and Mickey set several constables to search for the petrol can – though without much hope of finding it. Mickey was likely correct and it was by now at the bottom of the dock.

He was curious also about the man with the pushcart loaded with chimney sweeps' brushes that George Tullis claimed to have spotted. It seemed like a strange time for a sweep to be out and about his business. He had asked his informant, Betty Moran, if she knew who the sweep might be and where he might be found, but it seemed she'd not even seen him.

Tibbs was right when he said that Betty would not make a good showing in the witness box. Not even if Mickey got Belle involved in scrubbing the heavy make-up from her face and dressing her like a respectable lady. Betty had too many convictions against her name for that to stick. The fact that her information, alongside the complaints that had already come to the attention of the local constabulary, had led them to the three youngsters would count for something, as would George's confession, but Mickey would like something firmer – and preferably something that went some way towards explaining the dead man.

Constable Higgs came over to speak to him and Mickey automatically looked for the younger officer who had accompanied him the day before. Higgs interpreted his look. 'Leonard didn't come into work, Inspector. He was mad as . . . not best pleased by what you said to him. Vowed he was set on leaving.'

'Well, if that's his mind,' Mickey said, 'it might be as well he finds his path elsewhere.'

'He's no worse than most,' Higgs said, but Mickey felt that his protest was half-hearted and more for form's sake than because he really cared.

'I've been asking about the sweep,' Higgs continued. 'Seems it might be a man by the name of Hezekiah Jenkins. The landlord at The Maid reckons he's not been about for a while, but that he comes and goes and turns up unexpected like, from time to time. Chimney sweep is just one of his occupations. He sharpens knives and mends whatever needs mending. Old soldier,' he added, looking meaningfully at Mickey. 'Still wears his army greatcoat. I believe that Inspector Johnstone might have been acquainted with him.'

Vague bells rang in Mickey's head. Although he had worked intimately with Henry for many years, the two of them had also been in the habit of cultivating a separate set of informants, some of whom were known to the other, some who were not. Both took the protection and confidentiality of such information-gatherers very seriously, and Henry had some intelligencers dating back to when he had still been in uniform before the war. It was possible that Hezekiah Jenkins, a name Mickey was certain he had heard, was among them.

'And where might I find this Mr Jenkins?' he asked.

'That I don't know, and neither did the landlord. I'll ask around, but the landlord at The Maid said that Jenkins is a man who appears and disappears according to his own whims and on his own terms. If someone comes looking for him, he's as likely to disappear as not.'

Mickey thanked him. He must speak to Henry, he thought.

Tibbs, he noticed, had wandered back into the yard behind the warehouse and Mickey joined him. 'What are you thinking?'

Tibbs mounted the steps up on to the loading bay so he could see through the warehouse doors and back into the yard. He pointed across to where the fire had been set. 'The boys came in through the little side door over there, set the fire, left the same way. Our witness, Betty Moran, saw them enter and leave and estimates they were inside for perhaps ten minutes. That would be enough to make a pile of timber and old sacking, spread the petrol around and light the fire.' He paused. 'They're lucky not to have been burned – it was a really stupid thing to do.'

Mickey nodded agreement.

'We know that this main door was supposed to have been padlocked. But the fire brigade had no trouble getting in when they arrived, and there's no mention of them breaking locks to do so.'

'No mention of the small side door being locked either. There's a bolt on the inside, but if the boys came in that way then you can bet it wasn't shot.'

'No, so someone must have made life easy for them by leaving the door unbolted. We know the vagrants who slept in the front offices got in through a broken panel in the front door, but they seem to have remained in the office space where I suppose it's more comfortable. The door between the warehouse and the offices is locked and the lock doesn't seem to have been interfered with.'

'So, the lads came in and left the same way. Why leave the loading bay doors undone?' Mickey said.

'Unless someone wanted to gain entry in order to take advantage of the fire.' Tibbs shrugged awkwardly. 'I know that sounds improbable, but it occurs to me that someone could have waited for the boys to leave and then come in through the loading bay doors . . .'

'Deposited a body and left again?'

Tibbs frowned. 'I know it sounds improbable, but if you accept that the boys did not kill our man, that his body was not there when they came to set the fire – and they'd hardly have missed it; there's a clear view all across the area – then there is a small space in which he could have arrived, been assaulted, set on fire and left to die.'

Mickey could not fault the logic of that. 'Why not simply push him into the dock?' Mickey felt the need to play devil's advocate.

Tibbs smiled. 'You know as well as I do. Bodies have an awkward tendency to float, and even well-weighted bodies tend to catch on anchors or propellers and be discovered that way. A body destroyed and an identity obliterated in a fire – well, that's another thing entirely. Most people assume that a body in a fire will be utterly destroyed. That all evidence will be gone. Our killer was unlucky in what happened here, the alarm being raised, the fire put out; but even if the fire had taken hold, there might have been evidence remaining that he couldn't guess at. Even hot fires fail to burn teeth.'

'True,' Mickey agreed. He remembered a case from several years back when a fire had been set to conceal a strangulation. The body had been badly disfigured, but the marks of the ligature could still be made out on the neck of the victim. There had been another occasion when the jawbone had been charred to the point of fragility, but the teeth had remained. The police surgeon, realizing the value of the evidence, had taken time to mark and draw and label each tooth in situ so that even if the jawbone had disintegrated before it arrived at the mortuary, the body might possibly be matched to dental records.

'My betting is he was killed here,' Mickey said. 'It would be easier to get a man into the building walking on his own two feet than it would be carrying a body across the yard and up the steps.'

'Whoever did the killing had cold bones,' Tibbs said. 'To strike a man down, stab him, then set him ablaze, probably knowing he still lived.'

Mickey nodded. He liked the description. Somehow it was more solid than mere cold blood. 'That,' he said, 'would indeed take cold bones.'

They returned to Scotland Yard with no sign of the petrol can and with more questions for the three boys. Who had paid them, how had that transaction taken place, and had they been told where to set the fire and perhaps to leave the petrol can behind?

Dan Trotter had been desperate for news. He had bought every paper he could find that might have a report of the fire, taking care to buy his news at different stands and newsagents so as not to look suspicious when he collected all the papers. There were stories about the fire and about the murdered man – not yet identified – and reports that three boys had been held for questioning about the fire, but little information that Dan did not already have. He tried to work out what the police did not yet know. There was no mention of anyone having seen him leaving with the petrol can, nothing about the woman who'd shouted after him. Did that mean that the police were not aware of her? How likely was it that a woman as low as she was would voluntarily speak to the police?

But what, he thought suddenly, if a reward was offered? The police and the insurance companies often offered a reward for witnesses, didn't they? The idea grew in Dan's head until it was overwhelming. She might come forward if there was a reward.

His housekeeper bustled in to collect his supper plates and bring his coffee. Mrs Mead was the only member of staff employed these days. She still lived in, cooked breakfast and the evening meal, kept the rooms Dan still used tidy and the rest covered down with dust sheets but, as he was now the sole occupant of this over-large house, there was no need of other staff. It had crossed his mind lately that he could sell this house – even though that would mean losing his beloved garden. He could buy somewhere small, out of town, perhaps with an even bigger garden. But that would have meant Mrs Mead losing her place and her home and he worried about that. She, alone, had always been kind to him. Never made fun of his struggles. He would have to ensure she was fairly dealt with before he went anywhere.

'You've not eaten your supper, Master Dan. Are you not well?'

He would always be Master Dan to her, he thought, even now he was officially master of the house and should have been Mr Trotter. No, that would have just sounded foolish. He could never fill his father's shoes. 'I just didn't feel hungry. Perhaps cover it down and if I want it later, I can warm it through.'

'Right you are,' she said. 'I'll set the plate on top of a saucepan of water. You can just let the water simmer for a while and that should serve.'

'Thank you, Mrs Mead.'

She set the coffee down and glanced at the paper he had been reading. 'That's a bad business,' she said. 'Some poor soul losing his life to violence.' She clucked her tongue disapprovingly and then left him to his coffee. She always brought him biscuits, always had, even when she'd had to sneak them to him in her apron pockets. Now he could have eaten all the biscuits he liked, but the three on the little plate next to the coffee pot suited him admirably. It was, as Mrs Mead would say, sufficient for a treat.

What to do? Dan thought. The woman had seen him, the woman would know what he'd done. Perhaps she would even know who he was. He took a deep and quavering breath, and told himself sternly: Dan Trotter, you've done it once, you can do it again. He had no hatred or anger towards this unfortunate woman, but she would have to go. She surely would.

# TWELVE

They had arrived at Helen Church's cottage just after nine on Friday morning, as Fielding had arranged. Helen opened the door wide when she saw the car pull up. She was surprised to see that it was a woman driving; slender, dark-haired, in a smart blue summer dress with fluttering sleeves.

She was even more surprised to see that ex-Inspector Johnstone was in need of help to get out of the car. She stood aside as he made his slow way up the path and into the cottage. The woman, she noted, greeted her with a friendly nod.

Henry made the introductions. Miss Malina Beaney, Helen thought. That sounded like a Romani name.

She couldn't help herself. She stared at Henry. 'You look old,' she told him. 'Old and broken.' In truth, she was shocked by his appearance, by the weight he put on the stout walking stick, the lines of pain on his pale face.

And she didn't know what to make of the woman who stood close by, her face calm and almost unreadable, though she was unable to conceal the anxiety as she watched this man. The anxiety, or the love.

That shook Helen. Who could possibly love this man? 'What happened to you?' she asked sharply.

Henry Johnstone, no longer Inspector Johnstone, managed a faint smile. 'My life got complicated,' he said.

'You'd best sit down before you fall down,' she told him. She could see him bristle at the suggestion of weakness, caught a glimpse of the man she had encountered almost four years earlier, but it was just a flash. He took the seat she offered, the woman with him came to stand closer, and when Helen brought her a chair she seated herself as well.

'You'd like some tea, Miss Beaney?'

'Thank you, Mrs Church. I'd like that very much.'

Church, Helen thought, as she so often did. By rights she

should have been Helen Samuels. By rights none of this bloody mess would have happened.

'Malina,' she said, looking at the woman more closely. 'That's a Gypsy name.'

The woman nodded. 'My people are from Kent. Most of them on the boats now, though some still travel.'

'What are you doing with the likes of him?' Helen demanded. She knew she sounded rude, but the woman just laughed and, echoing Henry Johnstone's earlier reply, she said, 'Sometimes life really does get complicated.'

Frowning, Helen turned away and set the already half-boiled kettle on the stand close by the fire. She stroked her belly as the child inside of her flipped and turned. Like a little fish, she thought, this baby was more active than her firstborn had been. This was Frank's child; her first had been Ethan's and Frank had known that. To give credit where it was due, he'd been a good father, and little Sam had loved him. He'd not even said a word when, though Samuel was the child's second name, the first being Charlie, she'd always called him Sam. That must have hurt him, she knew, echoing as it did her lover's family name. She knew now that it was guilt that had led to his acquiescence.

The kettle had begun to steam, and she realized belatedly that she had been ignoring the others in the room – she could not think of them as guests; that was a word that implied her welcome. She poured water on the tea, stirred the pot.

'So why are you here?'

He had been staring into the fire. He looked up now, and for a brief instant she was reminded of the man she had met when he had come to arrest Ethan. The man with eyes as hard and grey as river pebbles, who had run, broadcloth coat flapping behind him like crows' wings, keeping pace with the bloodhound pack as they had followed Ethan's trail. He had, she'd been told, kept pace with the dogs with less effort than it had cost their handler.

They had not found Ethan, he'd been far away by then, but she still cursed the man for trying.

'Why are you here?' she asked him again.

He nodded as though aware of all that was going through

her head and that he somehow agreed to her remembering it. 'I had word from Doctor Fielding that Frank Church had made a deathbed confession. That Ethan Samuels had not, after all, struck the blow that killed Robert Hanson. Though,' he added, 'it still seems that Samuels beat him senseless before Frank Church decided to finish the job. Ethan Samuels may not be guilty of murder, but of violence with intent to kill, perhaps.'

'So, you'd still string him up?'

'No, I'd find him and hear his story. Then let the judge decide. He'd no doubt be imprisoned, but he'd not hang; not on the evidence we now have from your husband's confession.'

Helen stared at him. 'What makes you so bloody vindictive?' she said. 'I've lost Ethan, God keep him wherever he's fetched up. Now I've lost Frank and I've a child to look after and another on the way. And you come up here, sit in my kitchen and tell me that you now plan to start the hunt for Ethan again because it's fine now, he won't hang, he'll just be locked away for years?'

Henry Johnstone opened his mouth as though to speak, then shut it again. It was the woman who spoke, her voice soft but confident, as though she was used to speaking out and used to being heard. 'I did put the same argument to you before we left,' Malina said.

'I wish to see justice done.'

'Justice for whom?' Malina asked quietly. 'For the dead man, Robert Hanson? For his family? Robert Hanson is long past caring and his family now know that his killer is also dead and, if you believe in that sort of thing, facing God's judgement.'

'And do you believe . . . that sort of thing?' Helen asked. She found, somewhat to her own surprise, that she was challenging Malina rather than Henry.

The woman appeared to consider for a moment and then she said, 'Not generally, no. Most of the time it's my opinion that God turns a blind eye or is perhaps too busy amusing himself elsewhere. Not that I'd tell my mammy or my aunties that,' she added. 'They still see fit to speak to him in church every Sunday.'

Helen studied the woman, wondering if she was being mocked, but she saw no trace of that in Malina's face.

'And so, your man here, he sees himself as purveyor of justice in God's absence, does he?'

Malina looked mildly surprised but then said, 'Perhaps he does. All I know is, when once he's set on a course, a London bus crashing into the side of him wouldn't divert him from it. He plans to search for Ethan Samuels and clear his name of the murder charge. I'm not sure he's thought beyond that yet.'

Helen looked at Henry, who was doing his best to scowl angrily at Malina and not making a good fist of it. Helen shook her head. 'You should get on and marry her before she gets a better offer,' she told him.

'If you have quite finished,' Henry's voice broke in tetchily.

'I've not,' Helen told him. She turned her back, arranging teacups on a tray. She heard Malina get up from her chair and was somehow unsurprised when the other woman followed her to the table, carrying the teapot and stand. The sugar and the milk jug had already been set in place. Helen set down the tray and moved her hands to the small of her back. She ached, and the tension in her shoulders had not abated for days.

'Will you let me do this while you sit down?' Malina asked.

Helen nodded and took a seat beside the fire, poking at the logs before placing another in the embers. 'I'd wish to know he's safe,' she said reluctantly as Malina handed her a cup.

Malina nodded when the woman asked her if there was sufficient milk and told her no, she didn't want it sweet. Even since the morning sickness had passed, she'd found it hard to stomach sugar. Instead, she craved sharp and bitter things – something her mother saw as a bad sign. She'd taken to pretending to sugar her tea, just to keep her from fretting.

'Yes, I'd wish to know he's safe,' she said again, 'but beyond that it's best left alone. I know full well what he did and why he did it. Ethan couldn't bear to see any man treat his beast the way Robert Hanson treated his.'

'It was more than rage over a horse, though, wasn't it? From what I hear it was also rage over Robert Hanson's jibes and threats,' Henry said.

'And who told you that?' Helen demanded.

'As a matter of fact, it was his father. Elijah Hanson was under no illusions about the kind of man his son was. Had they simply come to blows, matters might have been different. But Ethan Samuels beat him hard and did not cease even when the man lay helpless.'

'You do not know that,' Helen told him. 'No one but Robert Hanson, Ethan and Frank knew what happened that day. And Frank has confessed to the killing. The most Ethan did was—'

'Beat seven shades out of a drunken man.'

Henry held her gaze now, and something of that adversary she so hated was still present in that gaze. 'No,' she said firmly. 'Ethan would have stopped when he believed the man had learned his lesson. Robert Hanson fell from his horse and clouted his head on a stone. That was bad luck, nothing more. Ethan cannot be blamed for bad luck. He ran because he believed the fall from the horse had killed his boss's son, and that none would believe it was just an accident. Frank Church told him Robert was dead, and Ethan, fool that he was, believed him. Frank testified, on his deathbed, facing judgement, as he saw it, that Robert Hanson had been alive when Ethan ran. Knocked senseless, but that was all. It was Frank who kicked him in the head, again and again while he lay helpless on the ground. Who killed him stone dead. If Ethan is guilty of anything, it's of losing his temper and striking a man down.'

Helen glanced at Malina. She was sipping her tea, regarding them both with what looked like wary interest, as though not sure how this would play out and ready to intervene. Was it her role to keep this irascible man out of trouble? Helen wondered. Last time he had come, that task of ameliorating the situation had fallen to the shorter, sturdier man who had accompanied him. 'What happened to that sergeant of yours? He at least managed to do his job without all and sundry loathing him.'

There was a twitch of a smile as Henry replied. 'Sergeant Mickey Hitchens is now Inspector Hitchens,' he said, 'with a sergeant of his own to train. I left the police force shortly after his promotion.'

'Because no one else would put up with you?'

'That was one of many reasons,' he agreed. 'Mrs Church, believe me when I say I have no malicious intent towards Ethan Samuels, but surely you'd rather he did not spend the rest of his life on the run.'

'Better that than caged.'

'He'll serve a prison sentence, that's true. But he has people to speak for him, including, perhaps, the victim's father and brother.'

'And you'd trust them to testify on his behalf if it came to it?'

'I will endeavour to persuade Elijah Hanson to give me his word.'

'Best get it in writing then,' Helen spat back.

He seemed to consider for a while and then nodded. 'If it eases your mind then I will try to do that. Do you know where he is? I'm told he's been in contact with you.'

For a moment she considered denying it, then sighed. In a small place like this, everyone would know about the letters, no matter how careful she was. Frank had known. So had Frank's mother, and she'd never been one for making any allowance, not where her daughter-in-law was concerned. So far as Mrs Church senior was concerned, her son should never have married a woman she regarded as no better than a whore.

'Two letters, and a postcard,' she said finally. 'Frank insisted I burn them.'

'And did you?'

'Of course not,' Malina said. 'How could she?'

Helen remained silent. She turned her head, staring into the flames of the open fire. The cooking fire was kept lit even in the warmth of summer. It made the room stuffy and sometimes unbearably hot, even with the doors and windows flung wide. But Helen was glad of its warmth just now, as Henry Johnstone had seemed to be earlier. 'He sent a postcard,' she said, 'from Lowestoft, further down the coast. In Norfolk. He sent that through the regular mail. It was sent to his parents but they let me have it. Frank did throw that into the fire.' She paused, remembering. She had never felt such rage, not with anyone, but as she had watched that little piece of card burn, she had hated her husband and with such a passion that it was as though everything she had ever felt for Ethan had been turned upside down. Inverted, converted into loathing for this man whose ring she now wore, whose bed she shared.

And now, whose child she carried. Helen laid a hand on her belly, feeling the child move and knowing that although Ethan was not the father, she would still love it and care for it as much as she loved and cared for Sam. The babies were the innocents in all this; she could have said no to Frank's offer, gone away somewhere, had her first child and . . . then whatever. She'd never thought that far. Instead, she'd agreed to marry him, knowing that although it would not still the wagging tongues, it would at least allow her to remain as a respectable member of her community.

The truth was Helen had been just seventeen. She'd been so scared and so desperate when she'd realized she was with child that she'd just been grateful for Frank's offer.

'And the letters,' Malina asked gently. 'Were they handed on?'

Helen glanced at Malina, intercepting Henry's questioning look at her turn of phrase. She nodded. 'There were two, that's all. The first took two weeks to get to me from when he wrote it and the second three months. But they got here, and I was glad of that.'

'They weren't posted?' Henry asked.

'No,' Malina said. 'Messages are often sent with those travelling in a particular direction. You ask, they carry the message on, then maybe pass it to someone else going closer to their destination. It can take time, but they rarely go astray.'

'I don't understand; we have a perfectly good postal service—'

'For people who have an address. You know how it is when I write to my brother. I send letters to the hostel or the Seamen's Mission he's likely to call at. Or to the hostel he uses in London, if I know that's where he'll be next. But for our family that still travels, this is the surest way. You know what stopping places they might use in a particular season, where they're most likely to get work picking or dealing, what fairs they might be at, so families help one another out by taking messages and news and sometimes parcels.'

Helen saw Henry nod. 'I hadn't thought about that,' he said.

'For a man supposed to be blessed with brains, it seems to me there's a lot you've not thought about,' Helen told him tartly.

His response surprised her. 'So I'm often told,' he said. 'Sometimes I even agree with the assessment. So, will you show me these letters?'

Helen shook her head. 'No, and you can't demand, not now you're not a policeman.'

He looked as though he might argue, but Malina stood and indicated that they would be taking their leave. Helen watched them from the window as they made their way back to the little blue car. Malina helped Henry Johnstone to get into the passenger side and then slid into the driving seat. It would be nice to be able to drive a car, Helen thought. To be able to point the car in any direction and just go, not ask for or wait for anyone's permission. Ted Hanson had been teaching his little sister how to drive. Their father wasn't keen, but from what Ted had told her, Elizabeth was finding it easy enough and Ted had convinced his father that it was a skill that would prove useful to the farm if Elizabeth could run errands further afield and more quickly than on horseback. As though Elizabeth did not already have enough responsibilities.

She got up and went up to the small bedroom she shared with her son. Little Sam had been asleep when the visitors called but he was rousing now. She lifted the rag rug beside her bed and, from a hidden pocket stitched into the backing, she withdrew the two precious letters and, for a moment, held them close to her heart before slipping them back into their hiding place. She didn't need to read them to know what had been written.

Sam was awake now, rubbing his eyes and smiling at her. He was a cheerful little soul. Up with the lark at five in the morning, he usually settled back to sleep for an hour a little before nine and allowed her time for working. She had set the time for the visit knowing that her son would not be a distraction.

As she returned with him to the kitchen to give him a drink and a piece of bread, she thought about that first letter, the words sorrowful but resigned.

*This place I fetched up in, it should have been a place for passing through, but some of us, we got caught like flies on honey paper and we stayed. For many of us, I suppose, exiled from home and anyone we cared for, this was as good a place as any to make our journey's end and anyway, a few months of this town's hardships and the strength to leave gets buried somewhere in the earth we mine.*

*To look at, Helen, this little village is like the place we grew up in. A valley with steep sides and the houses nestled at the bottom of it, but this is not a place of farms and hedges and growing fields. The hills are tree-covered in thick, scrubby growth and outcropping rocks, that showed the seams of coal and minerals that men took as a sign that they should dig down into the ground.*

*We don't plant the earth here, apart from the thin soil we've dug and sowed into gardens at the valley bottom, and where we grew a little fresh stuff to make our diet bearable and maybe keeping a run of chickens or an occasional pig, ready to be salted down come winter. These are things that remind me of home and family.*

*Here, my love, we cut our living from the earth. We dig deep into the hills and sometimes it seems, instead of ploughing the furrow and sowing with seed, we've ploughed great pits and passages and sowed them with live men.*

*I suppose we all fancy that our lot will improve in time. That our labour will bring rewards and the conditions of our lives improve. But it's the same the world over, isn't it? Those of us who do the work, who throw our labour into the deepest holes and shafts and dig the black gold, we're not the ones to benefit, any more than we did when we worked in the fields and with the cattle. But what else is there to do about it? We've washed up here, we've stuck ourselves to the fly paper, we lack the reason to move on and the rest of the world just goes marching by.*

Henry had noticed that Malina was very quiet after the visit. They drove back to Fielding's house in near silence and twice he asked her if something was wrong. It was only after they had returned and gone upstairs to refresh themselves before lunch that he asked again and she responded.

On the broad landing outside their rooms was a window seat set into the alcove where a large window looked out on to the countryside beyond. Malina took off her hat and sat down, patting the cushion beside her. Obediently Henry took his place. Her face seemed clouded and troubled, and he didn't like to see that. Malina was by nature a cheerful person, a problem-solver too; she would look at a situation and seek to resolve the issue. It was only when she could not that this expression of loss and solemnity appeared. He realized that it had been a long time since he'd seen such sadness in her eyes.

He took her hand, not sure what to do. Mickey had once told him that a gesture of affection and the patience to wait until a woman had her say usually sufficed. He remembered that Belle, Mickey's wife, had laughed at that, but Henry, at a loss for what else to do, held Malina's slender hand in both of his own and counselled himself to patience. He remembered another piece of advice, this from Belle. 'It doesn't hurt to ask if there's anything you can do,' she said. 'And even if there's not, sometimes you just have to sit and be present.' Once upon a time, Henry would have been baffled by such advice. He was a man who had to be doing, sorting, solving, organizing. But months of illness, of being grateful to wake from disturbed sleep and see Cynthia or Malina and, on occasion, Mickey sitting by his bedside had taught him the value of presence. Of knowing that another human being had the time and the concern to remain at his side. So he sat now and finally asked, 'Is there anything I can do?'

Malina sighed. 'I feel like a fish out of water,' she said eventually. 'Visiting Helen reminded me so much of where I come from, of the life I'd have lived if I hadn't decided I wanted more, and if chance hadn't brought Cynthia into it and then you. Here I am, dressed like a lady, engaged to a man whose sister gives me the run of her house, her friendship, her love, even—'

'Oh, Cynthia thinks very highly of you,' Henry told her. 'We all do.'

'And I'm a guest in the house of a man who, nice and well-meaning as he is, would probably make Helen Church and her family use the kitchen door, that's if he allowed them into his house at all. Mrs Fredericks certainly wouldn't. She sees the lot of us as thieves and dross.'

'Malina, you don't know that.'

'Yes, I do. Absolutely I do.'

Henry listened as she told him about the overheard conversation the evening before. The housekeeper's attitude and Fielding's response. At least, Henry thought, he had stood up for Malina, though she was probably also right in her assessment of Helen Church being made to use the tradesmen's entrance.

Henry had frequently encountered the same response to a policeman coming to call. He'd lost count of the number of times he'd been directed 'round the back', or the number of times he'd refused that order. But for the likes of Helen Church there could of course be no refusal.

'I'm sorry,' he said. 'We could leave, find ourselves a hotel for the rest of our stay.'

'No,' Malina told him. 'I would not want to offend Doctor Fielding. I understand the line he's treading and I'll not insult his hospitality. But, Henry, I'll be relieved to go home. I've lived long enough in Cynthia's and Albert's house, been accepted as a valued member of the team, I suppose, that I'd almost forgotten what it was to feel like an outsider. To be reviled.'

He leaned in and kissed her gently. Below them there was a sudden bustle in the hall and the gong was sounded to announce that lunch was ready. Malina took her hat to her room and they went down together to join Fielding, just back from his morning rounds.

Lunch was set out on the sideboard, much as breakfast had been and dinner the night before. Of Mrs Fredericks there was no sign.

# THIRTEEN

When Mickey and Tibbs returned to Scotland Yard, they made another brief attempt at interviewing the three miscreants who had set the fire.

It appeared to Mickey that the two older boys, Mal Eagen and Marcus Reynaldi, had reached that stage of being no longer frightened but now merely bored with the whole process, believing Mickey could do them no real harm. They seemed prepared to wait him out. George Tullis had insisted he had told them all he knew, and Mickey was inclined to believe him.

Tibbs was concerned, but Mickey counselled patience. 'Leave them alone,' he advised his sergeant. 'In the end boredom will turn to anxiety, once they start to be afraid of being forgotten.' Neither of their families had come forward to intervene; no legal representation had been offered or asked for. 'In time they'll crack open like a mussel does when it's cooked.'

Tibbs looked dubious. 'And if they don't?'

'In a few hours we'll hold up the possibility of release for their consideration,' Mickey told him. 'And remind them both that they'll be returning to streets frequented by those who thought they were such damned nuisances that they were prepared to give their names and location over to the police. To families who've been made to suffer their neighbours' anger because they couldn't control their boys, and to an area of London run by gang bosses who took a very dim view of them encroaching on their territory. If there's to be a warehouse fire, then it's those higher up the societal ladder who will organize it and who will take a cut of the insurance payout or whatever else might be forthcoming. None of those three youngsters is protected; none of them can claim membership of a gang or a cabal, not even by loose association, and whatever we do to them in here will be as nothing to what might happen to them out there. Eagen and Reynaldi both know that. Young George can easily be frightened into knowing it too.'

'We can't actually release them,' Tibbs pointed out. 'We've as good as got them on the arson charge with the information got from Georgie Tullis.'

'No, but we can hold out that possibility as though it might be possible. We have enough evidence to bring charges, maybe, and while we might be able to remand the other two quite swiftly, it's likely, due to his age, we'll be advised to bail Georgie to his family in the interim, until he's summoned before the court.'

'Pity we don't have a better eyewitness,' Tibbs said bitterly.

'We've got a solid enough witness in terms of information,' Mickey said. 'Trouble is, the law doesn't rate the word of prostitutes and street-walkers. No, we need our man with the pushcart.'

'The man with the sweeps' brushes? What makes him better?'

'If he's who I think he might be, then he's an old soldier, served Queen and country and has the medals to prove it. From the description I recognized that it might be a man called Hezekiah Jenkins, and the landlord at The Maid confirmed that. Henry used him as an informant from time to time. I'll need to contact Henry and find out how to get hold of the man. Henry used to leave him a message somewhere, I believe.'

'I'll organize a telegram,' Tibbs said.

'You do that. I'll write the message for you and then I'm going to take another look at our dead man's clothing, see if we can find some identifying marks.'

A few minutes later, Tibbs went off to deal with the telegram – Mickey had telephoned Cynthia for Fielding's address – and Mickey fetched out the brown-paper-wrapped parcels containing the murdered man's clothes. He had asked if they could be sent for more expert analysis to one of the professors who sometimes helped out with such stuff at the University of London but was told an unequivocal no. The calling in of expert witnesses was fraught with irritation and cost and should only be done when a result was likely to help in the courts. Mickey had not been surprised. It was often difficult to find anyone who could take the time out of their working day in order to do analysis on behalf of the police, and who would furthermore be willing to explain that analysis in court. Police and medical men grew used to the often aggressive interrogation they might meet in the adversarial setting of a courtroom, but other experts had little experience of such questioning, and Mickey had seen even experts at the top of their field fall apart in such circumstances.

So, he would take a leaf out of the 'Body in the Trunk' investigation from 1927, when Detective Sergeants Clarke and Burt had broken the case by their discovery of a burnt match, with a fleck of blood on the shaft and, more importantly, a check duster, dirty and bloodstained, which when washed through in the men's cloakroom, had revealed the name of the Greyhound Hotel, a piece of evidence that linked their suspect, Robinson, to the murder of Minnie Bonati, the woman in the trunk.

He took the dead man's shirt and washed it carefully in a bowl to which he had added a little soap to help break down the soot and blood. Then carefully examined the garment for labels and laundry marks that might help them identify the dead man.

The shirt, he noted, was of good-quality linen, well-worn and carefully mended here and there. Men often made holes in their shirt tails, in Mickey's experience, with too much enthusiasm when tucking in, and there was indeed a small darn close to the hem.

Two buttons, surviving presumably because they were tucked tightly behind the waistband of the trousers, had been replaced with two very like but not an exact match to the original. Both replacements were at the bottom of the row, as though the original buttons might have been moved to conceal the loss; these two were unlikely to be seen in the normal run of things. At some time the collar had been removed and turned, the old wear now hidden underneath when it was folded down. It had been expertly done, probably taken to one of the little shops or private seamstresses that did repairs and refurbishment and were to be found all over the East End.

The label, he was interested to find, was not original to the shirt, but a small tag bearing the word 'Josephs'. He wondered if this might be the name of the repairer. Something to set the constables to finding out. If the place could be found, then the shirt could be shown. It was possible they might know for whom the repair had been made.

Possible, but how likely? Mickey wondered. The turning of a collar must be a commonplace and popular repair adding considerable life to a shirt that was otherwise still sound.

He turned his attention to the hem, hoping for a laundry mark. Even those women who simply took in washing for their neighbours usually insisted on some distinguishing initial to be sewn in, just so that disputes could be avoided. He found it eventually on the wet fabric at the back hem. The front of the shirt was all fragile rags from the burning, but the back was remarkably intact and there, neatly stitched at the bottom curve of the hem, were the initials WP.

Tibbs had returned and come to find him. He looked astonished at his boss's antics until Mickey explained what he had discovered.

'That's if the initials are in fact his,' Tibbs said. 'If the shirt was bought second-hand, as so many of these things are, then the initials could have belonged to the previous owner.'

'True but unlikely,' Mickey said. 'Young Tibbs, tell me, what clothing are you most comfortable buying after someone else has worn it?'

'A coat, boots, a jacket.'

'And what would you rather have new?'

'Um, I'm not sure?'

'Underclothing and shirts. Socks too,' Mickey said. 'Shirts are cheaper than many other items of clothing and they wear less well than a jacket or a coat or even a pair of trousers. A shirt or three can be bought for very little money, so that and underclothing is what most will choose to buy new, if they can.'

Tibbs grinned. 'One to wear, one in the wash and one in reserve,' he said.

'Indeed, together with a few too old and shabby to be worn out of the house, kept for off-duty times when no one is looking. Besides why would you leave someone else's laundry mark on your clothing, when it is easy to remove and will save any trouble if the laundress refuses to believe that it is yours?'

Mickey squeezed out the excess water and then hung the shirt to dry on a hook behind the door to the men's toilets. It dripped on to the concrete, but he considered there was little to be done about that.

'You've sent the telegram?'

'I have.'

'Good, then let's hope Henry gets it swiftly and replies by return.'

# FOURTEEN

That afternoon Henry elected to rest for a time. His body still ached from the effects of the journey and he desperately needed to lie down. Malina had said she would go out for a while. He had expected she would walk, so he was surprised when he heard the car engine and, looking from the window, he saw her heading out of the gate.

A little puzzled, but too exhausted to trouble about it – she was entitled to take the car and perfectly capable of looking after herself – he lay back down on the bed and closed his eyes. He had hoped for more from Helen, but the more he thought about it, the more he realized that hope had always been a vain one. Of course she would not trust him with the letters. It had been hard for her even to admit that she had received any communication. He wondered how angry Frank Church would have been and he doubted Helen would have been able to keep the letters secret. In such a small community there were eyes and ears everywhere. In all likelihood, she had pretended to destroy them.

So, what now? His investigation had already stalled and he was uncertain where he might gain more intelligence regarding Ethan Samuels and where he might have gone. No one had found him three years before when he'd been wanted for murder and there had been bulletins with his description circulated to all ports and all police forces. So, what hope did Henry, acting practically alone, have of finding him now.

Malina had not really thought about where she might be going, but the day was bright and the countryside beautiful. The road wound through hills between high-hedged fields. She slowed her pace, noted elder, hawthorn, bramble, the last remnants of wild roses and the first black berries of sloe, not yet ready for picking. Occasional glimpses through farm gates or over the tops of lower hedges showed her a landscape that rolled and flowed, richly green or gold or furnished with sheep and cattle. There had been rain here for the week before their arrival, Fielding had told her, and the pasture was lush and verdant, though she doubted the rain had been welcomed by those trying to bring in their wheat harvest or the maincrop potatoes. She had childhood memories of working on the potato harvest with her mother and aunts and brother. It was considered easy, unskilled work, fit for the women and the young, but actually it was backbreaking. The men went along ahead, lifting the crop with wide-tined, blunted forks; the harvesters followed on behind, picking the potatoes from the soil, and tossing them into baskets ready to be sorted and weighed. She remembered the hours spent bending over the rows. If the weather had been dry, great clods of dried mud stuck to the crop and had to be broken free. If the weather had been wet, slick mud would coat everything: crop, basket, hands, feet, clothing.

Her bones ached with the memory of it. She would not willingly return to that life.

Malina was not entirely surprised when she reached the crossroads and read the sign for Thoresway. She turned right, heading down the hill, then, on impulse, she pulled the car on to the verge and got out. A little further on was a stile and – if she was not mistaken – a footpath that led into the field at the back of the cottages where Helen lived.

Malina crossed the stile and began to walk.

Malina let herself in through the garden gate, noting the well-tended rows of vegetables and the edging of chives and mint, thyme and marigolds against the path. She knocked at Helen's back door, thinking wryly that now she was the one to use the tradesmen's entrance. Helen's face appeared at the kitchen window, her look of puzzlement changing to one of surprise and then momentary hostility before resignation gained the upper hand and she opened the door. Malina stepped inside.

'I didn't hear the car. I don't see your man?'

'He needed rest, I parked the car close by the stile and walked down. I noticed the path this morning.'

Helen laughed. 'You don't miss much, do you?'

'It's best to know the lie of the land,' Malina said. 'You

never know when you might need to make a quick escape. I hoped we could talk.'

'He sent you here, did he? But no,' Helen decided, 'I don't think you get sent anywhere you don't want to go.'

'I try not to let that happen. I had enough of that as a child.'

Sam was sitting in a patch of sunlight playing with some carved wooden toys. He looked up and smiled at Malina and, curious, she went over to look at the wooden animals.

'These are lovely,' she said.

Helen nodded. 'Would you like some tea? Frank made them. Carved them with a pocketknife from bits of firewood. He was good at that kind of thing. And despite everything he loved Sam. Though he always called him Charlie. Charles Samuel, we agreed on, and I tried my best to call him Charlie.'

'And now?'

'Now I suppose he's Sam.' Helen shrugged. 'Nothing's ever simple, is it? I did try and be a good wife to Frank. He tried to be a good husband to me. He did manage to be a good father, even though he must always have known.'

'Children shouldn't be blamed for what their parents do,' Malina said firmly. 'Credit to him that he felt that was right, regardless of the rest.'

'Small credit considering what he'd done,' Helen said bitterly. 'But none of us came out of this exactly smelling of roses, did we?'

'Sometimes life forces us into corners,' Malina said.

A tall terracotta water-cooler stood on the table beside the window. Helen opened the spigot and filled the kettle. 'He brought this back one day from the market,' she said. 'Proud as punch he was. Said we could fill it up in a morning from the pump in the garden and I'd have water for the day. He got it cheap on account of the sprigs being crooked.' She pointed at the decoration of sheep and trees and Malina could see that one of the sheep must have slipped after it had been applied.

'It's still a fine-looking thing,' Malina said. 'Useful too. Men, in my experience, don't often do well with gifts.'

'Is *he* good with gifts?' Helen asked.

'No, but his niece and his sister are a dab hand and usually put him straight.'

'And his family accept you, do they?'

Malina nodded. 'They do.'

'Then I wish you happiness. It must be hard though, living amongst strangers.'

'I've been making my own way since I was fourteen,' Malina said. 'So, half my lifetime. Now it sometimes feels stranger to go back.'

'And you've never wed? You ain't widowed or anything?'

Malina shook her head.

'Seems odd to me,' Helen told her.

Helen's curiosity didn't surprise Malina. Amused, she got the sudden impression that Helen would have liked to ask her some more intimate questions, such as what she did for sex, seeing as she wasn't married. She decided to move the conversation on. 'What did the letters say?' she asked. 'Would you let me see them?'

She knew that she was being almost too direct, but Helen seemed to expect this of her now.

'Let me think about it,' Helen said. She wrapped a quilted cloth around the handle of the kettle and took it from the hook above the fire, warmed the pot and set the kettle on the trivet while she spooned the tea. 'I'm short on milk,' she said. 'Ma will bring me some later; she brings it over for Sam, mostly. You all right with it black?'

'So long as it's been brewed strong, I'll drink it any way it comes.'

'You want to sit outside?'

Malina nodded. She helped take Sam and his toys out into the garden, and a few minutes later they were settled on the bench by the back door. The sunshine slanted across the garden but the bench was in slight but welcome shade. Sam puttered down the garden path with a carved wooden horse in his hand, jumping it over his mother's flowers.

For a while they sat in an almost companionable silence, watching the child play, Malina enjoying the quiet and the sound of birds. That was the one thing she missed in the city. It was never quiet.

'Did he seem well when he wrote to you?' she asked at last.

Helen nodded. 'Well enough. Though he seemed sad. He regretted being so far from home, from all he knew. He said he'd fetched up with a crowd of others who had no place else to be. He said, he said he still loved me and wished he'd come to me, asked me to go along with him.'

'Did he say why he did not?'

Helen shrugged. 'He said he was afraid to take me away from everything and everyone I knew and cared about. That he was afraid he couldn't provide for me and feared that I'd be miserable.' She laughed. 'I've no doubt he believes that now; he's likely been telling that to himself for so long that it's come true.'

'But you don't believe him.'

'I don't think he's lying,' Helen said, 'just not telling the truth. He didn't come to me because he was running away and too scared to even think about that. I don't blame him,' she added. 'Mr Hanson would have had him before the magistrate and sentenced before he'd even had a chance to tell what happened. Who'd have listened to the likes of Ethan, especially with Frank as a witness? And what could he deny? He'd taken the riding crop off Robert and lashed him, just like he'd been lashing the poor beast. It was the drink that caused Robert to fall to the ground but it was Ethan's temper that led to it.'

'If Ethan hadn't run, Frank wouldn't have had the opportunity to kick Robert in the head,' Malina pointed out.

'Doesn't mean he might not have died. Doctor Fielding said he'd hit his head. He might just as easily have died from that. They'd have said Ethan had murderous intent or something – you just know they would.'

Malina drank the rest of her tea and watched little Sam gallop his horse up and down the path.

'You want kids?' Helen asked.

'I don't know. Perhaps. Henry is very close to his niece and nephews.'

Actually, that wasn't quite true. He cared deeply for all of them, but the boys had a love of cricket and adventure that Henry found hard to handle. Mickey Hitchens was a great favourite of both boys when they were home from school, playing cricket with them on the beach and teaching them to box. Before Henry had been so injured, that had been something he too could do with his nephews. A common point of interest that might have led to others, but even that door was closed to him now. His niece Melissa, with her bookishness and her passion for science, was a better fit, and they spent long hours browsing bookshops and in deep discussion about the latest scientific theories. Melissa had introduced both Mickey and her father to the joys of microscopy and, though Albert left the making up of slides to his far more capable daughter, he had even convinced the boys that this was something to indulge on a wet afternoon.

'I think he would make a good father,' she said. 'I'd have doubted that when I first got to know him, but life changes us all. It's changed him more than most.'

'Looks like life nearly broke him,' Helen said. 'Just as well he's not trying to survive in our world.'

'Almost,' Malina agreed. 'And it is. Will you show those letters to me?'

'You don't give up on a thing, do you?'

'No, I'm a persistent type.'

Helen laughed, then looked more seriously at Malina. After a moment she went inside, taking both tin mugs with her. Last time they had come, Malina remembered, she had given them tea in the bright Imari patterned cups that sat on a high shelf out of little Sam's reach. She was slyly pleased that this time Helen had chosen to give her an everyday cup. She had been uncertain at first if this was intended as an insult or as a gesture between equals. She was now inclining towards the latter.

Helen had left the still half-filled kettle on the trivet to keep hot. Malina heard her pour more water into the pot to refresh the tea. She smiled. So the meeting was not yet at an end. She heard the young woman go upstairs, her tread heavy and almost reluctant. Minutes passed and then she came back down, refilled their mugs and came back outside.

Malina thanked her, sipped at the hot tea. Helen set her own mug beside her on the bench and drew two envelopes from her apron pocket. 'I'll not let you take them away from here, but you can see them.'

'Thank you,' Malina said.

For a minute more, Helen sat with the letters in her hands, as though still doubting her decision. Malina sipped her tea and waited her out. She doubted Helen had shared these fully with anyone else. She might have told Ethan's family that she'd had news, that he was safe, but more than that?

'He liked to write,' Helen said at last. 'He actually liked school. Our teacher used to make us write stories. Ethan was good at that. He liked to use words, liked to make them dance to his tune.' Abruptly, she thrust the envelopes at Malina. 'Here,' she said. 'Sam needs me.'

Malina closed her hand on the letters and glanced towards the little boy. He was still focused on his play but wriggling now in the classic style of a small child that has a full bladder but is reluctant to interrupt their game. Helen opened the privy door and ushered her small son inside. Malina set down her cup and began to read.

She began with the first letter *This place I fetched up in, it should have been a place for passing through, but some of us, we got caught like flies on honey paper and we stayed.*

Then moved on to the second, reading quickly in case Helen should change her mind and take the letters from her.

*I wanted you right from that first moment, Helen love, and I knew, from the way you looked at me, that straight off you felt the same. I could no more have let you go or have stopped feeling the way I did than I could have taken a knife and stabbed you through the heart.*

*Keep away from her, my Dar told me. He had his reasons, but they were none of them good enough for me and, since you met up with me every which way and when you could, it seemed it weren't good enough for you either.*

*If I had to do it all again. If I could be put back then and know that all the time we'd have would be that summer, that few short weeks of loving and laughing and, yes, hiding from folk that disapproved, I'd do it all again. Even knowing the rest of my life might be spent away from you and all the others that I love.*

*I'd do whatever it took, love, to have you there for even that little time, warm and eager and so much wanting me, and if I must spend the rest of my life away from you, then let it be so. I had you, I knew you. I called you mine and I only wish now that I'd had the nerve to come to you that day when it all fell apart and asked you to be gone with me, to run away to wherever fortune took us, you and me.*

*But if I'd done that, would you always be wondering about the ones we left? About your mam and your dad and your brothers and all the others that had more claim on you than just a few weeks of loving could deserve.*

*You'd cherish the autumn here. One of the men who takes the samples from the ground tells me it's the minerals in the soil that make the birch and oak and elder turn so deep red and gold and canary yellow. The pines on the top ridge, in the forestry, they look black against the sky even on a summer's day, and in the autumn the fog takes them as it rolls down on to the valley floor, so even the blackness disappears into nothing. Sometimes it feels like this whole valley has been separated from the rest of the world, we're lost somehow, the whole world moving on without us.*

*The colours remind me of you; you had that same red gold, burnt into your black hair by the summer sun, shining against the dark. I remember that, the way it shone with the sun on it like you'd drawn the sunset right down into yourself and it had poured out through your hair.*

Later, when she had returned to her car, Malina took a notebook and pencil from her bag and began to write. She had always had a good memory for words, and Ethan's were easy to recall. In another place . . . in another world, she thought, Ethan could have made something of his skill with words, his evident intelligence, but then, so could Helen. Instead, they and their families were kept in their place by poverty, by the likes of Elijah Hanson and yes, even those akin to the essentially good-hearted Dr Fielding. Mrs Fredericks had a good position in his house, but her security and well-being were utterly dependent on her satisfying the domestic role Dr Fielding demanded of her. She, in turn, keenly felt her own superiority over the likes of the Samuels and the Churches and Malina herself. It must really rankle that Mrs Fredericks could not tell Malina directly that she was getting above herself, pretending to be so much more than she really was.

But then, Malina had never really been one for knowing her place and, she acknowledged, she'd been lucky in where that had taken her. She could just as easily have taken a tumble from which she'd have never recovered. She paused in her note-taking and looked at the small square sapphire on her left hand. It was a pretty thing, not large or ostentatious but of a colour that reminded her of evening skies in summer and, somewhat surprisingly, Henry had chosen it himself.

Malina's mother had always taught her to be mistrustful of men. Marrying had done nothing to improve her life; apart from the birth of her two children, she had definitely nothing to show for it. After Malina's father had been killed, her mother had been sought out by several who would have been step-father, but her mother would have none of it. Malina and Kem had largely grown up in the company of woman – aunties, grandmothers, those vaguely designated as cousins – and she felt she had probably benefited from that.

Neither she nor Kem had contemplated marriage, and she was aware of just how unusual that was. Until she had met Henry and a friendship had grown between them that had slowly but surely developed into something more.

She glanced at her watch. It was after four, time to be going. She turned the car in the lane and headed for Dr Fielding's house. As she crested the first rise, the sun disappeared behind fast-gathering clouds. Thunder heads massed on the horizon. There would be a storm.

Henry was waiting for her when she returned, sitting on the window seat on the landing and looking down into the garden as the raindrops splattered hard against the window. He must have heard the car, she thought. He smiled at her as she shook the droplets from her hat.

'How was your afternoon?'

'Useful, I think. Yours?'

'I read through Mickey's file and then fell asleep.'

'You needed the rest.' She sat down beside him and took out her notebook. 'I went to see Helen Church.'

'I thought you must have done. What did she say?'

'She let me read the letters. When I left, I sat in the car and wrote down all I could remember. That young man has a poetic turn of phrase, I'm not surprised he turned her head.'

'I'm not good at poetry,' Henry joked.

'Just as well. I'm not inclined to have my head turned. I'd as soon face life straight on.' She handed him the notebook. 'You read while I get changed. I got wet just coming from the car.'

She left him reading, the memory of Ethan's words echoing in her mind.

Was there anything there that would help them find him? she wondered. And was that even the best plan, if they could?

# FIFTEEN

A telegram had arrived for Henry late on the Friday afternoon. Mrs Fredericks had taken it upon herself not to give it to him immediately and so, much to Henry's annoyance, he'd not had the opportunity to send a message by return with the delivery man. She gave it to him only when dinner was being served.

Mrs Fredericks had been miffed that Henry had seemed put out. 'I thought you'd gone off in the car, sir,' she had told him indignantly. 'I thought there was no one home but me and Biddy.'

So, she'd not even come to knock on his door. Henry was furious but, for the sake of peace, Malina persuaded him to let it go. There was nothing to be gained by creating a scene. He was desperately curious as to why Mickey would want to find Hezekiah Jenkins and tried telephoning Scotland Yard, but was told that Inspector Hitchens had already left. For now, Henry would have to wait.

'So, what now?' Dr Fielding asked as they sat in the parlour after dinner.

Henry accepted the offer of more coffee and leaned back in his chair. 'I think we go and speak to the Hansons in the morning and perhaps the Samuelses. It's possible they know more than they think about where Ethan might have gone. We know that Helen received letters from him, passed hand to hand; it's possible that those who brought them would have some clue as to their origin.'

'You'd need to find them first,' Fielding pointed out. 'And you'd have to assume they told their right names. These Gypsy types, they change their names as frequently as the rest of us change our socks.'

Henry flinched and glanced at Malina. She sipped her coffee, her face expressionless. Fielding realized what he had said. 'No offence meant, my dear. I do understand the difficulties they face, the—'

'I'd rather not go with you to see the Hansons,' Malina interrupted.

Henry frowned. 'Why not?' he asked, a little more sharply than he intended. 'Besides, I'm not sure I can drive myself there.'

'I can drive you,' Fielding said quickly. He seemed relieved to be able to offer something that might cover his rather thoughtless insult. 'It's Saturday and I'm free. Perhaps Miss Beaney would like to go into Louth? She can perhaps send your telegram from there. It's a lively little market town with some very nice shops. And a cinema; there might be a film that would appeal to you. I can recommend an eating place where a lady lunching alone would not feel uncomfortable.'

'I think I might,' Malina said. 'Henry, you won't mind, will you?'

Something in her tone caused Henry to look at her more carefully. 'No, of course not,' he said. 'If Fielding can drive me, then I'm grateful. And yes, you could telegraph Mickey for me while you're there.' That way he could keep his appointment with the Hansons – though it rankled that he might not perhaps be able to quiz Mickey about Hezekiah before they returned home.

He was grateful that Malina's smile seemed genuine as she said that of course she would. She set her coffee cup aside and announced that she was heading up to bed, that she planned to read for a while. Henry rose and kissed her cheek.

'She's a fine woman,' Fielding said as the door closed. 'I'm sorry for what I said. Out of line. I never meant . . . I mean, she's different, isn't she?'

Malina is unique, Henry thought. He interrupted Fielding before the man could dig an even deeper hole. 'Could I trouble you for some brandy?' He didn't want brandy, didn't even particularly like it, but it did the trick of diverting the conversation from Malina. What he really wanted to do was tell Fielding what a prejudicial fool he was, but that would have been unfair and counterproductive. Mickey would have been proud of his tact, Henry thought wryly.

He thanked Fielding for the brandy. 'Just how important is Hanson around here?' he asked.

'Ah, good question.' Fielding settled himself in his chair, glass in hand and a look of relief on his face that the awkward moment had passed. Henry almost wished he *had* told Fielding he was a fool.

'Hanson owns land, and around here land is power, perhaps even more than out-and-out cash. Land needs people to work it. Those people need to be housed and fed. Hanson owns both houses and the means by which they're fed. They are utterly dependent on his goodwill. They must wait for the quarter-days to be paid – by Hanson, or whatever other landowner you care to name – and then pay a substantial amount back in rent for the cottage tied to Hanson's land. If they displease him, Hanson can dismiss them at a moment's notice, but they are not permitted to leave on their own account until the term of their contract should be up. Usually on the next quarter-day. Should they renege on their end of the deal, the constable will bring them back.'

'Even now?' Henry questioned. 'That sounds almost feudal.'

'I suppose it is,' Fielding agreed. 'Oh, things are changing of course, but the change is slower to come in such a rural area as this, and the financial troubles the country has faced since the financial crashes of Wall Street and London have retrenched the old ways.'

Henry nodded. Even prosperous families had been adversely impacted; he could well imagine the effect on those who started out with nothing.

'And this new means testing proposed by the government will not help. Unemployment relief is little enough as it is without being forced to sell the few bits you have before you can hope to receive it. Oh, that's been the way of things for years with parish support, but to have a government directive effectively compelling those in need to be stripped of all they own before they can receive a penny in help will only harden attitudes and further diminish the already poverty stricken. It was often the way for those applying for parish relief, but to have the directive come from the government is bound to make the welfare boards take a harder line.'

Henry nodded.

'Most of the cottages have gardens big enough to help

support a family,' Fielding went on. 'Around here, it's usual for a family to plant on Good Friday, after church. Hanson and others still give the men the day off to do this, though they have to work the Saturday as usual, of course. Most families supplement their diet with rabbit meat. Hanson has no objection to them taking rabbits from his land – the darned things are pests, after all – but some landowners insist that their workers pay for what they see as their property.

'He's better than most,' Fielding added thoughtfully. 'The men still get their breakfast in the kitchen at Home Farm, though by that time they'll have been working since daybreak this time of year. I've no doubt Hanson gets the worth of the food out of them in other ways, but they at least get a decent meal. Young Elizabeth's taken on that job and much else besides since her mother's death.'

'How did Mrs Hanson die?' Henry asked, not because he was particularly interested, but because he felt the question was expected.

'Oh, she caught a chill, it went to her chest, she got a fever and she was gone within a week. There could have been some underlying cause we were not aware of, but her death was a shock. I tended to her, of course, but sometimes there is little anyone can do.'

Henry nodded. 'Was she badly affected by her son's death?' he asked.

'Perhaps she was. Mothers often are, even if the child is a wastrel. I don't believe that impacted on her death, though. As I say, spring fever often takes its toll where you'd least expect.'

Henry nodded absently. 'And the Samuels family have moved out of the village.'

'Hanson had them out within days. He could have turned them out completely, of course, but I don't believe he blamed Dar Samuels or Eliza for what had happened. Besides, Dar is far too valuable an asset to just cast aside. So, he sent them to look after the sheep on Bogle Hill, just a few miles away. He has land at Caistor and at Brigg. This particular holding is too steep for ploughing but the sheep do well there. There's a cottage and a garden and the Samuelses are a resourceful lot.'

'You say he's valuable?'

Fielding laughed and tapped his own head. 'Valuable for what he's got up here. He's often better than the vet, is Dar Samuels, when it comes to treating the beasts. Knows the bloodline of every bull, every horse, probably every child born in this county, and if Dar tells you it's going to rain, even if the sky is clear and blue as a Meissen vase, you'd best listen to him. No doubt in less enlightened times he'd have been hauled up before some witchfinder.'

Less enlightened times, Henry thought. Were these really that much better?

'What would have happened to them if Hanson had thrown them out?' he asked.

Fielding shrugged. 'The Samuelses would have managed that better than most, I would have to say. Dar has skills to sell that are well-known and recognized, and the boy, Ned, is old enough to be useful. Someone would have taken them on. Failing that, they have kin who would have taken them in; they might even have decided a travelling life might suit them. Liza's family still make the rounds of the horse fairs, and there's work in plenty at this time of year. Of course, had Ethan committed . . . done what he had done in winter, the story might have had a harsher ending. That's not a time to be on the road without shelter.'

Henry nodded. He was still holding his untouched glass when Fielding went to refresh his own. Henry sipped at the brandy, allowing the spirit to evaporate on his tongue. He knew that here Malina felt herself somehow caught between worlds. He was beginning to feel the same. What could he really hope to accomplish? Ethan Samuels was long gone, and if Henry did find him, he was condemning the young man to arrest, trial, imprisonment which, yes, was what he deserved but . . .

'You look weary,' Fielding said. 'Are you certain you're not overexerting yourself? I could provide you with a tonic?'

Henry shook his head. 'Thank you, but I slept for a time this afternoon. The journey was more of a strain than I anticipated.'

And that was the problem, wasn't it? If Henry did manage to find a lead, if someone did come up with evidence to suggest where Ethan might have gone, Henry would be obliged to follow that lead, to consider that evidence. Not so very long ago, he would have risen eagerly to that challenge, he would have been impatient for some break in a case like this so he could forge ahead and find the solution, bring the guilty party to justice.

The trouble was, Henry admitted to himself, right now he didn't know if he could even summon the energy to try.

# SIXTEEN

On the Saturday, Malina had set off for Louth mid-morning and Henry wished he could have gone with her. She was wearing the blue dress he really liked, with all the little pleats at the bottom of the skirt that swished and skirled when she walked, and a small brooch in the shape of a marcasite fan pinned to the shoulder. Her dark hair was twisted into a knot in the nape of her neck, and she had added just a touch of lipstick and a tiny hint of shadow on her eyelids, barely there but enough to accentuate their colour and shape.

Malina's brother, Kem, had very dark eyes. Malina's were shot through with hazel. She looked beautiful, he thought, and felt suddenly that time spent interviewing the Hansons when he could be stepping out with her was wasted time.

He caught his breath; this was not a normal Henry Johnstone thought. It was not a thought he'd have had even a twelve-month before, but so much had changed in that time and this woman had been at the heart of that.

He caught Dr Fielding appraising her, his look approving. Too approving, Henry thought, the sudden feeling of jealousy or possessiveness or whatever it was taking him by surprise. What was getting into him this morning?

They watched as Malina tripped down the steps, the blue pleats flipping provocatively. She got into the Model A Ford and drove away. Leaning heavily on his stick, Henry followed Fielding to his larger Wolseley Super Six and settled in the passenger seat. It was a larger vehicle than Cynthia's Ford and, to Henry's relief, he could settle his leg more easily. He had been grateful for the loan of his sister's car, but his body had suffered in the cramped space over the long miles.

He was thinking about the letters that Helen had shown to Malina and wondered if she could be persuaded to share them with him. He didn't doubt Malina's excellent memory, but it would be useful to see the originals. He realized that Fielding was telling him something but that his mind had drifted.

'Slid down the blasted hill sideways,' Fielding was saying. 'Hit a snowdrift at the bottom and had to be dug out, then borrow a horse to get to where I needed to be. Fortunately, she was a first-time mother and the baby was not in a hurry to arrive in the world. And the midwife had got through ahead of me. Perfectly capable of dealing with the birth as it turned out, but as the mother had been ill . . .'

Henry murmured something about not wanting to be in the depths of the country in a bad winter and allowed his mind to drift again. This time Mickey Hitchens was the subject of his reverie. He had given Malina a message to cable to Mickey, instructing him as to how to contact Hezekiah Jenkins, where to leave his message and what wording to use. He had chafed at the necessity for condensing his message into so compact a form when what he really wanted was to speak at length to his friend and discuss the case properly.

'Pardon?' he said as Fielding directed some comment his way.

'We're almost there,' Fielding told him.

Henry apologized for his mental absence.

'You seem tired this morning,' Fielding said.

'I think the journey took more of a toll than expected,' Henry said, reiterating what he had told Fielding before. And I'm constantly tired, he thought. It doesn't seem to be getting any better.

Fielding drove between wooden gateposts and into a yard. Henry remembered the house and the yard, and the stables and barn beyond, from the last time he had been there. It had changed little, but then, it had only been three years; it just felt as though a lifetime had passed. Getting out of the car he glanced down the hill, between stables and barn, to a length of fence that delineated the field where Robert Hanson had died. The land dropped away at that point; the vista across the Wolds countryside was spectacular, but that closest field was effectively obscured from view, even from anyone who might be standing in the yard. How long had Frank Church stood over Robert Hanson's body, mere yards from the help that might have saved his life? He had until that point been prepared to make some small allowance for Frank Church's actions. Perhaps he had been afraid, perhaps he had been racked by indecision, but that reminder of the proximity of field to farm, of help, of the opportunity to hand over those decisions into the hands of someone better placed to deal with them changed Henry's mind. No, Frank Church had calmly and coldly waited for the young man to die and then, when he had taken too much time about it, had hastened the unfortunate man on his way and laid the blame squarely at Ethan Samuels' feet.

Henry straightened, though he still leaned heavily on his stick. He felt a sudden determination that Ethan Samuels should at least be apprised of the true situation. That the young man should not have to live his life with murder on his conscience. Henry still despised his decision to run, his failure to face the consequences of his actions, but then, who would not have run from the certainty of a hangman's noose?

'Doctor Fielding, how are you this morning? And,' the girl hesitated, 'Mr Johnstone. Father is waiting for you, so is Ted. I'll bring tea for everyone.'

Henry looked with interest at the girl who stood in the kitchen doorway. No one in this house, he remembered, used the front door, apart from on such major ceremonial occasions as marriages and funerals. Hanson daughters, he imagined, left through the front door to go to their weddings, Hanson brides would be welcomed across the threshold. Robert Hanson's coffin had been carried out that way; the rest of the time the door was locked, bolted and a curtain drawn across to guard against draughts. This kitchen door was the usual entrance into the house. This girl, he realized, was Elizabeth Hanson, now fifteen, who had taken over her mother's work on the farm. She was small and slightly built, her dark hair in a long braid. To look at, she was still a girl, but she carried herself with a woman's confidence and looked him straight in the eye when she spoke to him. He was reminded again of Cynthia at that age.

She led them through the large room, dominated by the long table where, he recalled, the workers would gather in the morning for a welcome breakfast. The room still smelt faintly of fried bacon and fresh bread. Elizabeth directed them into the parlour. This was not the formal, frigid little room where Henry and Fielding had examined Robert Hanson's body. A room kept for best, used probably, he reckoned, as often as the front door. For the rest of the time, the curtains were kept closed to prevent the furnishings from fading, and the furniture itself shrouded in dust sheets, just in case some unwanted light should filter through and threaten the fabric.

It always struck Henry as an odd thing, this preservation of one room 'for best', which in practice meant it was scarcely ever used. And it wasn't just the likes of the Hansons that kept the habit. Front parlours of terraced houses were often kept for Sundays, or for esteemed visitors, the family using the kitchen and the middle room for their everyday living. Of course, those like the Samuels who had just the one room for everything didn't have that kind of luxury, though he found himself recalling the rag rugs set aside in a wooden chest and kept as extra covering for the children's beds in winter.

Perhaps everyone had need of a special thing, a room or an object set aside, so that whoever they were they could still possess a special, almost sacred something that—

'Henry?' He realized with a start that Fielding was speaking to him and that both Hanson men were staring in puzzlement and – in Elijah Hanson's case, outright hostility – in his direction.

'Mr Hanson.' Henry switched the stick to his left hand and extended his right. After a momentary hesitation, Elijah Hanson shook it.

Ted Hanson smiled and followed his father's example. 'Mr Johnstone,' he said. 'Well, it's a strange set of affairs that have brought you back to us.'

Elizabeth appeared in the doorway carrying a large wooden tray. She set it down on a table beside the window and Hanson motioned Henry to sit in one of the fireside chairs. Elijah Hanson took its twin. Fielding and Ted settled in a pair of old leather armchairs draped with antimacassars, the arms protected with linen covers. Elizabeth served everyone with tea and then, Henry noticed, took up a position close beside the door, out of her father's line of sight.

Hanson expected her gone when she'd done her duty, Henry thought. Elizabeth clearly felt she had the right to hear what was about to be said.

'I don't see the need for you being here.' Elijah Hanson's tone was frosty. 'What good can come of you being here?'

'As you know, the fault for that is mine,' Fielding said. 'I believe that the young man should not continue to believe that he's guilty of murder. If he can be found, then he should be told.'

'And to what end? My son is dead. It's chance and chance alone that Frank Church killed him and not the Samuels boy. You can't tell me that wasn't his intent.'

'We have no means of knowing his intent,' Henry said coldly. 'We do, however, know Frank Church's intent. That was to kill. He was mere yards from the house, standing over the body of your son, waiting for him to die. When he did not, then Church kicked him in the head until he died. That, Mr Hanson, is murder in anyone's book. What the Samuels boy did was undoubtedly criminal, but it stopped well short of that.'

'Then why did he run? I ask you that?'

'You know why he ran,' Ted said, and Henry guessed from the weariness of the tone that this was a conversation reprised many times and always with the same end. 'Frank Church told him that Robert was dead and that he'd be sure to hang for it. While I agree that his running away was reprehensible, it was at least understandable.'

'It's the fault of that girl, all of this. If she'd not thrown herself at the Samuels boy, none of this would have happened. Everyone in the village knows—'

'And she's suffered for it, as has everyone else involved,' Ted said quietly but firmly. 'Father, please, hear what Mr Johnstone has to say. What harm can it do?'

'Harm! What good will it do? Raking over the scandal yet again.'

'And I've told you, I take full responsibility for that,' Fielding said. He sounded slightly bored and spoke, Henry thought, with the assurance of a man who knows that even if his decision is disagreed with and resented, he's still too much needed for that to lead to any real consequences.

Hanson scowled in his direction then drained his cup and set it aside. 'I'll have none of it,' he said. 'You will all no doubt do as you see fit. I have better things to do with my time than to sit here debating on a closed matter.'

'They need to find him,' Elizabeth said, and all eyes turned to look at her. Elijah's eyes had narrowed and he regarded his daughter with what Henry could see was barely controlled fury. Elizabeth was undaunted. 'Ethan did wrong, he lost his temper, and yes, he deserves punishment for what he did, but he's no murderer and he deserves to know the truth of what Frank Church did, to him and to Robert. He deserves to get his life back and he can't do that unless he knows the truth.'

'You stay out of this, girl,' Elijah Hanson said. 'You're still a child, under my roof; this is none of your concern.'

'I've been woman enough to take on the running of the house and Home Farm. I work from daybreak until dark, running about after you and Ted and the men that need providing for and the accounts that need doing and the marketing and preserving and the cooking and the cleaning . . .' She broke off, drawing breath, calming her tone. 'I've earned the right to have my say.'

Hanson had risen from his chair, his hands clenched into fists at his side. Elizabeth took a small step back, but she was, it seemed, determined not to be silenced. 'Robert was a cruel man and a stupid one. If he hadn't died the way he did, he'd likely have been killed in a pub brawl or been beaten to death by someone he owed money to.'

Elijah took several steps towards her, his hand raised now. Henry began to rise but Ted was ahead of him and had stepped between his father and his sister. 'You should not speak ill of family before strangers,' he said to her. His tone was gentle but there was no mistaking that he was also very much put out.

'It's true though, isn't it?' Elizabeth said. She turned then, making what seemed to be a tactical withdrawal. For a moment it looked as though Elijah might follow her but Ted's presence in the doorway seemed to dissuade him. He sat back down.

'See what your meddling has done,' he growled at Henry.

'Was he in debt?' Henry asked.

'None of your damned business. You're not even a police officer now, so you've no right to even ask. This is family business, not yours.' He gestured angrily, the sweep of his arm taking in Fielding and Henry and even his own son. 'You'll do as you will, I suppose. You don't need my permission to go on a wild-goose chase. But don't think you can bring that boy back here. You do and I'll break his rotten little neck for him.'

'It probably will be a wild-goose chase,' Fielding said as they got back into the car a few minutes later. Ted had walked them out; of Elizabeth there was no sign.

'Where will you even begin?'

'I don't yet know. There were certain clues in the letters and we know that a postcard was sent from Lowestoft. It may be that the trail can be picked up from there.'

'A trail that is three years cold? Following a man who knows all too well how to disappear, whose people have had generations of practice in not being found, identified or registered?'

Henry shrugged. 'I will at least try.'

He was not entirely surprised when, rounding a bend in the lane, they spied Elizabeth perched on a farm gate. She must have cut across the fields, Henry thought. Fielding stopped the car and she came over.

'I took the letters to Helen,' she said. 'It was easier for me to do than for the men that carried the letters this far. I may be woman enough to work like my mother did, but I'm disregarded the rest of the time. No one takes notice of where I am, or if they do they don't remark on it.' She smiled grimly. 'Being a Hanson means no one has the right to question me. Anyone else tried to give Mrs Church her letters, it would have been noted and questions would have been asked. I know Frank Church later found out about them, but she'd have not got them at all if I'd not intervened to give them to her.'

'And the messengers, you know them?' Henry asked.

She nodded. 'And I know where they're likely to be found this time of year. What stopping places they might use.' She paused. 'I hear you've got a Gypsy woman with you. That you're to be married.'

Henry nodded.

'Helen says at least you treat her like she's got a brain in her head.'

'Malina has a very fine brain,' Henry said.

'That's why I'm telling you. Helen says she still doesn't like you, but she's willing to give you a chance, because your woman believes you've got some worth. That and we've all heard rumours and stories about you, Mr Johnstone, from the travelling people down south, about how you've dealt fair with them. So deal fair with Ethan when you find him.'

She thrust a piece of paper into his hand and took off across the fields.

'If her father doesn't change his attitude, he'll lose that girl,' Fielding said as they drove away. 'And he'll lose a valuable business asset into the bargain. The loss will be all on his side. He'll turn around one day, demanding she do some task or another, and find her gone.'

'Where would she go to?'

'There's plenty of work for a young woman in nearby towns or on the coast, though my guess is she'd hop on a train one day and take her chances somewhere far away.'

'As Ethan Samuels has done.'

'As so many of the young are doing and will do. What do they have to gain in a place like this? You can't expect every new generation to do as their fathers and mothers have done, especially as they do worse now. Most are at best just scratching a living, and I don't see the situation getting better.' He laughed shortly. 'Of course, I doubt she'll go to sea, as Ethan did. It might have been better for everyone if he'd stayed there. He'd survived two years of it before he came back.'

'Why did he come back?'

'He came back for a visit. Then Hanson started to talk about him following in Dar Samuels' footsteps. There's a long tradition of the Samuelses being stockmen on Hanson land. They hand their skills down the generations; I think Elijah realized he'd have a hard time replacing Dar when the time came. Young Ned's got his father's hands and eyes, but Ethan was of an age where he could be immediately useful, especially as the Hanson business was set to expand.'

'Expand?' Henry asked.

'Hanson didn't lose money when the financial world crashed around so many ears. His wealth was in land and stock and crops and hard cash. He had a mistrust of banks, used them only when he had to. There're rumours he keeps his cash in his mattress, and maybe he does. I think there are great numbers of people over the past few years wishing they'd done the same. Anyway, it turned out that Hanson was in a position to buy up cheap land when others went under. They say he kept the labour, but cited financial constraints that meant they kept their jobs but took a cut in pay. I don't know. I *hear* gossip, I don't make a practice of listening to it.'

Henry nodded. He unfolded the piece of paper Elizabeth had given to him. There were two names and a list of locations that made no sense to him. Perhaps Malina would be able to interpret. And the information that Ethan may have been travelling under the name of Hayes, that being his mother's maiden name.

'Why *are* you involving yourself in all of this?' Henry asked as the car turned into the narrow road leading to Fielding's house.

'You mean other than the pure-and-simple desire to see justice done?'

'We are both old enough and wise enough to know that nothing is pure and simple, and even justice is oftentimes a muddy relict,' Henry said.

'Then I suppose curiosity. Or boredom. I'm kept busy but I sometimes worry that my mind will stagnate for lack of proper stimulation. I suppose the puzzle of the matter appealed to me.'

Thinking about his new role as a private investigator, his fear that all the hard-gained knowledge he had won at such cost over the years would be lost, Henry thought he understood what Fielding meant.

But this wasn't just a puzzle, was it? Not an academic exercise from which something might be gained and nothing lost. In his mind's eye he could imagine Mickey sitting across the table from him, papers spread across their shared desk, mug of tea in his massive fist. These are people's lives, Mickey would have reminded him. And in Mickey's absence it seemed that Malina had taken on that role, telling him gently but firmly that Henry Johnstone was not what mattered here. That his satisfaction was secondary.

'Now you have had time to think about this matter, what would you do about Ethan Samuels?' Henry asked.

Fielding appeared to consider the matter. They had drawn up outside his house now and he cut the engine, staring thoughtfully out through the windscreen. Henry got the feeling that the doctor had already given this matter much thought. That his appearance of consideration was more about demonstrating that fact, rather than that he actually needed more time for it.

'I believe he should be found,' Fielding said at last. 'Told what really went on that day. Then I believe that he should be punished for his actions. They were reckless, and though it turns out did not cause Robert Hanson's death, they could well have done. Then I think I would buy Helen Church a train ticket for herself and one for her little boy and I'd send them to be close to where Ethan is, even if that means she can only visit him in prison until his sentence is served. I think I would also provide her with a little money, just to tide her over until she can find work enough to support herself and her children, along with references so she can get that work, even if that means telling a small lie about her employment with me. Though she did once remove bloodstains from my shirt, so perhaps that counts for something.'

Henry eyed the doctor thoughtfully and then he nodded. 'I will find him,' he said. 'Even now that I have left the police force, I've more resources that I can draw upon than you or Helen Church or her community. I agree he should be punished for what he did – but no more than that. Speculation regarding what the outcome might have been is not within my remit. He struck Robert Hanson, who then fell from his horse and was knocked unconscious. That is the extent of what Ethan Samuels can be held responsible for. So, common assault.'

'Hanson would not agree with you. He'd have additional charges brought; would settle for nothing less than attempted murder.'

'So, it's as well he can't be called as a witness, and if Ethan pleads guilty to the lesser charge then the matter will be settled quickly.' He sighed; he still had to find Ethan Samuels and the boy had evidently hidden well.

'You'll keep me apprised of developments?'

'Of course, and I'll be depending on your discretion. Then on you paying the train fare for a woman and two infants. I will help with the other expenses, and my sister may be able to find me a decent lawyer to defend the young man.'

'Why the change of heart?' Fielding asked. 'When you came here before, you were quite happy to send him to the hangman.'

Henry felt his anger flare briefly, but he had no energy and no desire to sustain it. 'That may have been true,' he said. 'But I was not in possession of all the facts at that time. And I'm tired, Fielding, bone tired of nothing good coming out of what I do.'

Fielding laughed, disbelieving. 'You have had a long and illustrious career,' he said. 'Bringing miscreants to justice, protecting the innocent—'

'No.' Henry said this more loudly than he had intended. 'I and those like me are brought in when the innocent have already suffered. Nothing I do can rescind that suffering or even mitigate it. Yes, I have made arrests, I've seen men and women hang because I've found sufficient evidence of their crimes to condemn them. Often to condemn them many times over. In the main, I don't regret their deaths any more than I regret the deaths of the men I killed in the war. I've done what was required of me and—'

Mrs Fredericks had appeared at the front door, obviously wondering why her gentleman was still sitting in the car with his guest.

'Would you like me to bring you some tea, sir?' she called down from her lofty position at the top of the steps.

'Thank you, Mrs Fredericks, we will be in presently. Serve it in my study, if you please.'

Henry had taken the opportunity to gather himself. 'I'm sorry,' he apologized a little stiffly. 'I seem still to be in a bit of a funk.'

'Not at all, old chap; happens to the best of us,' Fielding said. 'At least you now have a plan in mind, what!'

Henry nodded. At least that. His thoughts were clearer now, and the action required laid out before him.

'I'll have Mrs Fredericks bring you some tea and perhaps some biscuits up to your room, shall I? Best you have a rest before dinner.'

Henry nodded gratefully. He wanted to lie down and be quiet. He felt ashamed of his sudden outburst and that Fielding, this man he had known for so short a time, should have been the witness to it. 'Kind of you,' he said. Then eased himself painfully out of the car and made his slow way up to his room.

For all the confidence he had put into his intention to find Ethan, he was beginning to realize that this might be an impossible task and that hurt him a great deal. He could go to the local police and ask if the men who had brought the messages for Helen had a record, but they'd not tell him, not now. He was no longer Inspector Johnstone of Scotland Yard, he was merely a member of the public, at best a very insignificant private detective. A one-man band with no influence or authority. He was fortunate that the goodwill he seemed unexpectedly to have retained with ex-colleagues had helped him towards cases that did not fall particularly within the purview of the police, but which could still make use of his skills. And that Mickey had persuaded his superiors to make occasional use of Henry's abilities and to allow him to review old cases. But beyond that?

He would have to ask his friend to ask questions on his behalf.

He sat down heavily on the side of the bed. He could, he supposed, get Malina to drive him to Lowestoft, from where it seemed likely Ethan Samuels had boarded a vessel, probably under the name of Hayes. He could ask at the Seamen's Mission there, could interrogate the masters of the fishing boats and small cargo vessels for whom that was the home port, see if any had a memory of Samuels?

The sound of china rattling on a tray brought him to his feet, and he opened the door to Mrs Fredericks. She set the tray down on the bedside table and asked, 'Will that be all, sir?' her tone cold and disapproving now her master wasn't there to hear.

Henry thanked her. Then added in his frostiest tone, 'You may be assured, Mrs Fredericks, that we will be gone by Monday.'

He saw her eyes widen, and the realization hit that she might have gone too far and that he could cause trouble for her. 'I'm sure you are welcome to stay as long as you and the doctor might wish it,' she said, her tone now friendly and placating. 'It's always a pleasure to have guests.'

I could destroy you, Henry thought almost absently. I could tell Fielding that what you were overheard saying about Malina was a disgrace, that he shouldn't even countenance having a woman of your sort in the house, spiteful and bullying and . . . but what would be the point of that? She was a woman who needed work and a secure place to stay in a world that had those things in very short supply.

Instead, he thanked her once more for the tea and she left. Henry eased off his shoes with the toes of his other foot, not bothering to undo the laces, and then stretched out on the bed. Was he letting Malina down by not saying more?

Perhaps. But if he made a scene, it might lead to this woman losing her position and Malina would not wish for that. He recognized also that Fielding's attitudes, though more liberal, still carried a degree of prejudice that he could not shake. He was, Henry considered, a well-meaning sort who did his best, within certain parameters, to alleviate suffering and improve the lives of those he considered deserving of it. He had no doubt Fielding would help Helen Church, perhaps even going so far as to buy her the train ticket as he'd suggested, perhaps with a reference so that she could get work, but only so long as he could do so secretly, not lay himself open to disparagement by others of his own class or – almost worse – by those like Mrs Fredericks who needed to perceive herself as a cut above the 'Gypsy types' that Fielding's comments at dinner had derided.

Henry sighed. As he had told Fielding the evening before, nothing was ever pure and rarely simple. Life was a complicated mess. With that thought in mind, Henry, his tea forgotten, fell asleep.

*Letter to Helen, unsent*

*I so much want you to see this, my darling, but I'm afraid to risk the sending of more letters. I know the trouble it would cause should your mother catch sight of them, how the village would talk and what that would mean for you. So I write all of this down in the hope that one day I can show you what I wrote and you can know all my thoughts.*

*I never told you everything that was running through my mind the night after Frank and I had fell to fighting. Dar barely gave me the time to dry off before he'd gone out and come back again with your ma and da and the Churches. Frank didn't come, nursing his pride and his bruises somewhere, I suppose. But Dar soon made it clear that this wasn't something we younger folk were entitled to discuss. Soon as they arrived I was sent from the room, like I was still a child. Looking back, it seems the strangest thing, to be sent away and not be party to what our families decided for us, but back then, even that few short years ago, it was just the way it was. The older women would sort it out while the men listened on. It was always the women who dealt with matters concerning other women and marriages and kids, that was the way it had always been.*

*I waited with the young'uns in the bedroom, hoping they wouldn't take long to decide whatever it was they were going to decide and I remember, Helen love, that I felt empty inside. So much longing it seemed to have eaten its way out and left a great damned hole.*

*I remember too that I was hungry and so were the children. It was long past suppertime and Mam wouldn't let them eat until Dar and I had had our fill. Alice's belly growled and gurgled all the time we sat there but she said not one word to me. Neither of them did. They just sat on the bed, watching me like I'd turned into some stranger who'd done wrong and they couldn't figure out what to do or say to be right.*

*I suppose in a way I was a stranger. I mean, I'd been gone two years before then and to walk back into their lives the way I had and turn everything topsy-turvy . . . It must have been more than they could understand.*

*I heard Frank's mam holding forth. She has a shrill voice, that woman. Harsh and high and bitter. Or maybe it's spite that makes me remember her that way. When we were all little kids she was kind enough. I suppose she just wanted to protect her own.*

*Then I heard the door slam and voices in the street and Dar called us down.*

*'It's been decided,' he told me. 'I know you won't like it, but it's for the best. You two will not meet for a full seven days. If you see her on the road, lad, you walk on by. After seven days, we'll talk again, when tempers are cooled and you and her have had a chance to think on.'*

*I remember his voice softened and he tried to take the sting out of his words. 'Look, lad,' he said, 'they're worried about you both, we're all concerned. What do you have to give a woman yet? Wait until you're signed on with Hanson, proper like, then we can discuss things. Meanwhile, a week apart and time to think will do neither of you no harm.'*

*'What will one week change, Dar? I'll still love her and she'll feel the same for me.'*

*'If that's true, then seven days out of either of your lives will make no matter. If this is just a pash, a whim on either part, it'll give the pair of you time to consider. Now, no more. Eat and keep quiet.'*

*I suppose I respected him and Ma too much to say more. I suppose too I knew without them backing me I'd have less than nothing, not that it would have been a steep fall from what I had to what I would have had. But I thought about losing you, about having no means to keep you fed and cared for. If Dar didn't speak up for us with Elijah Hanson, or if the village wanted me gone, there'd be nothing I could do. I knew I'd have to go along with what had been decided and I knew you would too.*

*Seven days out of your lives, he'd said. What's seven days? But I worked it out. The fraction of it and seven days was one tenth part of all our time, like taking maybe eight or nine years out of an ordinary lifetime and, for that, I'm bitter. I could have been with you, held you, kissed you so many more times, had so much more than we had.*

*I missed you with a great ache, knowing you were so little distance away and yet we must be separate. Can you imagine, my love, how heavy and sore that ache has become now? Has it been like that for you?*

*In the end, we lasted a bare five days apart and I know now that Dar knew that. How could I hide such joy from any man?*

# SEVENTEEN

Mickey had received Henry's telegram about how to contact Hezekiah Jenkins. Leave a message at the Workers' Circle, at Circle House on Alie Street. It was, as Mickey had mentioned to Tibbs, a familiar place to both of them. The Circle was also a Friendly Society and Belle paid into an insurance fund there, in case either of them fell too ill to work. Henry had a liking for music and Mickey for politics, often playing devil's advocate in some lively debate or other, over a plate of warm bread and pickled herring.

He recalled that Kem and Tibbs had arranged to meet to listen to the concert but that would be taking place next Sunday. Saturday evenings tended to be quieter; the club was Jewish in its origins and before sunset on the Sabbath it was still unusual to see the usual clientele there in any numbers. Later on, it would be as busy as always. Mickey arrived just after seven, helped himself to a cup of strong tea from the samovar, and dropped his money into the jar provided for the purpose. He asked two elderly men playing dominoes what the procedure was for leaving a message on the communal noticeboard and was told he should date his note and then pin it up. If the board became too crowded then the oldest or obviously outdated notices would be taken down and left in a box on the small table set under the noticeboard, just in case anyone needed to retrieve them.

Mickey thanked them and did as advised.

Mickey knew Hezekiah to be a man with itchy feet. His home base seemed to be the area around Leman Street, but he was often to be found further afield and indeed well outside London. Hezekiah moved as the mood took him, Henry had once told him, and so it had occurred to Mickey that he might not have realized Henry had retired. He also had a suspicion that Hezekiah Jenkins would be more likely to answer a summons from Henry Johnstone than from Mickey Hitchens.

Accordingly, he left a message asking if Mr Hezekiah Jenkins could contact Mr Henry Johnstone at his earliest convenience. The wording had been suggested in the telegram; Hezekiah Jenkins apparently liked things to be done properly.

After that, there was little Mickey could do.

He cast a final glance around the main meeting room but, seeing no one he knew well enough to join for supper, took himself home. Belle would be late back tonight; her performance would not finish until well after ten and she was having a late supper with a friend who was leaving with a repertory company and would not be back until pantomime season began.

Mickey tried not to mind, but he missed her tonight. He missed Henry too. Tibbs would turn into a fine officer, Mickey had no doubt of that, but if Henry had still been around they could have passed the evening somewhere, perhaps even at the Workers' Circle, getting a bite to eat and indulging in one of those long, meandering conversations that mark ancient friendships. They would have been at ease with each other, and Mickey missed that sense of ease more than he could say.

# EIGHTEEN

Henry had not heard Malina return and woke only when she tapped on his door to tell him that dinner would be served in fifteen minutes. He washed the sleep from his face and the sweat from his body and changed his shirt. Malina was already chatting to Dr Fielding when he went into the dining room. They were discussing her impression of Louth and its array of shops.

'Is that a new dress?' Henry asked. 'It suits you well.'

She smiled at him. 'I saw it in the window of Eve and Ranshaw and couldn't resist. It's such a lovely shade of green.'

Fielding didn't dress for dinner, merely, as Henry had done, freshened himself up, and they had taken their lead from him, relieved that their host settled for informality. Malina's new dress, Henry thought, bridged that gap perfectly. It was not a workaday dress, the green silk and pleated bodice too fancy for that, but it was not formal dinner dressing either. A garden party frock, perhaps? Whatever, it suited her well and brought a moue of distaste to Mrs Fredericks's lips when she brought the soup. Henry caught sight of the slight twitch of Malina's mouth, half smile, half something else, as she noted the woman's reaction.

'Thank you, Mrs Fredericks,' Fielding said. 'We can manage. I'll ring when we're ready for the next course.'

The housekeeper departed, a heavy cloud of annoyance gathered around her. 'Shall I serve?' Malina asked, and earned herself a dartlike glance.

After dinner Fielding asked if they would excuse him for an hour. He had some paperwork that must be dealt with. Henry wondered if he sought to absent himself, just in case Henry should want to pick up the conversation of the afternoon.

'Can we walk in the garden?' Malina asked. 'It's still light enough.'

At the back of the house was a small walled garden, with espalier apples trained against the wall. A garden bench had been set between them. The evening light was golden and the wall, bathed in sunlight all day, now gave back a warmth that felt good against Henry's back. He was aware of a restlessness in Malina, a discontent. 'I think we will go home soon,' he said. 'There's little more we can do here.'

She nodded. Then said unexpectedly, 'I almost went into the register office today to get us a special licence.'

Henry blinked. He was acutely aware that she was watching him carefully. He weighed what his next response should be, then said, 'The only objection I would have to that is that Mickey and Cynthia would not be present as witnesses.'

'The only objection.'

'Yes.' He hesitated, wondering how to frame the next sentence without causing offence. 'Can I ask why, particularly, today? Did something happen?'

It was, he realized with a little shock, now her turn to be trying to formulate her next sentence. Finally, she said, 'I suppose it occurred to me how much easier life would be if I was Mrs Johnstone and not Miss Beaney. I think being here brought that home to me. It made me think that perhaps much of my life is a sham.'

He felt truly shocked. 'How can you think that? I'm not sure I even understand. Cynthia values your work and your friendship because of who you are; the rest doesn't matter to her. I love you because—'

'Well, perhaps it should matter,' she snapped. 'I have been fortunate—'

'You have deserved any good fortune. And, if I may say so, I have benefited from that far more than I can ever deserve.'

She looked at him with tears in her eyes. 'And how about the likes of Helen Church: don't they deserve better?'

'Yes, yes they do.' He sighed. 'Truthfully, they deserved better than they got from me the last time I came here.'

He took her hand. 'I want you to be Mrs Johnstone. I don't know that I'm going to be the best husband, but at least you know me well enough to be aware of my failings.'

She leant her head against his shoulder. ‘I’m out of sorts,’ she said, ‘and I have no idea what to do about it.’

For a time they sat in silence. Henry, because he didn’t know what to say. He hoped his presence would be enough; knew that she probably needed more.

‘We should set a date,’ Malina said. ‘For when we get home.’

Henry felt a surge of relief. ‘I’d like that,’ he said.

# NINETEEN

On the Sunday morning, when they judged the church services might be over, Malina drove Henry to see the Samuels family. They had said their goodbyes to Fielding, with promises to keep one another updated as to progress. The original intent had been to set off early on the Monday, but Henry was restless, out of sorts, and wanted to be on his way. Malina had suggested that they could break their journey in Lincoln, after seeing Mr Samuels, and start afresh from there.

'We've no need to tell Doctor Fielding we're stopping so close by,' she said. 'Or if you wish, we can tell him I've a desire to hear evensong in the cathedral.'

Henry recalled a pleasant little hotel, The White Hart, close by the cathedral court, from a previous stay in the city with Mickey Hitchens, and a call using Fielding's phone secured them rooms for the night.

He felt better now that he was on his way.

Cynthia's little car coped with the steep slope of Bogle Hill well enough, though Malina announced herself relieved when they reached the top. The sound of an unfamiliar engine had brought Dar Samuels to his door, his two younger children behind him. The scent of food drifted from the kitchen.

'We must not stay long,' Malina said. 'We'll be interrupting their Sunday and I'll not put them to the pain of offering us dinner. Lunch,' she amended quickly.

Henry nodded. He got out of the car but made no move to go towards the cottage. Instead, Dar Samuels came to stand beside him. His expression, Henry noted, was wary rather than outright unwelcoming. He nodded politely to Malina. 'Miss Beaney,' he said. Then added, 'We've just got back from chapel—'

'And I'll not keep you,' Henry assured him. Now he was here he was suddenly uncertain as to why he had come. Was it likely Samuels could add anything to his small knowledge of Ethan's whereabouts? Was it likely he'd tell Henry even if he could?

He sighed. 'Truthfully, Mr Samuels, I'm here to ask you a question you'll likely not give me a straight answer to. So, I'll make this brief. I think your son should be found, punished for what he did, relieved of the burden of believing himself a murderer. So, I'll ask you, can you help me in this task? Do you know where your son might be?'

Dar Samuels regarded Henry with thoughtful eyes. Henry felt himself being weighed and considered and found wanting. Frankly, he wasn't sure he could blame the man. Henry was finding himself much wanting.

'Helen allowed me to read the letters,' Malina said softly. 'Your son had a smart turn of phrase.'

Dar Samuels laughed suddenly. 'He did that,' he said. 'You know, when he was a young lad, he fancied he might one day be a writer. He read everything the school teacher could find for him and she helped him get a ticket for the library in Binbrook. He even went to the Sunday school, just so he could read the Bible stories and all the lives of the saints and such. Hagiography, they call it? Did you know that?'

'I did, Mr Samuels.'

He nodded. 'He even got himself a prize for a story he wrote. A proper, money prize. He gave it to his mother so she could buy the young ones winter boots. I wish I could have told him, Ethan lad, you can do that, you can write your stories and get them made into books, just like that Jack London he thought so much of, or that D.H. Lawrence bloke, who came from coal-mining stock and so, Ethan always reckoned, was an example to the likes of us. Or the man what wrote the story of Noah's Ark.'

He must have caught Henry's quizzical look because he smiled and said, 'You don't fancy those stories just appeared on the page, do you?'

'No, of course not.'

'No, someone, sometime, thought it was worth writing down. They thought the story mattered and so they fixed it to a page, so it could be shared. Our Ethan should have been able to do that. He used to read to us of an evening, from the books he'd borrowed, and he'd get old newspapers from whoever could be persuaded to give them to him so he could read about the world.'

'Something you still do,' Henry said.

Dar nodded. 'I fancy it keeps me close to my boy,' he said.

'We should be on our way,' Malina said quietly. 'We've a long way to go. I wish you and your family well, Mr Samuels.'

'And I wish the same to you, Miss Beaney.'

Henry slid back into his seat, acknowledging that there was nothing to be gained from staying and trying to press the matter. Dar Samuels stood back to give Malina space to manoeuvre the car around and they headed back down the steep hill. He felt her relief when they reached the bottom.

'So,' she said, 'Lincoln, a decent meal, evensong, and then head for home in the morning. Then you can call Mickey and tell him what you need to know.'

Henry nodded disconsolately. What else was there for him to do?

*Letter to Helen, unsent*

*That should have been a sign, my love, that quarrel with Robert Hanson. I should have known that he wouldn't let up after that. He'd go out of his way to rile me or to insult Frank, make him feel worse about losing you, especially after our families announced that we'd wed in the autumn, after the harvest was done and when there'd be proper time for folks to take stock and celebrate.*

*I never quite knew what to think about Frank. In his place I'd have fought tooth and nail to keep you. I'd have been there, nagging and whittling after you until you'd got no choice but to give in and agree to be mine, but I suppose that was never his way. I suppose too that he'd got his pride and, like he said that day, what good would it do any man to take a woman to his bed and know she was wishing herself with another.*

*You know, or maybe you don't, that the night Dar made his announcement about us, I went to see Frank and his parents and I told them, as fair as I could, that we meant no disrespect. I think Frank's father understood but his mam never did, never could, I suppose. She had her plans for her family to marry with the Lees and I'd come along and sunk them all.*

*Frank, well I never could tell what Frank was thinking. He was a man who shed his thoughts only when the wind that shook him was gale force, like that day he caught us kissing in the barn. If Robert Hanson hadn't been close on his heels, I reckon we could have sorted that out between us. Come to blows, maybe, but sorted it. As it was, Robert Hanson was always on at him, prick, prick, prick, like an old maid with a needle. Wouldn't let it go. No man can be expected to put up with that and stay quiet.*

Dar Samuels watched as the little car made its slow and careful way back down the hill then he turned and went back into the house. Liza was watching him.

'Everything all right?' she asked.

He nodded. Then went up the stairs to their tiny bedroom. The two children shared the other, the room now divided by a curtain to give each a modicum of privacy now they were growing. In a box at the foot of the bed, beneath blankets and linens, lay a book. The scent of lavender from the folded sheets rose to greet Dar as he reached into the depths of the box and drew out the little book, with its green cloth covers and scuffed spine. He sat for some time on the side of the bed just looking at it, half hearing the voices of his wife and children from the room below, the chirruping of birds through the open window, the distant sound of cars on the road that curved around the bottom of the hill.

The book was called *Clater's Farrier* and it had been given to Dar by his father, who had received it from his. It talked about horses, mostly. Their quirks and diseases and the tricks used by horse traders to fool the buying public. The second part of the book contained recipes and more general advice. How to make wine from elderberries, how to brew simple beer, to make bread, to cure the croup. The margins of the book were filled with notes written by three generations of Samuels men; Liza had a notebook filled with her own memories and lessons and receipts, copied from her mother and her gran and her aunties, and she'd go nowhere without it, but this, in Dar's mind, was even more precious. It was an heirloom.

He flicked through the pages, noting the entries made in his own neat hand. Those from his grandfather, in swirling copper plate. Those of his father, less certain and in printed capitals, marking a generation when family circumstances had interrupted his schooling. He'd never quite caught up, but that didn't stop him making his mark. The Samuels family had always prided themselves on their literacy; it was just the way they were. On that and on their knowledge, half secret, passed by word of mouth, by observation, by keeping one ear open to those who might know more than they did, written in this book.

He'd given it to Ethan that last summer he had been with them, when it had looked as though all might after all be right with the world. Ethan and Helen would be married, Hanson would give the boy employment. Eventually, Ethan would take over from his father, or if not with Hanson, then with some other landowner who knew the Samuelses' reputation. And make no mistake, the family was proud of their reputation.

Dar had received the book back the Christmas after. He'd been astonished by this, having assumed that was the last he'd ever see of both these treasures: his son, his book. A man he didn't know had come over from a winter stopping place near Grimsby. The weather had been closing in and he'd declined the offer of hospitality, saying that he was going to take the bus back while they were still running. It was as well he had, Dar remembered; snow had fallen heavily for days after and marooned them with the sheep at the top of what he thought of as their mountain.

He turned the pages again now, looking at the flyleaf and the unprinted endpapers, now covered in Ethan's handwriting, tight cramped as though he was eager to get as much on to the page as he could.

Dar drew out a scrap of paper from the book's spine and set the little green volume aside. He went back down the stairs and found a pencil, envelope and sheet of flimsy in the kitchen drawer. Liza glanced at him. She was putting dumplings, spoonful by spoonful, in the top of the stew pot. He could smell that she'd added fresh thyme to the suet mix and his stomach rumbled in anticipation.

By the time Dar had finished the letter, the meal was ready. He addressed the envelope, copying the words he had no idea how to pronounce, letter by letter on to the envelope. Liza handed him a stamp.

He looked up at her in surprise.

'I bought it ages since,' she said. 'Kept it for when you decided it was time.'

Dar sighed. 'I thought it safer not to write to him,' he said. 'You know that. Someone might have seen me posting it, might have wondered who I'd got to write to. But with all this new business going on. The lad has a right to know he's not a killer and the right to know that man is hunting for him. I've to go into Market Rasen midweek with Master Ted. I can post it then, while he's busy having lunch with his father's cronies.'

Liza nodded. 'He should be warned,' she agreed.

*Letter to Helen, unsent*

*It's strange and painful, my Helen, to think that after the incident in the barn half our time was gone. Our folk got together after that and set a date for a wedding that would never come. There was still some bad feeling, but after that was settled it was in everyone's interest to accept what was and make the best of it. The old folk decided it was a closed matter and the rest followed their lead.*

*There was sympathy for Frank, of course, and I think a lot more for his mother. She felt so wronged, so snubbed, as if your rejection had not been of her son but of her. But she never said nothing to me or to Ma when they met up after church and chapel were over and all the women stood a while to gossip as they always did. I never understood what women who lived so close to one another that they must know all of each other's business, and in so small a place that nothing different happened from one week to the next, would have to talk about and, what's more, be able to say it at such length. But I've come to think that's the way of women all over the world, or at least the parts of it I've seen, and I've learnt something since then about their talk. That it can be that talk which binds a community together. That they share the trials and the troubles of their whole community and that they solve them, standing outside of a church on Sunday or sitting on the porch steps on a summer evening, or in talking on the walk to market. They get things done and often their means of getting things done remains a mystery to everyone else.*

*Though at its worst, talk also kills as surely as a knife-blow to the heart or a stone against the head.*

*I'll admit, love, I was afeared their talk would be hateful after Hanson came and lectured both our families. I hated the way Dar had to stand and take it all, and me, I never dared to say a word, though my fists itched to do the talking for me. Though once Hanson said his piece, all parties had to bow with the wind and let things be and he made a point of coming up to Dar after church and congratulating him on the match.*

*I wonder, often, what would have happened if I'd gone to him and confessed. In my dreams he sometimes speaks up for me, tells folk that Robert brought it down on himself. Then I wake up and I know that he would never have said that. Robert was his son. Elijah Hanson would never have forgiven what I'd done. What man could?*

# TWENTY

Hezekiah Jenkins was a tall man who held himself like the old soldier he was, though his hair was white, long and flowing, very clean, tied back with a piece of garden twine. He wore the same greatcoat Mickey remembered from the last time he had seen him, long, army-issue green though a little faded, and mended here and there with careful stitching. His boots were polished and his pushcart wheels ran smoothly, without a single squeak or complaint, sweeps' brushes packed neatly and tied along the side, the rest of his belongings folded into and beneath a heavy tarpaulin.

There was, Mickey thought, a pride to the man that belied what others might think of as his straitened circumstances.

He had come on the Monday morning, much to everyone's surprise, into the reception area at Scotland Yard, having left his pushcart outside but within view, and demanded to see Inspector Johnstone.

Mickey had of course been summoned.

Hezekiah stood to one side of the reception desk, feet apart like a soldier at ease, and hands clasped behind his back, surveying the scene with the interest and acuity of a man committing every single thing to memory.

'Mr Jenkins, thank you for coming.' Mickey extended a hand and Hezekiah shook it gravely.

'I came to see the guv'nor. He left a message for me to come at my earliest convenience and as he never set a place, I come here.'

'And I thank you for it,' Mickey said. 'Henry, Mr Johnstone, he told me what to put, said you might be able to help me with something.'

Hezekiah's eyes narrowed and he peered closely at Mickey. 'And why ain't he here hisself?'

Mickey sighed. This was going to be more complicated than he had thought. 'Inspector Johnstone had to retire,' he said.

'He was injured in the line of duty and is unable to continue with his work here. I have reason to believe you may have witnessed something a few nights ago that might help with our enquiries. A man was murdered, and it's possible you might have seen—'

Hezekiah had begun to walk away.

'Mr Jenkins, please.'

'I'll speak to the guv'nor, no one else. He knows as how I'll speak to no one else. You remind him of that.'

'I could have arrested him, I suppose,' Mickey said to Tibbs later. 'Though I don't know on what charge. As it is, we'll have to wait on Henry's return and hope he can get the old fool to talk.'

'Vagrancy,' Tibbs suggested. 'He could be brought in for being a vagrant.'

'And then he really would refuse to speak to us. Besides, from what I remember, Henry told me our Mr Jenkins always has enough in his pockets to pay for a bed, even if he camps out under the stars most nights. So long as he's got the means for that, no one's going to hamper him. And he earns an honest enough living, sweeping chimneys, sharpening knives, doing odd jobs. I should have known he'd not talk to me.'

'Why will he only talk to Mr Johnstone?'

Mickey shrugged. 'I suspect he sees Henry as a kindred spirit in some way,' he suggested. 'I'll leave word with Cynthia that I need him to contact me and then I'll leave Mr Jenkins another message and hope he responds to it. And that he has something useful to tell us when he does.'

They had been going through missing persons reports to see if there might be anyone matching the description of the dead man. Although his face had been burned, it was still possible to guess his age at being late forties or perhaps a little older. His hair had been neatly cut in a short back and sides. At the post-mortem, Mickey had noticed flecks of grey among the brown. The colour of his eyes they had guessed as blue, but the action of the fire had made that difficult to gauge. He was five feet seven inches in height and of an average build, not flabby but not muscular either. After the post-mortem, Dr Keen had informed Mickey that he had been able to take a single fingerprint impression from the little finger of the left hand. He'd got about two thirds of the print, showing a half whorl, and had been rather pleased with himself for his skill.

Mickey had thanked him and the print had now been passed on to the bureau, based up in the tower of Scotland Yard. Little fingers were not the most useful, as they were least involved in the casual picking up, touching and clasping actions from which prints were often derived, but Cherrill of the Yard had instituted a means of categorizing and searching single prints so that might give them a lead. If they were very lucky.

'So,' Tibbs said, 'it looks as though we have three possible missing persons from the area close to the warehouse. If these don't prove useful, we may have to extend our search over a wider area.'

Mickey nodded. He glanced at the addresses: two were within a mile of the warehouse. He assigned one to Tibbs, taking the second for himself and arranging that they should both go to the third, as it was on the way back to Scotland Yard. All three men had been reported to the local constabulary. One had been reported at Leman Street, the man having gone missing from the next street. Tim Brading was known to be a drunk; he had just lost his latest job and had stormed off after a row with his wife. That had been a week before. Mickey fully expected to find him back at home after an extended pub crawl. He suggested Tibbs look into that.

'I'll take Smith from Commercial Road,' he said. 'Like as not, you'll have done with Brading before I have and you can come and find me. Then we'll attend the Fincher residence together.'

'Any particular reason?' Tibbs asked.

'Because the old woman, Mrs Fincher, is a blasted harridan. The last time I had reason to be there, she threw a tea kettle at my head. The missing person is her son-in-law, and if you ask me he's just done a bunk, and good luck to him.'

Tibbs half closed his eyes, thinking. 'Fincher. Didn't she or some member of her family get done for receiving about a year ago?'

'That would be one of the daughters. I believe there are five and a couple of sons, all in the same broad business. But a missing person is a missing person, even if they do have the misfortune to be related to the Finchers.'

Two hours later, Mickey's predictions had largely proved to be correct. Tim Brading had indeed returned home, though not as flat broke as Mickey had anticipated. He had arrived with cash in his pocket, the winnings, he said, from having backed a horse – though he was reticent to explain which horse and had no betting slip to show when Tibbs had asked.

Mickey had fared no better at the Smith residence. Rodney Smith was not there, though Mickey was able to eliminate him. He was definitely not their dead man. His very furious wife and her equally furious mother berated Mickey with the news that the man had returned, gathered up his belongings and then left again. He'd let slip that he had another woman; Mickey hoped, for her sake, that the wife and mother-in-law never found out her name.

Tibbs was waiting on the pavement outside when Mickey departed. 'I heard angry voices,' he said. 'I thought I'd leave it to you, sir.'

'Oh, did you now?' Mickey said. 'And why is that?'

'I thought I'd bow to your greater experience,' Tibbs told him. 'I'm not at my best with angry women.'

'Well, you can start to hone your skills with Mrs Fincher,' Mickey told him. 'She's permanently angry.'

The Fincher house was larger than most of the others in the terrace. It occupied a corner plot and instead of an entryway between two houses, a broad arch led through to what had been a stable yard. This had been built as a manager's residence, one step up from the mill workers he managed and close enough that he could oversee their leisure time as well as their working hours. It was in that stable yard that crates of stolen tea and bales of cloth had been discovered the previous year. The tea was from a van theft, though that theft had not been pinned successfully on any of the Fincher clan. The cloth was from a draper's and clothier's shop in the West End, removed from said shop by Dilys Fincher and a number of other young women who had gone into the shop slim as willow wands and come out again several sizes larger. It was a ploy that depended upon two others keeping the assistants occupied, and was generally more successful in the winter months when warm overcoats covered a multitude of sins and no one looked twice at a woman bundled up against the cold.

It was in actual fact years since Mrs Fincher had chucked the kettle at Mickey's head. Mercifully it had been cold and empty, and he'd made more of a dent in it than the kettle had in his head, but even so it had stuck in Mickey's mind as an incident he'd not want to repeat.

The missing man was Wilfrid Benning, married to Maisie, the third of the five girls, and he'd been absent since the night of the fire. It was Maisie Benning who met them at the door.

'That good-for-nothing decided to come back, has he?' Mrs Fincher's croak lanced through from the back of the house.

'No, Ma, it's the police.'

'What the hell do they want?'

'Don't worry, I'll deal with it.' She pushed them back outside and then led them under the arch and through into the yard. 'Sorry,' she said. 'She doesn't know I reported him missing. She's happy he's gone.'

'You're evidently not,' Mickey said.

Maisie sighed. She was a mousy-haired young woman, pale skinned and with big violet eyes. 'I wish he'd taken me with him,' she said. 'He promised he would. I knew he wouldn't be able to stand being here, not when we had to move back in with her. I knew he wouldn't be able to stand it, but I wish he'd taken me with him.'

'He'd been planning to go?' Mickey asked gently.

Maisie nodded. 'I tried to make him wait for a bit. He'd lost his job and couldn't seem to find another. Ma said he was good for nothing. We had to move back here, to my old room. I was grateful but—'

'But hard after having your independence.'

'You've not found him, have you? I mean, I heard about that man found dead in the old Brinton place. I heard about the fire.' The violet eyes were wide with fear.

Gently Mickey asked, 'Had your husband just got new boots? I mean a good pair but likely second hand? The man we found was wearing almost new boots and a shirt with a laundry mark of WP, of good linen, which had the collar turned not so long ago. The seamstress put her own label back in the collar.' He could already see the relief in the young woman's eyes.

'No, nothing like that.'

'The man we found had dark brown hair, cut short back and sides, and with the start of a little grey running through it. He was likely in his forties?'

She shook her head even more emphatically. 'No, it's true he's older than me but he had no grey and, besides, he's got fair hair.' She sounded glad but Mickey fancied he could also hear the resentment in her tone, free to make itself known now that he wasn't the dead man. He'd simply gone and left her, and she wasn't about to forgive him for that.

Well, he thought, there wasn't a great deal he could do to make that better. Maisie would have to make her own decisions over what to do next. He thanked her for her time and then turned to leave. A thought struck him. 'It's not my place to say, but if you're looking for work, there's always jobs posted on the noticeboard at the Workers' Circle. Some of them for live-in staff, I believe.' He'd noticed several when he'd posted his own message to Hezekiah Jenkins.

She looked dubious. 'Ain't you got to be a Hebrew to go there?'

'Not at all,' Mickey said. 'And they have a women's chapter too, so it might be worth your while taking a look.'

He and Tibbs left, aware that Maisie was staring after them. He doubted she'd go looking for work at the Circle, but he sensed that he had sown a seed in her mind. The suggestion that she didn't need her man's permission to leave her mother's house. He'd gone off and left her to deal with the old harridan – and Mickey found it hard to blame him for that – so now she could do the same.

'So,' Tibbs said. 'We've eliminated those three.'

'So, we'll set the constables to continue their sweep of the neighbourhoods around the warehouse. Not everyone reports a man missing immediately, especially if they've a habit of wandering. For now, we've done all we can, and must plough through the other work piling up on our desk, at least until Henry speaks to Hezekiah Jenkins. It's possible that might throw up another lead.'

'We should pay a visit to the Tullis family while we're in the area,' Tibbs said. 'We're only two streets away. If any of those lads is going to give us more information, it will be young George Tullis. He might have mentioned something to his family now he's had time to think.' George had appeared before the magistrates at Toynbee Hall and had, as Mickey had predicted, been remanded into the care of his parents until his fate should be decided. What sentence George might serve would probably be dependent on what was handed down to the two older boys.

Mickey nodded. 'Might as well while we're so close,' he said.

But when they arrived at the Tullis house, an ordinary terraced house in a street of ordinary terraces, they were in for a surprise. The house was empty, no curtains at the windows and, when Mickey peered through the window, not a stick of furniture to be seen.

The next door opened and a woman came out. 'You'll not find them there,' she said. 'A van came, early hours of this morning. They packed their bits inside and they were gone. Did a flit, I shouldn't wonder.'

'What kind of van?' Tibbs asked. 'Did it have a name on the side?'

The woman glared at him. 'A van,' she said. 'That's all I saw. And that's all I saw because once I realized what was going on I shut my curtains tight, and I went back to bed. No business of mine where they go.' She went back inside and shut the door firmly.

'Should we?' Tibbs gestured towards the door.

'Lad, you've worked these streets as a constable. You know what it means when a woman shuts the door in your face. It means she's not about to open it again.'

'True,' Tibbs said reflectively.

'We'll get the constables to canvas, see if anyone saw anything more than a van. Meantime, I think we should check on the Eagen and Reynaldi clans, see if they've had the sudden urge to move too.'

By the time they returned to Scotland Yard, Mickey and Tibbs had confirmed that the other two families were still in residence. Neither had greeted Mickey and Tibbs with any enthusiasm. Their sons were locked up, waiting for their day in court, and no one wanted to talk to the police.

Back in Central Office, refuelled by tea and a doorstep sandwich, Tibbs seemed restless. He got up from the desk, paced to the window and then back again. Mickey waited him out. Sometimes Tibbs reminded him of Henry.

'So,' Tibbs said finally. 'The three set the fire and then leave. Our killer comes in, with his victim, and most likely dispatches him in the warehouse. We know the boys are well away by then, but someone, probably the killer, has paid them to set the fire. Why? Why not do it himself?'

'Good question,' Mickey said. 'Why not kill his man and then set the blaze to cover his tracks. Perhaps the fire was an excuse to get the man into the building? They spot smoke, they go running in.'

'Why not summon the fire brigade? Why run into a burning building?'

'Concern that there might be other people inside or a vain notion that they could tackle it themselves before it takes greater hold.'

'Why should they care? Why take the risk?'

'Civic duty, perhaps. The wish to play the hero? Odd things do motivate certain fellows.'

Tibbs looked unimpressed. 'The owners are dead. We don't yet know who benefits from the will. Does insurance continue even after the payer of the premium dies?'

Mickey shrugged. 'Presumably arrangements can be made for someone to take over the payments. Presumably whoever the property has been left to.'

'And we still don't know who that is.'

'No one's come forward with a will. Old Mr Brinton was reportedly not in his right mind when he died. The place had stood empty for years; the solicitor who had handled the business had ceased to be when the final partner died. We're still waiting to see who inherited their archive.' Mickey shrugged. 'The workings of the legal profession can be opaque, so we're awaiting the verdict of the Law Society as to who might be responsible and then for someone to lay hands on the relevant records.'

'So why fire the building? No one will benefit.'

'Why continue to pay the insurance? It's a conundrum, I'll grant you that.'

Mickey rummaged through their notes until he found what he wanted. The address for the woman who had seen the boys go into the warehouse that night, while she'd been busy with her client. 'We should check on the whereabouts of Betty Moran,' he said. 'The boys in H division can take care of that, as she's usually on their patch. I would like to check that she's got nothing more to add to her statement.'

Tibbs nodded. 'And Hezekiah Jenkins should be warned of trouble. He's not known as a witness, but if one of the boys mentions a man with a pushcart to the wrong people, they might recognize the description.'

Mickey nodded. 'I'll have an eye kept out for him,' he said. 'And hope that he can tell Henry something to our advantage.'

# TWENTY-ONE

It was late on the Tuesday evening when Malina and Henry arrived back at Cynthia's house in Bournemouth. Both were exhausted and hungry. Henry was given Mickey's message but was weary enough that it didn't take a lot of persuading that he should wait until morning before acting on it.

After he'd retired to bed, Malina sat for a time in Cynthia's bright little sitting room with its wall-covering of yellow Chinese silk, decorated with flowers and butterflies and birds. Malina loved this room and only regretted that there was no fire set in the hearth. She felt she could have done with the cheer. It was now September but the evening was still warm and the windows were open. Street noises drifted in along with the scent of roses, the salt tang of sea. She was glad to be home.

Cynthia poured them both a hefty measure of scotch and came and sat beside her. 'Was he a nightmare?'

'Not so much. But the journey took it out of him, and I think the frustration of not being able to wield his usual authority. No one takes as much notice of an ex-inspector.'

Cynthia grimaced. 'He was a fool to go.'

'I think he had to, for his own peace of mind. I think he also realized it was doing no good, that all it did was stir up ill-feeling and bring no one any closer to justice.'

'Will he pursue this Ethan Samuels further?'

'He has a few leads, three years old and stone cold, but . . .' Malina shrugged. 'What else does he have to occupy him? He needs a challenge, Cynthia. He's lost his sense of who he is and I'm damned if I know what would fill the hole.'

They drank in silence for a while and Cynthia said finally, 'Well, we've a wedding to plan. That is, I hope you'll let me help you?'

'Willingly, though if Gretna Green was closer, I think I'd

be heading there, just to keep things simple. So long as you and Mickey could come along, of course.'

Cynthia laughed. 'Poor love, you really are feeling jaded, aren't you?' She stood up and headed for the door. 'I'm hungry,' she announced. 'I'm going to raid the pantry. You come and find a bottle of fizz and we'll chase the blues away. We can both sleep late in the morning.'

'I could sleep for a week,' Malina said. But she got up and followed Cynthia down to the kitchen, knowing that her friend, her employer, her protector, her soon-to-be sister-in-law was right. If she went to bed now, she'd just brood, likely toss and turn until morning. They made themselves a picnic and returned to Cynthia's sitting room.

'Now tell me all,' Cynthia said, unceremoniously pouring wine that sparkled and fizzed into their whisky tumblers. 'I need to be prepared to head my darling brother off at the pass if he looks to be ready to do something really stupid.'

'Really stupid?' Malina asked.

'Like taking you off on any more wild-goose chases,' Cynthia said.

# TWENTY-TWO

Henry had called Mickey at Scotland Yard first thing on the Wednesday morning and Mickey had promised to put a new message on the board at the Workers' Circle. Henry would meet Hezekiah there on the Friday lunchtime.

'I've a little information regarding the Samuels business,' Henry said, 'but I don't hold out much hope. He sent a postcard from Lowestoft about a week after he ran away. I don't know what it said exactly; Helen Church insists it just told his family that he was safe and well. They passed the card on to Helen but Frank Church insisted she burn it. The two letters arrived later – one in September and one in November of the following year. They were hand-delivered by men passing through and, I think, working on Hanson's farm as casual labour. They passed the letters on to Elizabeth Hanson who saw them safely delivered. Of course, nothing like that could stay secret for long. Frank Church found out about them and insisted they be burned, but Helen managed to deceive him, and the letters were kept.'

'You've seen them?'

'Unfortunately not; she wouldn't be persuaded.'

Henry sounded bitter, Mickey thought.

'But she did show them to Malina, who noted down everything she could recall.'

Which, Mickey knew, being Malina, would have been a good deal, though it crossed his mind that she might have been selective in her memory if she believed that would be for the best.

'He talks about having fetched up in a mining village, in a steep valley. Though he gives no clue as to what they might be mining. The rest is just flim-flam intended for Helen Church's gaze only. His family claim to have no knowledge of where he might be.'

'You don't believe them?'

'I don't, but there's nothing I can prove and no leverage I could apply.'

Again, that bitter note, Mickey thought.

'The only remotely solid leads I have are from Elizabeth Hanson, who acted as a go-between. She gave me the names of the men who carried the messages and made a guess as to where they might be found. The stopping places they use at different times of the year. They are unfamiliar to Malina, being north of where her family used to travel, but it may be that local constabularies in Lincolnshire and Derbyshire and even further into the Midlands would be able to assist. I'll collate everything and bring it to you when I come for my meeting with Hezekiah. Oh, and she thinks he may be travelling under the name of Hayes, rather than Samuels.'

'Do that,' Mickey said, with as much cheer as he could muster. When the call had ended, he stood beside the phone for a moment or two after thinking the matter through. From what Henry had told him there was little to be done. The trail was not so much cold as frigid. The young man was now clear of the murder charge, so pursuing him would not be a priority and, as Henry well knew, even when he'd been reported as a murderer and the pursuit been fresh, they'd turned up no solid leads. Ethan Samuels would have known where casual work was likely to be found, that few questions were ever asked as long as you earned your pay, that vanishing was only dependent on your will to do so, provided you did nothing to draw attention to yourself.

Even the description they had put out – there being no photographs of Ethan apart from one taken at the village school when he had been perhaps seven or eight years old – was generic. Slim build, medium height, dark hair, blue-grey eyes. This last being the only feature that made him stand out, and even that was only in contrast to the darker eyes of most of his community.

'Is something wrong?' Tibbs asked, and Mickey realized he had been standing motionless, one hand on the telephone. He collected himself. 'Only that I must let a friend down carefully,' he said, 'and without seeming to do so.'

'The old case,' Tibbs said. 'Does Mr Johnstone have any leads?'

'Nothing less than two years old, and scanty. Besides, what good will it do? The man in question is no longer thought to be a murderer. He'd be fetched before the judge, charged with battery, and perhaps serve a short term in jail. What would be gained? But my friend Henry hates loose ends, as do I, I suppose, but there are more pressing and longer loose ends that need tying up just now.'

# TWENTY-THREE

Early that Wednesday afternoon, a woman came to the front desk in Scotland Yard and said she wished to speak to whoever was in charge of the murder enquiry. It took a while to sort out which murder enquiry she was interested in, but eventually Mickey Hitchens was called down to speak with her.

She had just returned from a visit to her younger sister, who had just had a baby. Her third – so Mrs Peters had been staying to help out with the other children and the cooking and the laundry while her sister got back on her feet. She'd returned home to an empty house, food on the table that had moulded and milk that had soured, post on the hall floor and no sign that her husband had been there in days. Enquiring of the neighbours, it seemed that they had assumed he had gone to join her or perhaps to fetch her home. Further digging revealed he'd not been seen in over a week and he'd not turned up for work either.

He was, she told Mickey, a man who kept himself to himself anyway, and didn't really socialize with the neighbours. His work didn't exactly endear him to most people. He was, she told Mickey, a rent collector, working for various local landlords. Landlords who were not always sympathetic to those who could not keep up with the rent.

This last, Mickey thought, was told with a touch of defiance, as though she was used to people disapproving of her husband.

And is he responsible for enforcing evictions, Mickey wondered. But first things first.

He settled her down on a bench set between the two great doors leading into the reception area and asked for a description of the missing man.

He was forty-five, dark hair, usually cut short at the sides, but it had been becoming a little long when she'd gone away, and she'd urged him to see his barber. His eyes were grey and he was five feet and seven inches tall. 'A solid man, not running to fat as a lot of men do when they turn forty. But of course, he walked a great deal. I'd got him some good boots just before I left. A better quality than we could have afforded buying them new. Some people discard quality goods into the second-hand market and don't think twice about it.'

'Indeed, they do,' Mickey agreed. 'My wife found me a fine overcoat last winter. Mrs Peters, did your husband take pride in keeping his boots well polished?'

'Indeed, he did.' She stopped, stared at Mickey, her hand flying to her mouth as she took in the implication. 'You think it might be him? I must see.' She got to her feet, looking ready to march down to the mortuary and check for herself.

Gently, Mickey tugged on her sleeve and sat her back down. 'Mrs Peters, let me describe what our man was wearing and see if that makes sense to you. There's also some dentistry that might be familiar to you.'

'Mr Peters had all his own teeth! Well, apart from one at the very back that he had taken out last winter, when it pained him. And a gold filling he had done years ago before we met. He was in the navy at the time.'

Mickey nodded noncommittally but his mind was busy. Those details fitted with their dead man. 'He was wearing a good linen shirt; two buttons had been replaced but they had been added at the bottom of the button band so the ones that showed all matched.'

He watched her as her world began to crumble. 'And the collar had been turned and the seamstress added her own label so we wouldn't forget where we'd had it done. I could have done it myself, I'm skilled enough with a needle.'

'I'm sure you are.'

'But she's a young woman, just starting out, and I thought she could do with the work. She's cheap enough and does a good job.' She had begun to cry now, and Mickey had the strange impression that she was weeping as much for the fact she'd not made the repair herself as for the fact that her husband might be lost. The one thing was too big to comprehend so she was dealing with the other.

'I'm sorry, Mrs Peters. It does sound as though it may be your husband that we've found.'

'I want to see him.'

'I'm sorry, Mrs Peters, it wouldn't be a good idea for you to see your husband. You see, there was a fire.'

She stared at him and suddenly the tears began and there was nothing Mickey could do to comfort her. He left the widow for a moment while he went to the desk and had the sergeant summon one of the matrons employed to look after female suspects. Then went back to sit beside the distraught woman.

'Now, I'm going to need to find out about his work and his friends and anywhere he might have gone. Can you tell me that, or is there someone else, his employer, perhaps, that I'd do better asking?'

By the time he'd returned to the Central Office, he had names and addresses of several associates. The matron was arranging for a taxi to take Mrs Peters home and Mickey had suggested she go back to her sister's. No, he was sorry, she couldn't arrange the funeral just yet, not until enquiries were done and the body could be released.

Tibbs took one look at his face and a moment later a great mug of tea had appeared on Mickey's desk. He took his hip flask from the pocket of his jacket and poured a measure of whisky into the tea. 'Well,' he said, 'we now have a name, and a woman now knows she's widowed. I suppose that might count as progress.'

Tibbs nodded. He picked up the notes Mickey had made. 'I'll make a start,' he said.

# TWENTY-FOUR

Thursday had been a day of footslogging, Mickey thought. He had spoken again to the insurance company that had the policy on the Brinton warehouse. This time he spoke to an older secretary who, it turned out, knew more than her employers about the day-to-day running of their business.

'It's no mystery as to who paid the premiums,' she told him, peering at him over the top of her glasses. 'The policy was paid, as usual, for the twelve-month from June each year. Mr Brinton's bank sent the cheque to us two weeks before it became due, so even though the old gentleman died shortly after, the insurance had already been renewed for a year. What will happen next year, I can't possibly tell you, of course. I believe the estate is in probate, so the solicitors should know more.'

'And is this usual practice,' Mickey asked, 'for the bank to pay directly like this?'

She sat back and studied him carefully, as though wondering how much she was going to have to explain to this man who obviously knew nothing about finance. 'It's not particularly unusual for an arrangement like this to be in place,' she said. 'But I think Mr Brinton was perhaps a little unusual. He was a lovely old gentleman, and I had many dealings with him over the years, but in the last eighteen months of his life he developed a somewhat morbid fear of being unable to, well, keep abreast of his affairs. You see, his health had not been good and it was in his nature to keep his affairs organized, so I believe he had an agreement drawn up by his solicitor that, at the start of each financial year, a certain number of cheques should be drawn up, to cover those regular payments such as his insurance. These were then held by the bank and paid as instructed, crossed so that they must be paid into an account and not to the bearer, for the sake of security, and not dated until they were due. The chief clerk at the bank was given authority to add the date. You have to understand, Inspector, that Mr Brinton was a wealthy man, and wealthy men can afford to pay for such arrangements. He could have afforded a business secretary to take care of his affairs, of course, but he preferred for the bank to be his executor.'

'I see,' Mickey said. 'And you don't happen to know—'

'Who benefits from his death or from the insurance policy? No, I'm sorry, and I've already been less than discreet in telling you as much as I have. I doubt the bank will help you, your best bet is to go to see his solicitor.'

'Who also passed on this summer,' Mickey said. 'The office is closed and no one seems able to tell me who took over the affairs of Mason and Tonks.'

She smiled then and removed the heavy glasses. They hung on a beaded chain against her crisp, white blouse. 'Well,' she said. 'There I can help you. Mason and Phelps, great nephews of the original Mr Mason, I believe, are handling all of the residual affairs of Mason and Tonks. If you give me a moment, I'll find their address for you. If you like, I can even telephone to let them know to expect you.'

That had at least seemed like progress. Until his visit to Mason and Phelps. He was ushered into the office of a cheerful young man who introduced himself as Richard Phelps and who told him, in an equally cheerful manner, that he was unlikely to be of help.

'Unfortunately, Mr Brinton drew up his will some years ago. He left all his worldly goods, apart from a few small bequests, to his sister and thence to her family. Sadly the sister died some years ago. She had two children, one of whom, the daughter, we know left for Australia in 1922, and so we've set enquiries in motion there. Unfortunately we don't know her married name. The son we can find no trace of, though it's possible he died in a car crash in 1923. Again, we've got our investigators looking into the matter, but until one or the other turns up, we're no further on. We can't, unfortunately, even dispose of the house or the warehouse or any of the other holdings, and that's always a problem.'

'Why?' Mickey asked.

'Oh, because sometimes these things can drag on for

months or years, and meanwhile the inheritance goes to rack and ruin. It's a great pity. If we had permission to liquidate the assets, then at least the money from the sales would be safe in the bank and still be intact when the relicts did turn up. In the meantime . . .' He spread his hands in a gesture of helplessness. 'It does seem odd though, doesn't it? That someone should set fire to a heavily insured building, presumably to profit from the insurance, but then no one appears to benefit. Are you certain this was not a case of accident, or of someone playing the fool and it getting out of hand?'

'The evidence indicates otherwise,' Mickey told him. 'But yes, it is a strange state of affairs.'

What Phelps had said nagged at him as he walked back to the Central Office. Truthfully it had bothered him right from the beginning, when it had swiftly become clear that there was no obvious beneficiary had the building burned down. Besides, it was so damned amateurish. The three previous fires under investigation, if they had definitely been arson, had been professionally done, and it was only the fact that there had been similarities in the second two that any serious investigation had begun. This; three kids and a can of petrol . . . No, it was all cock-eyed. It suggested desperation and yet, so far as Mickey could tell, there was no one involved who was likely to feel such desperation.

Tibbs was waiting for him when he returned. He'd been tasked with interviewing Mr Peters's employers and tracking down the list of friends they and the widow had provided.

It was, Mickey thought, a sadly short list.

'Apparently he wasn't one for socializing,' Tibbs said. 'Didn't drink, didn't gamble, didn't go to the theatre or the music hall. Did attend church but, as the vicar couldn't initially place him, was perhaps not a regular attendee. Unlike his wife, who attends service each week and is involved in various social and charitable groups connected to the church. Everyone describes him as a quiet, efficient sort. Unremarkable, smart, well turned out . . .' Tibbs ran his finger down his notes. 'Affable; they had been married for twenty years but had no children. Inspector, I don't think anyone really knew him. He seems to have done his job, gone home, little else.'

Mickey nodded. 'He must frequently have carried a good deal of money with him,' he said thoughtfully, 'and yet there was no sign of a nightstick or blackjack on the body. It's unusual for any money collector to be without the means to defend himself. It might have been better for him if he had carried something.'

'Unless that's what the killer used against him and then took away,' Tibbs suggested. 'He was hit about the head and then stabbed. He could have carried a knife and a blackjack. He could have been handy with his fists.'

'It's possible . . . Did his employer cast any light?' Did you think to ask? Mickey added silently.

'He said that Mr Peters always collected his money with seemingly no difficulty. He got quite sniffy when I asked if Mr Peters went prepared for trouble. Said,' Tibbs flicked through his notes again, 'that the clients Mr Peters collected from weren't the sort to make trouble over payment of rent, and that Mr Peters did not attract trouble to himself.'

'And were you supplied with a route for his collections and the addresses he collected at?'

'Reluctantly,' Tibbs said. 'But I think it might prove interesting and perhaps explain why Mr Peters experienced so few difficulties in doing his job.'

Mickey scanned the list Tibbs gave to him. 'Ah,' he said. 'I thought that might be the answer.' The list did not detail a single area or a simple round such as might be expected from a landlord with a row or two of houses. These addresses were spread across a number of streets, and in some reasonably affluent areas. And all of the tenants listed were female.

'At the very least we could charge the landlord with profiting from immoral earnings,' Tibbs suggested.

'We could, but by the time we get the warrants issued, many of these women would have been warned and moved on. Others will claim they are sharing flats for the sake of economy and taking in typing or some other work. Some of them will even be capable of typing and perhaps even shorthand. And to be frank, Tibbs, if we eject them from these apartments, there's a very real danger of them ending up plying their trade on the streets, and what benefit will that be to anyone?'

Tibbs opened his mouth as though to argue, and then closed it again. A twelve-month ago, Mickey thought, he would have declared that those living by immoral earnings deserved to be on the streets. Mickey was pleased with the changes in his sergeant, by the fact that he no longer viewed the world in such black-and-white terms. Mickey set the list on the desk and Tibbs placed it back in the file.

'Do you think Mrs Peters was aware of the nature of her husband's job?' Tibbs asked.

'You mean that he was a rent collector?'

'I mean—'

'I know what you mean.' Mickey smiled at his protégé. 'I doubt he told her, and I doubt she asked. I think she cared for him and that she is genuinely distressed both by his death and – more so – by the manner of it.'

Tibbs nodded. 'Did you learn much from the insurance company?' he asked.

Mickey brought him up to date on his own frustrating day. He returned to the comments the solicitor had made about setting a fire that no one would benefit from.

'Mark my words,' Mickey said. 'We're missing something here. Something so obvious it'll be a slap in the face when we do stumble across it.'

Tibbs looked thoughtful. 'What would have happened had the fire spread?' he asked. 'It was only because the vagrants raised the alarm and the brigade was able to arrive so quickly and pump water from the dock that the fire was prevented from spreading. What would have happened had that not been the case?'

A slow smile spread across Mickey's face. 'What indeed?' he said. 'Tomorrow I must attend Henry and Hezekiah Jenkins but, while I do that, see what you can find about the warehouses next to Brinton's, who owns what, and if there's gossip about their financials.'

# TWENTY-FIVE

Mickey and Tibbs' plans for Friday were to be derailed. Betty Moran, who had been witness to the three young men entering the building with their can of petrol, was found dead in an alleyway, just a street away from the Brinton warehouse. Mickey and Tibbs arrived just after six that morning to find Dr Keen already there.

Mickey crouched beside him as he examined the body, confirming death, pointing out the obvious wound to the unfortunate woman's head. 'Someone stoved in the side of her skull with a brick or a stone, I'd say. Whoever did it used considerable force.'

'Not that she'd be a difficult target,' Mickey added sourly. Betty Moran had been a small woman, five feet tall at most and of slender build. A wisp of a woman that the wind might blow over. Her bag lay close by, the clasp still closed; when Tibbs opened it, using the tip of a pocketknife to lift the spring latch, so as not to disturb any prints, the contents seemed to be in place. A small purse containing coins and two ten-shilling notes, a compact and a lipstick, a handkerchief and a comb.

'Hop back to the corner shop,' Mickey instructed, aware that he had nothing in the murder bag he carried with which to wrap the bag. 'See if they have a sheet or two of butcher's paper, or a sheet of brown that we can wrap the bag in.'

Tibbs moved to obey.

'She'll have lain here all night,' Mickey said. 'It began to rain about one and the clothing is soaked through. The ground beneath looks to be dry.' He lifted the woman's outstretched arm and indicated the relative lack of dampness on the ground beneath. 'Rigor's not fixed, though the first signs are there,' he added, 'but the night was warm, despite the rain, so—'

'So, we should get her moved before it sets in,' Dr Keen agreed. 'I would suggest she met her death around midnight, allowing for the rain and the state of rigor. The jaw is rigid, the rest of her will follow soon enough.'

Mickey nodded. 'There's not much guesswork in cause of death, but let me know anyway when the post-mortem will be. My guess, though, judging from the way she fell, is that she heard someone behind her, began to turn, was struck and fell. Going by the contents of her bag, the motive was not robbery, and the attacker made no attempt to make it look as though it was.'

'It's possible he didn't see the bag,' Keen suggested. 'It fell close to the wall and might well have been in deep shadow. Her attacker might not have realized it was there.'

'Possible,' Mickey agreed. Betty Moran was wearing a summer dress and a light jacket. One shoe had been lost as she fell and lay a foot from the body. The other remained in place. Cream, summer shoes, he noted, with a small heel. She wore no stockings. He slipped two fingers into the pocket of her jacket, found nothing. Checked the other. 'A pawn ticket,' he said, and tucked it into his waistcoat, wondering what the woman had possessed that was worth pawning. The dress was thin cotton, the jacket cheap and well worn. He studied Betty Moran's face and wondered how old she had been when she met her death. Thirty-five? Forty, perhaps. Younger. Whatever, she'd not had an easy life.

Mickey stood and told the ambulance driver that they could take the body away. Tibbs arrived carrying a sheet of folded brown paper. He hooked the handle of the bag carefully and placed it on the paper, made a neat parcel.

'I doubt the killer even touched it,' Mickey said, 'but we might be lucky.'

Henry had also been up early, but that was largely because he could not sleep. The riddle of where Ethan Samuels might be had obsessed him for the past few days, though he had come to realize that this was now a purely intellectual puzzle rather than a desire to find the young man. Somehow, that had receded as they put the miles between Ethan's home village and their own home, and now the matter had become almost remote from its origins. He wanted to know because he wanted to know, much as Cynthia liked to tackle complex crosswords purely for the joy of setting her mind to something challenging.

Henry was often struck by the fact that Cynthia felt she was faced with few real challenges in her life, even though she ran a household, was the silent but executive partner in her husband's business and sat on various charitable committees. Cynthia was capable; she had often joked that would be her epitaph.

Henry had raided his sister's house for maps and any books on geology and geography they might have had. Then he had perused the public library and browsed the second-hand bookshops. He now had a stack of volumes laid out on his office desk that might give him a clue as to where the young man might have been when he wrote the letter to Helen and described the narrow valley with its outcropping rocks and some unidentified kind of mine working.

And that was Henry's problem. He'd had no idea just how many mineral deposits and of what different kinds and dispositions there were in the British Isles. Or how many glacial valleys – which, he had initially decided, was probably what Ethan had described.

Melissa had disagreed with him. Glaciers, she had said, created U-shaped channels. Water created the deep V. They had argued amicably over dinner the previous evening and he was slowly coming around to her way of thinking, though he was keeping both in mind.

He glanced at his watch, decided he should have breakfast and then get his train. He was planning to arrive in London well before his meeting with Hezekiah, scheduled for one o'clock. There were bookshops in London to be perused and the meeting with Mickey and Hezekiah Jenkins to be anticipated.

He had a liking for the old man. Hezekiah was surprisingly knowledgeable and could often be found in one public reading room or another, which was how he and Henry had met. That had been a decade ago, Henry realized with a little shock.

He realized something else as he drained the last of his breakfast tea and set the dishes in the kitchen sink. He felt content. Less agitated than he had been when Malina had first offered to drive him up to Lincolnshire. His mind was clearer and less fogged than it had been in many months.

Henry did not understand what had changed. He worried that the fog would descend again, and the mix of ennui and melancholy would return as abruptly as they had departed. He had, over the years, realized that both conditions seemed native to his mental state. That he oscillated between them. More and more he was grateful of those times when the melancholy lifted and his brain buzzed with life, though he always fretted about how long this might last.

'Come on, Henry,' he told himself as he checked the straightness of his tie in the hall mirror. 'Just be glad the funk has gone for a time.'

Mickey was early. He got himself a cup of tea from the seemingly bottomless samovar and added a little milk from the jug set beside it, then found a corner table and sat down to wait. Henry walked in at ten minutes before one. He had his stick in one hand and a heavy-looking bag in the other, which he set by his chair before fetching his own tea.

'You look better,' Mickey observed. 'And you've been buying books.'

'I'm afraid I have. I do feel better,' he added. 'Perhaps the change of scene did me more good than I realized.'

'Perhaps having something to challenge you.'

'Perhaps so. And how are things with you?'

'I've had better days. At six this morning I was examining the body of a dead prostitute. Our chief witness to the fire in the Brinton warehouse. One of the three lads involved and their family has vanished into thin air, and it turns out no one would immediately benefit from the destruction of the warehouse – had our three little toerags not been so inept – so we have lost our motive for the fire.'

Henry raised an eyebrow and listened as Mickey swiftly related the events of the past two weeks. Hezekiah arrived just as he finished his account and made his way over to them. 'They let me leave my cart in the yard,' he said. 'But I've brought my brushes in. A set of good brushes is too much of a temptation for thieves.'

The head of the main sweeping brush was swathed in canvas and he set the stack in the corner close beside Henry's bag. Seeing that it was full of books, he peeked inside, noting particularly *Structure and Surface. A Book of Field Geology.*

'Edward Arnold,' he commented. 'An erudite writer. Though it's a while since I had the pleasure. I found a copy in a reading room in Blyth Bridge, about two years ago.'

'When I'm done, you may borrow it – or any of them,' Henry said. 'I can leave them with Inspector Hitchens and have him pin a message to the board.'

'I would be obliged. May I ask what interest you have in mining science?'

'I'm looking for a location that matches a vague description of a place,' Henry told him. 'A narrow, V-shaped valley with mineral outcrops, scrubby trees, and what sound like forestry planted pines. There's mining being done there but I don't know what kind it may be.'

'Coal or iron I'd say.' Hezekiah nodded. 'Valleys like that are what you'd find in Wales, or maybe in Derbyshire. Though the deposits of both are deeper there, from what I remember; the outcroppings not so common, or at least not since Roman times.'

Mickey stared at the old man. Henry merely nodded and Mickey got the impression that this was the expected level of conversation between them.

Hezekiah finished his tea and went for a refill. He did not pay, but looked in Henry's direction and pointed to the jar. Henry nodded. 'You'd like some lunch?' he asked as Hezekiah returned.

'That would not go amiss.'

Later, when the thick vegetable soup and the fresh bread and obligatory pickled herring had been devoured, Hezekiah announced that he was ready for his questioning.

He's enjoying this, Mickey thought. But found he couldn't grudge the older man his peccadilloes. He was clearly relishing his conversation, discussing the latest news and the state of the world, the chaos likely to ensue from a National Government in which no one had a majority – neither of them held out much hope of cooperation, despite the King's avowed wish that this government should represent the best of all the nation – and the blessed feeling of having a full belly.

'That Friday night,' Mickey asked him, 'as you walked past The Maid with your pushcart, did you see a woman standing on the corner?'

'With a sailor. Ay. Betty, her name is. She's not a bad sort, for all that life's made her suffer.'

'Betty Moran was our witness to the fire and how it was set,' Mickey told him. 'Mr Jenkins, I should tell you that she was found dead this morning. She had been murdered.'

Hezekiah fixed him with his pale eyes. 'God rest her poor soul,' he said. 'So now you think whoever did for her might come for me?'

'If they saw you, then I think it's possible. Will you tell us what you saw that night?' Henry asked. 'Inspector Hitchens will need a statement from you later, but for now, if you could tell us what you saw?'

'Early morning it was. Maybe two; I'd not long heard the bell from St George-in-the-East church. There's a place I stay sometimes, an old barge left to rot. Sad old thing it is, but sound enough. I was headed there. I saw Betty and her fella in the entrance to the yard, back of the pub. I saw three boys carrying a big fuel can go into the warehouse by a side door. I stopped and I watched. I was worried, see, I knew other fellas that slept in the building. They got in through the rotten door at the front. It had glass in the panel, which got broken. Someone fastened a board across with a single big nail. You can swing it to one side and go in. The three youths – they were up to no good, all furtive-like and looking scared, like they didn't want to be spotted. I took a guess at what they were going to do and I didn't want to see no one burned to death. So, I waited in the little alley just beyond the corner after The Maid pub.'

Mickey nodded, visualizing the scene. He'd have been able to see the side door and would be able to see the boys come out. He would also have had a view of a section of the yard by the loading bay and the end of the road that led past the front of the property.

'I waited and I watched. Watched and I waited. I saw the

three young fellas coming out. No fuel can. They sneaked out and peered around and then ran back past The Maid.'

He paused. 'Betty, she called out to them: what were they doing, she wanted to know. The sailor, he pulled her back and away, I heard him tell her not to get involved. That he had better things for her to do. Been drinking, the two of them. The Maid sometimes has regulars in after it's closed its doors. I reckon they'd been in there until just before I saw them.'

Mickey nodded. The landlord of The Maid was well known for his flouting of the licensing laws.

'Then I saw a man walk through the loading yard at the back of the warehouse. I'd not seen him come off the street, so I figured he'd been in the yard somewhere. He'd be hard to see if he waited behind that low wall next to the dock. There's streetlights along the road, but even that's not well lit and once you get off the road you're mostly in shadow.'

Hezekiah emptied his teacup and Henry rose to fetch him more. Where did he put it all? Mickey wondered. 'I could smell smoke by now,' Hezekiah said. 'I was about to go and rouse the sleepers when I saw another man. He comes along the street, past the pub, sniffs the air and then crosses the street. He stops for a moment near the yard and then takes himself inside. I left my pushcart in the alley and I went to the front of the warehouse and I banged on the windows and I shouted, loud as I could. I told them, "Fire, there's a fire!" I was about to go in when I heard them shouting, so I went back over to my cart and I stood and watched. I never wanted them to burn, but those men, they're not the sort I want to be encumbered with.'

A look of unease seemed to pass over Hezekiah's face as he said this, and Mickey wondered about it.

'And then?' Henry said.

'I saw the first man come back out and I waited for the second man to show. The first, he had the fuel can with him and was in a rush to get out of there. Then I see Betty. The sailor'd gone, there was just Betty and she shouted at him, this man. Shouted something like "What you doing there?" and he turned and he looked at her. She was too far gone with the drink to understand, but I knew she'd marked herself, doing what she did. The men who'd been sleeping had come running out, but they didn't notice Betty or even look her way. The street they come out on is opposite The Maid.'

Henry nodded. 'And they raised the alarm.'

'Knew the landlord wouldn't be abed, so they hammered on the door. I watched the first man slip away, fast as night and just as dark. Then I went round the back and I looked inside and I seen him there, the second man. Dead as dead and on fire. Nothing to be done. The fire was all in a line from the far corner near to the door, back to where the man was lying, like the first man had spilt petrol and set it alight. I thought to myself, Hezekiah, that can must have been near empty by the time he'd got a hold of it. There can't have been enough left for him to make a good job. The three lads must have tipped most of it into the corner, but I'm thinking there can't have been a lot to start with. The fire didn't look fierce enough or big enough to have a whole can tipped over to start it off. But what would young'uns know? They did what they thought would work, but not enough to start a real big blaze.'

'And then you left?'

'I heard the sound of people shouting in the street, and I didn't want to get the blame for something I'd not done. So, I crossed over, quick as lightning, and I took my cart off down the alley and away. Slept under the tarpaulin that night, half under the cart. I've done it too many times for it to matter, when I couldn't find a better bed.'

He drained his final cup of tea and then stood up. 'And that's the lot.'

'You didn't recognize either man?' Henry asked. 'This first man, could you describe him to me?'

Hezekiah reached into an inner pocket of his greatcoat. He was still wearing it, despite the warmth of the day. He didn't look overheated either, Mickey noted. He removed a sheet of paper and gave it to Henry. Mickey leaned over to look as he unfolded it. A man's face, drawn in pencil, and skilfully drawn at that, stared back at Mickey.

'Thank you,' Henry said. He reached into his own pocket and withdrew a small cloth purse. 'An artist must have paper and pencils,' he said. 'I've failed miserably as your patron this last year or so.'

'So you have, but that can't be helped. You've not been here and I've not been here and so we've not met.' And with that Hezekiah took himself away.

'He's talented,' Mickey said. 'You think it will be a good likeness?'

'He'll not have seen the man for long and in the dim light, but he can catch the look of a person very quickly,' Henry said. 'Hopefully this man was not aware of Hezekiah being there that night and hopefully Hezekiah will now have the sense to go away for a while, though I'm sure he'll still call in to see you and make his statement, now the two of you are acquainted.'

'His patron?' Mickey questioned.

'He's a man who has his pride, Mickey. He found it easier to accept money if it was in payment for his art than if it was given for food or lodging. He works for those too. Knowing Hezekiah, I know that selling information sticks in his craw; accepting a donation from a patron to an artist was easier to swallow.'

The world never ceases to surprise me, Mickey thought.

# TWENTY-SIX

Dan Trotter stood in what had been his father's study, staring out of the window. Not that there was a view; the brick wall of the neighbouring building and a glimpse of the street, if you strained your neck, but that was the way his father had liked it.

'No distractions!' Dan could still hear his booming voice, feel his disapproval almost bleeding from the walls. The wall-paper in here was indeed a blood-red, making an already gloomy space even darker and more dismal. Two walls were decked out with wood panels to half-height, one other with floor-to-ceiling bookcases, stacked with books his father had never read and which, Dan suspected, he'd purchased by the yard just for the look of them.

Dan had always hated this room.

When his father had died two years before, he had thought it appropriate to move in here so that he could conduct business from the same space his father had used. It was as if he had hoped to imbibe his late father's acumen and administrative sense. Instead, he had found himself paralysed by the old man's presence, still dominating this heart of his small kingdom. This room that Dan had only ever entered to receive lectures or punishment. Dan's back and behind ached with the memory of the regular beatings he had received, even into adulthood, the physical memory revived of each and every one, just as soon as he crossed the threshold. There had never been any attempt on his father's part to teach him how to run the damned business, Dan thought, just his father's regular reminders that 'you're an idiot, boy. Bad blood on your mother's side, that's what it is.'

The constant reminder that his mother had taken poison, rather than remain one day longer with the monster she had married.

Or, at least, Dan believed that was the reason. He had been

only ten years old when he had discovered her, froth and blood at her mouth, her body twisted in agony. Prussic acid. He had overheard the servants talking about it later. Taken by accident, in mistake for her sleeping draught, the coroner had found. No doubt his father's money and influence being enough to create doubt about her suicide.

So, why had he come in here now? To be punished? What would the great Edward Trotter do, had he still been around to discover his son was a murderer?

Dan slumped in the chair set in front of his father's desk. The visitor's chair. He still could not bear to take his father's seat behind the desk; that was just too much.

A few weeks after the funeral, when it became obvious that this study was still not his, despite him now being the sole inheritor of the estate, he had set up his own study at the back of the house with a view of the garden, a view which caused him many distractions. Perhaps his father had a point in this at least. Maybe a window facing a brick wall would have been more profitable.

The truth was Dan didn't have a clue about the business and, it turned out, he didn't have a clue as to how to manage people either. His business manager, who had obeyed his father's minutest wishes, disregarded Dan entirely and the other staff took their lead from him. The old man was gone; his business was as good as dead and Dan had been the one to run it into the ground.

And if he was honest, he was not sorry.

He should never have even tried. It wasn't in him to make his father's enterprise work. He should have sold up, taken the money and bought a little place in some sleepy spot where he could have lived quietly, tended a garden, maybe even had a dog. And a library of books he actually read. Instead, he had employed more and more desperate measures to keep things afloat, to keep his father's kingdom intact, and the latest attempt had been his most stupid yet.

Dan's mind now felt split in two. One part telling him that he still had assets he could liquidate. The warehouse, the remaining stock of wine and Turkish rugs and strange artifacts from a dozen different lands. Items which Dan knew would have fascinated him, had he not been so conscious that they were part of his father's business and not his. Had he been brought up to understand the suppliers and the traders and the buyers and the history and origin . . .

He had tried, hadn't he? Had he? Dan no longer knew.

But these things could be sold off, the warehouse and the shares in the boats that his father held, and this house. Even after the mounting debts were paid off and the creditors appeased, there would still be enough for Dan to go away and start again.

This was what one half of Dan's mind was telling him.

The other half – oh now, that was full of dreadful things. The other half reminded Dan that he was now a killer. Now twice a killer. The first had been – almost – an accident. If that man had not walked in on him when he had; if he'd kept his nose out of someone else's business, then he would not be dead. For that death there might be mitigating circumstances. But for the second?

Dan, for all his faults and difficulties – or perhaps because of them – had never been anything but scrupulously honest with himself. The second death had been murder, pure and simple. He had gone out in search of that woman and he had struck her down.

He had even gone prepared, carrying with him the short but heavy iron from his father's hearth. There was no innocence, no mitigation in that.

And the worst of it was . . . No, the best of it was he had done what he set out to do with a directness and efficiency that was not at all common in Daniel Trotter's actions. The worst, and yet the best of it, and it both frightened and exhilarated him to realize this, Dan had returned home elated and joyous at what he'd done.

How, he asked himself, and why should he possibly feel that way?

He sat now, in the chair facing his father's desk, and he thought about what had happened and he realized, with a degree of shock, that the first death had also been well enacted. The man had come in and Dan had not given his actions a second thought. He had seen a threat and he had dealt with it, and when the man had not been felled by that first blow, he, Dan, had drawn the knife from his pocket, opened the blade, calmly and without fuss, and plunged it into the man's chest.

Only the failure to destroy the body in that ineffectual fire had spoiled the ending. But that had been down to the old Dan, the indecisive Dan Trotter, paying idiot boys to do a man's job. He would not make that mistake again.

Did this all make him crazy? Dan asked himself. He knew what he had done but he felt no real guilt, only a vague curiosity as to how this strength had been within him all the time and he'd not recognized it.

Dan Trotter got up, went around the desk and, after only a moment's hesitation, took his rightful place in his father's chair.

# TWENTY-SEVEN

Mickey Hitchens had spent the rest of Friday afternoon studying the photo books of known criminals. It had been a task just knowing where to begin. Could he start with those classified as arsonists? No, he decided, their man had not set the fire, merely in all probability caused it to be done. Could he begin with the classification by modus operandi? But no, again, he had nothing to dictate what that might be. Had he killed before? Most killers begin their career with wounding, and so Mickey began with the mugshots of those known for violence against the person, but after two hours had found no face that was comparable to the one in the picture Hezekiah had drawn.

Mickey found himself doubting Hezekiah's word. Was this really a portrait of the man he had seen or was it simply a figure from the old soldier's imagination? But Henry trusted him . . . and Mickey still trusted Henry's judgement.

When Hezekiah had left, the two of them had chatted for a while, settling companionably as they always did and discussing the possible outcomes of the projects each was concerned with. It had seemed to Mickey that the drive to track down young Ethan Samuels had diminished in his friend. That something had shifted in the past days, and Henry was now less concerned with applying the letter of the law and more sanguine about the fact that he might never be able to catch up with this particular miscreant. He had gained the impression that Henry was now more concerned with what course would do the least harm and with the hope that Helen Church and the Samuels family would eventually find some peace in the world.

Mickey would have raised a glass to that sentiment; he had raised his teacup instead.

They had discussed Mickey's case and Hezekiah's drawing. 'This is not the face of a poor man or a man who is out working in all weathers,' Henry had said.

'But it is the face of a killer.'

Henry had nodded agreement. 'And one who learns fast. It took three attempts to bring Mr Peters down, if you choose to include the fire, which I do, considering he was not dead from the stab wound before the fire reached him. The second time, from what you say, he brought Betty Moran down with a single blow.'

'She wasn't a hard target,' Mickey said. 'But I take your point. The worry is our man might find he has a taste for violence.'

On returning to Scotland Yard, Mickey had asked that a photograph be taken of the portrait and copies made. The plan was to canvass the area around the warehouse the following day. If Hezekiah's drawing was even partially accurate, someone might recognize their man.

In the meantime, Mickey had been studying the books and come up with nothing.

He glanced at his watch. It was after five. He would call it a day and go home; perhaps go and meet Belle at the theatre later on and they would walk home together.

Tomorrow, the search would begin again. The photographs would be ready by then, and hopefully this image would help to lead them to their man.

# TWENTY-EIGHT

Henry had phoned Dr Fielding to thank him again for his hospitality and see if there had been any developments. There had not.

'It's a strange business, strange and distressing,' Fielding said. 'I can't help but feel that I did everyone a disservice by contacting you. Perhaps Hanson was right, and I should have let sleeping dogs lie.'

Henry told him that he had passed all relevant information on to Inspector Hitchens, but both men knew that this was a long shot and unlikely to yield any useful results. 'I've been studying maps,' Henry said, 'and books on geology, to try and match a location with what Malina reported was in the letters. It's proving interesting but somewhat inconclusive.'

Fielding laughed. 'So I would imagine,' he said. 'Well, good luck, Henry old chap. I'll write if anything interesting happens at this end.'

Henry set the phone down in its cradle with the distinct impression that not only did Fielding believe him to be on a wild-goose chase – and Henry could not argue with that assessment – but that something had shifted at Fielding's end. That doubt in the rightness of summoning ex-Inspector Henry Johnstone had transmuted into outright regret, and Fielding now appeared to wish to distance himself from it.

Henry felt some small sadness at that. He liked Dr Fielding and had enjoyed his company. Could he have counted him as a friend eventually? Henry wondered, and found himself thinking that he probably could not, though he could not have said precisely why.

Malina knocked at the door of Albert's study, where Henry had been making use of the phone. 'Dinner is about to be served,' she said, and took his hand. They had set the date for the wedding and now just needed to make the booking. It was to be a quiet affair, mid-October, when the weather was still likely to be good but Bournemouth not so busy with visitors. A honeymoon would follow, but neither of them had any particular place in mind. Malina would continue as Cynthia's personal secretary and if children came along, the nanny who had cared for Cynthia's brood would come happily out of retirement. After all, she too still lived in Cynthia's house, a valued and much-loved member of her entourage, even though the children no longer really needed her.

Henry felt oddly content – and, as always when he felt content, fearful that the feeling would suddenly go away.

'Is there something wrong, Master Dan?' Mrs Mead asked. 'You've barely eaten a mouthful.'

Dan stared down at his plate and then at the dishes spread out across the table. He had barely even noticed what had been served. He felt a sudden guilt at the effort Mrs Mead had gone to. 'I'm sorry, Mrs Mead,' he told her. 'I seem to have no appetite lately.'

'Perhaps you should see the doctor,' she suggested, a look of very genuine anxiety on her face, and Dan felt an even deeper pang of guilt.

'I'll be fine in a day or two,' he told her. 'Just a small stomach complaint. It will pass.'

She set down the coffee and began to clear the dishes away. Dan said, 'Mrs Mead, I know you have holidays arranged in a few days. I've been thinking of taking myself off somewhere; a change of scene will do me good, I think. So why don't you go off a few days early? I'm sure your family will be delighted to have more time with you.'

She gave him a curious and concerned look. Then seemed to make up her mind. 'All right, Mr Dan, if you're sure. I can send a telegram to my niece tomorrow and see if it's all right for me to come down ahead of time.'

It would be, Dan knew. Mrs Mead had a large family down in Devon, and her niece in particular had urged her to leave London permanently and be closer to them. There was nothing to prevent her doing so, apart from a certain loyalty to Dan. A small bequest Dan's father had left would be sufficient for her to be comfortable, and Dan planned on making a gift of some of his mother's jewellery. It was his to give, and it would see her nicely provided for. He would draw up a formal letter to that effect so no one could question it. If the worst happened, he wanted Mrs Mead to be protected from any unpleasantness.

He poured his coffee, smiled at the three almond biscuits on the little plate, glad that he had settled that problem at least. The two halves of his mind continued to battle. One assuring him that all would be well, and the other screaming that he would end his days at the end of a hangman's noose.

Dan told them both to be quiet and ate his biscuits.

# TWENTY-NINE

On the Saturday morning, Mickey had continued with his perusal of the mugshots. He was getting nowhere fast. Sergeant Tibbs arrived just after ten in the morning and informed Mickey that he had ascertained the name and address of the owner of the warehouse next to the Brinton establishment.

'What manner of place is it?' Mickey asked.

'Well, the late Mr Trotter dealt in luxury items. Wines and exotic goods from Turkey and the Orient. He had shares in three cargo ships and owned properties, though some of these were sold off on his death. His son, Daniel Trotter, took over the business from his father but I got the feeling that he was not making such a success of it as his father had done. The clerk I spoke to was reticent. I interrupted him making an inventory of some newly delivered goods, but when I noted that the warehouse was half empty and that he was the only member of staff present, he admitted to some of the workers having been let go and made reference to how much a hive of activity it had been in the old days.'

'Interesting,' Mickey said. 'And did you get the impression that their new employer was liked?'

'I got the impression that he was, well, if not despised then discounted. Once I'd got the clerk speaking about the "old days", I could barely shut him up. I've listed all the goods that used to be handled there and taken down the names of dismissed staff and, as you'll see,' he turned his notebook towards Mickey, 'the tally runs to several pages.'

'So, likely a business in trouble,' Mickey said, retrieving his hat. 'We'll go and speak to the new boss, shall we, and then I think we'll call it a day. The post-mortem of poor Betty Moran is not until Monday. I'm still waiting for the photographs of our suspect to be ready, and it does seem as though things have ground to a halt for now. Unless this interview throws us a useful line, then I suggest we give thanks for a free remainder of the weekend.'

They were taken to their destination by a police driver, who waited for them while they knocked on the door of the Trotter residence. It was a tall, imposing house, left over from a time when the area had been home to many such residences, before the merchant class had moved further out from the noise and smoke of the centre of town and the slow decline, in status if not in busyness, of much of the docklands. Tall windows looked out towards the street, basement stairs leading down to the kitchen. Three main storeys rising high above Mickey's head, dormer windows on the attic floor above.

A narrow alleyway, barely wide enough for pedestrians, led to the back of the house next door, which looked to be of more recent construction than the Victorian edifice, whose massive front entrance was decorated with a large door knocker in the shape of a woman's hand. Mickey grasped the hand and knocked loudly.

On the other side of the house was an area of fenced-off land and the remnants of what had probably been a similar house. Mickey wondered what would be built there. A wider entryway led to a gate and Mickey could see trees beyond and so guessed at a substantial garden.

A woman opened the front door, the housekeeper presumably. She looked, Mickey thought, to be in her fifties, but had one of those faces that made it hard to tell. Unlined, milk-and-roses skin, blue eyes, thick and wavy greying hair caught back in a neat bun. She was dressed in dark blue with a wide lace collar and cuffs. He caught sight of a suitcase and lightweight summer coat on the hallstand.

The street was quiet, a car passed, a woman with a small child walked slowly by on the other side of the road. She glanced their way, probably curious about the visitors, and the housekeeper nodded to her in a neighbourly fashion.

'I'd like to speak to Mr Daniel Trotter,' Mickey said, waving his identification in her direction. She caught his hand, peered at it, then looked questioningly at the pair of them. 'And what would the police want with Mr Trotter?'

'As you may know,' Mickey said, 'the warehouse next to

the one connected with Mr Trotter's business had a fire a fortnight ago. It was arson, and not a clever job of it either, and a man was killed.'

'Of course I heard about it,' she said. 'A bad business. But that's no concern of Mr Trotter's.'

'All the same, we'd like to speak with him.'

'Then you'll have to come back. Mr Trotter isn't here presently. I'm his housekeeper, Mrs Mead, and I have a train to catch. It's my annual leave and I'd rather not start it by missing my train.'

'Perhaps we can offer you a lift,' Tibbs said, surprising Mickey.

Good idea, Mickey thought.

But Mrs Mead had other ideas. 'In a police car? No, thank you very much. I've made arrangements already, as you can see.' She gestured towards the cab which had just pulled up behind the police car.

'Now, if you'll excuse me. My taxi has arrived.' She retreated into the hallway and collected her coat and suitcase and a Gladstone bag that Mickey had not noticed. She closed the door firmly behind her and nodded to them both.

'Good day to you, gentlemen,' she said, and settled into the waiting cab.

She was, Mickey noted, still watching them as the taxi drove away.

'So, what now?' Tibbs asked as Mickey knocked on the door again.

'I think we arrange for an eye to be kept on the place,' Mickey said, 'but in the meantime, we go back to the warehouse for another chat with the clerk, see if the portrait we have is a picture of his employer. If it's not, we have a swift drink and a conversation with the landlord of The Maid, see if he can put a name to the mystery man Hezekiah saw. After which, we take the rest of our Saturday to rest, let our Mr Trotter think we've lost interest in him and see what, if anything, he does next.'

Dan Trotter was in fact blissfully unaware of the police interest in him. He had taken the day off to go on a tour of the museums and art galleries he would miss if he left the city, and had also taken time to lodge a letter and small parcel with his solicitor, leaving both with the secretary for attention on the Monday morning.

That done, he took the rest of his day for leisure, enjoying a slow tour around the National Gallery. Dan felt happy for the first time he could remember. He had made a decision: his father's shoes were not his to fill. He would, over the weekend, draw up a plan for the sale of his assets and the payment of creditors and then make appointments with his bank and solicitor to deal with both. If he continued with things as they were, it would not be long before others became aware of what dire straits the business was in, and if that were to happen he would never realize the full value of the properties and goods he had to sell. If, however, he acted now, there would still be some chance of equity being left in the sale for him to begin his new life. He already had the proceeds from the sales of various properties his father had been ready to let go and which had been sold on his death. That money was not in his business account, but had been deposited in a private bank in trust for Dan until he reached twenty-five. Dan was presently twenty-four years and eight months, so didn't have long to wait. It was as if his father had known he'd fail and wanted to make this extra provision, Dan thought wryly. Well, the old man had been right yet again. Not that he'd ever expected Dan to succeed at anything – or at least not at anything he counted as being of value.

The part of his mind that screamed accusations at him, for the murderer that he was, seemed to have quietened overnight. He had spent the small hours deciding what must be done and thinking rationally and carefully about what options might be open to him. Confessing to his crimes was not one of them. No, that business was done now – done and finished with – and it was time to move forward. He had finally taken control of his own affairs and Dan felt the better for it.

He was relieved that Mrs Mead was going away. By the time her holiday had ended, everything else would have been attended to and he could then send her a telegram, with a letter to follow, informing her that she need not return. He would pay her two months' salary and send on his mother's jewellery, or the solicitor would do so for him. The pieces were already parcelled up and left at the solicitor's office, along with two missives, one for the solicitor explaining his gift and one for Mrs Mead, assuring her that the jewellery was now hers to do with as she wished. That, he felt, would fulfil any obligation he might have had to the woman who had been such a faithful retainer, and by that time Dan would have left the city, left his old life behind, be a free man.

# THIRTY

As it happened, the clerk could not be found when they reached the warehouse. The door was sealed with a heavy padlock and the rear doors locked from the inside, so instead their first stop was at The Maid public house across the way.

It was just past lunchtime, and still busy with men whose hands and clothing suggested manual labour and who, to a man, looked as though they'd be able to handle themselves in a fight. Mickey, built like the heavyweight boxer he still was when opportunity allowed, felt quite at home in such company and, although the company examined him as he and Tibbs entered, they soon lost interest. Tibbs was another matter. Tibbs always seemed to lose what little coordination he had of his limbs when faced with men who made their living from managing theirs. He was coltlike at the best of times.

Mickey pushed his way over to the bar, opening a passage between the press of men through which Tibbs could follow. His sergeant kept close behind but, even so, Mickey almost lost him in the few yards between entrance and bar. He reached behind and caught his sergeant's coat, pulling him between two big bruisers, shirtsleeves rolled up over hefty forearms and hands like hams, who had crowded Tibbs out of the way.

'Now then, gentlemen, let me have my sergeant back,' Mickey said cheerfully. 'And I'll have two pints of Tetley's mild and enough of your time for a single question.'

The landlord regarded Mickey balefully but poured the beer into heavy glass mugs and set them down. 'I do like a glass with a handle,' Mickey told him. 'And the heavier the better. You can get more of a swing. Drink up lad,' he instructed Tibbs. 'We don't have long.'

The landlord now regarded the pair of them with more amusement than malice, Mickey noted. 'You'll have one yourself?' Mickey asked as the man sorted his change. He gave Mickey a brief nod of thanks or maybe just acknowledgement, separated the price of another pint from the change and dropped it into a tin mug set beside the till.

'One question,' he said. 'All I've got the time for.'

Mickey took the picture from his pocket and held it for the landlord to see. The man made to take it from him but Mickey pulled it back. 'I'd as soon not get it beer-soaked,' he said, and waited until the man had wiped his hands on a none-too-clean towel.

Some of the regulars had crowded in and were craning to see what this strange policeman had brought. Beside him, Tibbs was sipping his beer and trying to be invisible. Mickey would have to talk to him about that – again. He had been trying to convince Tibbs that what he lacked in heft he made up for in height and that he should use that to his advantage. He wondered again just how Tibbs had survived his years in uniform; that he had was apparent. The young man was standing at his side and had the makings of a fine detective. All of which proved that he had a certain tenacity and bloody-mindedness that others didn't always recognize.

The picture was being handed round now, causing Mickey some moments of grievous concern, but it came back to him soundly enough, with merely a crease at the corner and a smudge of coal dust at the edge.

'Hezekiah Jenkins draw that, did he?' someone asked.

'He did indeed,' Mickey confirmed. He took a good deep drink of his own beer and nodded approval at the landlord. 'So does anyone know the man?'

'Well, he doesn't drink in here,' another man announced, his comment met with laughter.

The crowd was starting to thin now as men prepared to return to work. A few said they'd seen him around. A toff was the general consensus. Two, crucially for Mickey's cause, suggested he had something to do with the Trotter place.

Mickey thanked them and downed the rest of his pint, then led his sergeant away. As they opened the door to leave, he was amused to note that the landlord was finishing Tibbs' barely touched pint. He raised the glass in Mickey's direction.

'You'll have to learn to drink faster than that, lad,' Mickey said. 'And it's in my mind that I should teach you how to box.' He regarded Tibbs' long limbs and wondered why this had not occurred to him before. 'Lord knows you've got the reach for it,' Mickey said.

# THIRTY-ONE

The weekend had arrived soft and golden and on Bogle Hill it was a quiet time for the Samuels family. The previous Sunday had seen the brief visit from Henry Johnstone as he headed for home, but this time the visitor was Dr Fielding.

Dar Samuels greeted him with the same wary friendliness as always, but Fielding assured him he would not be stopping.

'Had a birth to attend,' he said. 'As I was passing, I thought I'd bring you the newspapers before I get off home.'

'Thank you for that. You're keeping well?'

'I am, though I confess to being tired. Babies always seem to arrive in the dead of night or take all night to come. But I'm not as weary as the poor mother.' He laughed a little self-consciously at that. 'Well, I'll be off.' He paused with the car door open. 'There's been no news,' he said. 'Not from Mr Johnstone. I know he's made enquiries, but I don't believe they've amounted to anything yet.'

Dar Samuels nodded his understanding. 'I doubt they will,' he said. 'But the cards will fall where they might.'

Dar watched as the doctor drove carefully back down the hill. He would, he thought, miss this place, for all that it was inconvenient and out of the way. On clear summer mornings it felt as though he was lord of his own little kingdom, watching the early mist burn off the lower ground and he, sitting in rainbows above it. He shook his head free of fancies and returned to the house. Plans had been set in place now and Dar was happy with them. He had put the word out, telling a few good people he knew he could trust that he and his family would be leaving and might need a bit of help with transport and the like . . . and help also for Helen, little Sam and the baby yet to be born. The view from the hill might be pleasant enough but the truth was there was nothing for any of them here now.

It had become his habit to sit down with the newspapers in the kitchen and tell the news to Liza, when she was cooking. Sometimes he read from an article he knew would please her, sometimes he just summarized the content. The papers were a few days old, but no worse for that.

'It would seem Mr Ramsay MacDonald is to remain as head of the National Government, though he's been ousted from the Labour Party,' he told her.

'Oh, he's only been there two minutes and who's taken his place?'

'That's to be Arthur Henderson; he was Foreign Secretary. At least he's solid Labour, I suppose.'

'At least he knows what it is to work for a living,' Liza said.

Dar nodded. Henderson had been a mould-maker in a metal foundry before he'd started his political career. It was a good choice, perhaps, Dar thought. But what difference it would make to lives like theirs was scant. He was sceptical about this new National Government, which had been sworn in only days before. What hope was there that such a mix of parties and opinions could come to any agreement?

'And what did the doctor want?' she asked.

'Said he was passing and just wanted to drop the papers off.'

She laughed. 'Passing by from where? No, he's just nosing about again. Likes to be at the centre of things, does Doctor Fielding, and now the detective's gone he's had his nose put out of joint.'

Former detective, Dar thought, but he nodded agreement at his wife's analysis. 'Told me he'd had no news from him, that he'd put out enquiries of some sort but nothing's come back.'

'Or he's not seen fit to tell the good doctor if they had,' Liza said. 'He no doubt wondered if we'd had news.'

'No doubt of that.'

Liza turned back to her task of preparing vegetables and Dar went back to reading headlines from the newspapers. There would be no news about their son, they were both certain of that, and by Michaelmas everything would have changed and no doubt they would have provided the good doctor with another mystery to ponder.

Dar would not risk sending another letter to his son, Ethan would know soon enough and Dar had no doubt he would be happy with the outcome.

Dan wandered slowly back from church on the Sunday morning. It was the first time in months that Mrs Mead had not accompanied him. She enjoyed a good bout of hymn singing and was even quite partial to a sermon. Dan had been a little worried about the morning service, that part of his mind still ready to accuse him of breaking the sixth commandment causing him to feel that his sin might somehow be obvious to someone as trained in spotting sin as the vicar. But nothing untoward had happened. He had chatted to the usual people after service, accepted a supper invitation for later in the week, told old friends of his father that the business was fine, but that he was discussing some new options for the future. He had been vague, but they had looked suitably impressed.

He was within a hundred yards of his front door when he was hailed by a neighbour. Mrs Pickering was walking with her husband and their young daughter. He paused, wished them a good morning and was ready to move on, but Mrs Pickering crossed the road intent on speaking to him. Her husband and child followed more slowly.

'I'm so sorry you've had trouble,' she said.

'Trouble?'

'Yes, that the police had to come after that sad business with the warehouse and the man being killed. Yours didn't catch fire, did it?'

He managed a smile. 'No, the alarm was raised and the fire brigade came in time to stop the fire from spreading. But I don't quite understand. I know nothing about the police coming.'

'Did Mrs Mead not tell you?' Mr Pickering asked.

Dan shook his head.

Mrs Pickering laughed suddenly. 'Oh, I'm such a fool. Of course she won't have mentioned it. They came when she was about to leave for her holiday. Hasn't she gone a little early this year? Her taxi pulled up as she was speaking to the police officers, so she had to go. I'm afraid I overheard,' she said apologetically. 'Sally walks so slowly.'

Dan looked down at the child. She was, if he remembered correctly, about two years old, at an age when everything had to be examined and explored. He had often seen the child and her mother making their slow way along the street, often deep in conversation – or what passed for conversation with such a tiny child.

'I'm sorry I missed them,' Dan said. 'I could have asked if they had any news on the poor dead man.'

'I expect they'll be back,' Mrs Pickering said. 'I expect with you owning the place next door they'll want to know if any strangers have been seen about the place.'

They bade good morning shortly after and continued on their way, and Dan went inside, considerably disturbed by the exchange. There was nothing, he assured himself, that could connect him to the man's death. He had disposed of the witness, that stupid woman who had called out after him.

She had been with a man, he remembered, but thought he had left long before Dan could have come to his notice. Then, of course, there were the boys, but they would not know him. He had been cleverer than that. Dealing with the matter through the intermediary that his father had often used when difficult tasks needed seeing to.

But he would know, of course. Kimberlin would know. He would guess that the dead man was something to do with Dan. Would Kimberlin talk?

Dan set the kettle to boil and thought about his predicament. Kimberlin had never let his father down, and he had earned enough money from him over the years that he had been loyal and reliable. Though this was the first time Dan had asked him for anything. And Kimberlin had been stupid enough to employ those three idiot boys.

Abruptly Dan lashed out, knocking the kettle to the floor, splashing half-boiled water on to the stove and the sleeve of his jacket. Breathing heavily, Dan glowered at it as though it was the kettle's fault that it had landed on the floor.

Kimberlin, Dan thought, would have to go.

He leaned down and picked the kettle off the floor, filled it again and set it back on the stove. There was one more thing that would need his attention. He had brought the petrol can back with him, stowed it in the shed and then quite forgotten about it until now. What to do with that?

He could take it and throw it into the dock, he supposed, but if he was seen, how could he explain why a gentleman might be walking the streets with something as workaday as a fuel can. No, to Dan's mind that was absurd. He would have to think further about this. He could perhaps bury it, but that would mean disturbing his beautiful roses and Dan could not countenance that.

The kettle had come to the boil while he had been trying to resolve the matter, and he took it from the stove, warmed the pot, and then made the tea. While he waited for the tea to brew, he fetched the can from the tool shed and took it into what his father had called the junk room, high up in the attic space. There he tucked it safely behind an old steamer trunk, a tea chest full of books, and a suitcase that still contained some of his dead mother's clothes.

Then Dan shut the door on his problem and returned to the kitchen to pour his tea.

# THIRTY-TWO

The post-mortem on Betty Moran took place first thing on the Monday morning of the seventh of September. It was, Mickey thought, a sad affair. The woman was thin and malnourished and her body bruised and scarred, witness to the tough life she'd led. Her liver was already sclerotic, though Dr Keen was of the opinion that she was no more than mid-thirties in age.

'There's no doubt as to the cause of death,' he confirmed. 'Whoever hit her did so with considerable force and with a weapon that left no obvious trace, so no brick dust, splinters, anything of that sort. Perhaps a metal bar or something of that sort, though there are odd little indentations, here at the upper edge of the wound. You see?'

He handed Mickey the magnifying glass and pointed at what he had noticed. Then grabbed a piece of paper and a pen from his assistant and drew a rough shape.

'There's a roundness to the wound and then a narrow split that extends to skin and muscle but not through the bones of the skull. Is that what you mean?'

Dr Keen nodded. He showed Mickey the sketch he had just made. 'Now, it could be I'm being fanciful, but imagine a fire iron with a bulbous end and perhaps some feature for hanging, or even a decorative knob on the top. The blow was hard enough and at enough of an angle that it could be what tore the skin and made that mark.' He shrugged. 'Of course, it's pure speculation but I've seen something similar before. A husband who bludgeoned his wife to death with a heavy poker. It left a similar profile.'

'It's a deep wound, whatever made it,' Mickey said.

'Isn't it just? The weapon will be covered in blood and brain matter, fragments of bone.'

'And has likely been washed or disposed of by now.'

'Even so, it would be difficult to be rid of all contamination, even if it appears clean to the naked eye.'

Mickey said he'd take that under advisement. Dr Keen was clearly enjoying the detection element of his job. Mickey couldn't begrudge him that; he could imagine little more depressing than a continuous cavalcade of the dead, all waiting for the skilled knife, none of them capable of recovery.

He had arranged to meet Tibbs at the warehouse. There would be staff on duty on a Monday and it was possible they would know the man in Hezekiah's drawing. Tibbs had been commissioned with collecting the photographs and bringing them along, together with a couple of constables borrowed from Leman Street who could help with the canvassing of the area. If their man was local, Mickey now felt confident of flushing him out.

Tibbs had already set the constables to work. Mickey passed one of them knocking on doors as he arrived at the warehouse. He spotted the other going into one of the surrounding office buildings.

'Mr Edwards, the clerk I spoke to, arrived a few minutes ago, but I thought I'd wait on you before going back in. He'll like having an inspector call.'

Mickey laughed. 'Make him feel special, will it?'

'I think he might feel that rank equals respect,' Tibbs said. 'He's a man rather proud of his position and a mere sergeant did not fully satisfy.'

Mickey could see Tibbs' amusement but a moment or so of being in the company of Mr Edwards informed Mickey that Tibbs' assessment was correct.

Mr Edwards was a small, dapper man, with hands that were never still, particularly when he was talking.

'Inspector Hitchens.' He sounded delighted. 'I have read reports of you in the newspapers. This is a real pleasure. I was speaking to your sergeant the other day; I hope I've been helpful?'

Mickey assured him that he had. He asked Edwards about the stock the warehouse held, admired the antiquities and fine carpets that Edwards and one of his assistants were readying for delivery. Commiserated about the changes that were taking place in business.

'It's not like the old days,' Mr Edwards lamented. 'Time was this place would have been stacked up, floor to ceiling. Old Mr Trotter, now there was a man who knew the ins and outs of his trade.'

'And young Mr Trotter? Not so much?'

Edwards affected a look of sympathy, though Mickey suspected none was actually felt. 'He's young, I suppose he'll learn.' He leaned in confidentially and Mickey caught the scent of cigar smoke and bay rum. 'The trouble was, the older Mr Trotter, he never expected to fall ill so suddenly. He'd not fully . . . prepared his heir for the business side of things. I know it's not my place to say, but I did get the impression that he was worried young Master Daniel didn't exactly have a mind for business. That he might have been better in one of the professions or . . . well, something other than this.'

'You think that was a disappointment to him?' Mickey asked.

'I think it was a worry, certainly. And then when Mr Kimberlin announced his retirement, that was another blow. He'd been Mr Trotter's right hand for years.'

Kimberlin, Mickey thought. Could this be the mysterious Kim that young Georgie Tullis had claimed provided them with the petrol can? It was one hell of a coincidence if not.

'Anyway, is there anything else I can help you with, Inspector?'

Mickey wondered what Edwards thought he'd helped with so far. 'As it stands, there is. I've a photograph I'd like you and perhaps your staff to take a look at. If you could tell me if this man is familiar to you, that would be a great help.'

Mickey handed one of the photographic copies of Hezekiah's drawing to Mr Edwards. They'd come out well, he thought. Lacking some of the nuance, perhaps, but clear enough.

Mr Edwards stared at the picture and then back at Mickey. 'I don't understand,' he said. 'Is this some kind of joke? If so, it's in very poor taste.'

'I can assure you I don't joke around when I'm on police business,' Mickey assured him sternly. 'But I'm assuming that you may know this man?'

'Of course I know him. This is a picture of Master Daniel. What on earth are you doing with a picture of Master Dan?'

They left moments later, with directions from the warehouse to the Trotter residence, an address for Mr Kimberlin, and a promise – which Mickey did not expect to be kept – that Mr Edwards would not seek to inform his employer of the police interest.

Mickey intercepted one of the constables before he knocked on yet another door and told him to find his colleague and to follow after, quick as they might. 'But stay out of sight from the house. I don't want to spook the man and have him do a runner.'

The address was a ten-minute walk from the warehouse, through terraced streets and between factories and storehouses. Mickey, having been to the house before, now took time to take a proper look at the area. The street on which Daniel Trotter lived seemed to be from another age, when affluent merchantmen and those newly rich from trade had built their tall houses on what had been, Mickey guessed, still semi-rural land. Some had a Georgian look to them, a few even older, though the address they had been given led them to a house of Victorian splendour, rising above the neighbouring buildings and with a jutting roof gable that reminded Mickey of the prow of a ship. The large front door was set back a little from the pavement, but there seemed to be no steps leading down to a basement kitchen, only two very small, barred windows suggesting that there might be a cellar.

Once again, he grasped the door knocker shaped like a woman's hand and let it fall loudly. He caught a glimpse of the two constables standing at the end of the road, hopefully out of sight of the house. This time, no housekeeper opened the door to them.

Mickey knocked again.

'Could be there's no one home,' Tibbs said. 'Could be he doesn't want to speak to us.'

'Take one of the constables and see if you can find a back way in,' Mickey said quietly. 'Then leave the pair of them on watch and arrange for some proper surveillance. If we can't get hold of our chap now, I'm off to organize a warrant to search his place and then, while I'm waiting for that, to speak to this Kimberlin, see what light he can shed on the conundrum of three boys and a can of petrol.'

Mickey knocked again. Tibbs went off to do his master's bidding. No one opened the door and Mickey, stepping back into the street so he could see the upper windows, spotted no one looking out.

But I'll bet you're there, Mickey thought. I'll just bet you are.

Dan peered out cautiously through the attic window and down into the street. He had crept up to the highest point of the house but could not at first see who was hammering on his door. It was only when the man stepped back into the street and looked up that Dan got anything like a good look at him.

Was this, he wondered, the police officer who had come previously? Who Mrs Mead had spoken to?

Her family did not have ready access to a telephone, so Dan had been unable to speak to her on the matter. He had thought of writing a letter, but he was not much of a letter writer and a telegram seemed a little *de trop*. Now he wished he had, or had at least questioned the neighbour more closely about the police officers she'd seen.

He craned his neck, catching movement at the end of the street. A tall, thin man was walking to the corner to speak with someone, and Dan was certain he glimpsed a dark blue uniform and a constable's hat.

His heart began to race. What should he do? What could he do now?

Dan tiptoed away from the window and crept down to the next floor and along the corridor. His mother's old room would give him the best view. His own, on the first floor, overlooked the garden, but from his mother's room he could also see a portion of the street on to which the garden backed.

He watched for a while again, fancied he caught movement, but he could not be sure.

Dan slumped down on his mother's bed. Everything was covered with dust sheets, but the room itself had remained undisturbed since the night of her death. Dan had found her, lying on the floor, curled into a tight ball like a little child trying to hide. She was crying out in pain and retching, blood on her mouth and foam bubbling up from her lungs – though, of course, he'd not realized that at the time. It had made sense to him only as he'd grown older and was able to understand more.

Would everything have been different if she'd still been there as he grew up? Dan didn't know. His memories of her were of a loving but rather fey presence, all silks and perfume and, as his father always said, not a sensible bone in her body. Had that been true? Dan had no idea about that either. No one who had known his mother had remained a part of his life after she had gone. Even Mrs Mead had come after her death. She had replaced the old housekeeper three days after the funeral.

Well, he had no one to advise him now, Dan thought.

He got to his feet and went back into the attic rooms, but this time to the room at the back of the house. He unlatched the window and opened it wide, then left it open and went back down the stairs.

The knocking had ceased now and the man had gone.

# THIRTY-THREE

For the sake of speed, Mickey caught a cab back to Scotland Yard and set the issue of the warrant in motion. It was half past ten on Monday morning, and his experience of these things told him it might be mid-afternoon before it was approved.

He then procured a car and a driver and had them take him to meet the mysterious Mr Kimberlin.

Kimberlin's house was in St John's Wood and seemed, Mickey thought, an affluent place for a man who had effectively been a business manager. It had been built, he guessed, in Edward's reign, before the Great War, and was surrounded by a garden that, not large, was kempt and tended. A neatly dressed maid opened the door to him. Having asked if Mr Kimberlin would see him, Mickey handed her his hat and followed her through to a small room at the back of the house. Open French doors gave on to a closely mown lawn surrounded by tightly clipped hedges.

Kimberlin was not, to Mickey's surprise, an old man. Might he have taken early retirement? Mickey wondered. Perhaps he had accrued rewards other than his wages from his old employer. He was tall, straight and, though grey-haired, Mickey would not have put him past fifty.

'I was given your address by Mr Edwards, clerk at the warehouse owned by Daniel Trotter,' Mickey said.

'Indeed, Mr Edwards was good enough to telephone and warn me I might be getting a visit.'

Good of him, Mickey thought sourly. And had he also telephoned his employer?

'Now, what can I do for you? Some tea please, Dorcas,' he said to the maid, and directed Mickey into a chair set beside the open window.

Is she really called Dorcas? Mickey wondered. Or, as so commonly happened, did her employer call all his servants

Dorcas just for simplicity? A Dorcas had originally been a lady's maid . . . was there a lady of the house to tend to – a Mrs Kimberlin? Looking around, Mickey could see no evidence of a feminine presence in the tall leather chairs, the dark walls and heavy curtains. In fact, they seemed to have come from another age, more in keeping with the date of the house than with these times of lighter and less fussy décor.

'What can I do for you?' Mr Kimberlin asked.

'You can tell me about Daniel Trotter and about his father's business, how it's faring now his father's gone,' Mickey said. 'And perhaps you can answer an accusation: that you were the one who paid for the fire to be set in the old Brinton warehouse.'

Kimberlin raised an eyebrow and then laughed. 'Are you always so direct? One might say, so impertinent?'

'I probably am,' Mickey confessed. 'But particularly when my time is short. I'm sure you too have better things to do with your day than attending a police station to deal with awkward questions.'

'Attending a police station? I'm not sure I understand. Why would I be doing that?'

'You won't, for now, not if you give me straight answers,' Mickey told him. 'I have a problem, you see, Mr Kimberlin; a problem to do with the man in this picture.'

He handed the photograph of Hezekiah's drawing to Kimberlin.

'Mr Edwards warned me of this. Yes, it bears a passing resemblance to Dan Trotter, but I don't see—'

'It's from a picture drawn by a witness from the night of the fire. Someone who saw the three boys go in to set the fire, saw them come out, then saw this man enter, followed by another. This man then emerged and the other lay dead – bludgeoned, stabbed, and then set alight.'

Kimberlin stared at him. 'But you can't imagine that Dan would do such a thing? That's absurd.'

'And how is the business faring under his leadership, Mr Kimberlin? Because the impression I have is that it's not so healthy.'

The sudden change of tack had Kimberlin frowning, but he seemed more prepared to answer this question.

'Not as well as in his father's time,' he told him.

'And worse now you've left him to it, I'd guess.'

'Perhaps so. But I couldn't be expected to continue to hold the boy's hand. He has to learn to stand on his own two feet. That's what his father would have expected.'

'Did you leave before he ran it into the ground? Before you were impacted by that mismanagement?' Mickey asked mildly.

The maid came in with the tray and Kimberlin waited until he'd dismissed her before responding. 'I could see the way the wind was blowing,' he admitted. 'Dan is not a bad sort, but he's got no head for anything serious. His father knew that. I think he hoped that might improve as his son matured but . . .' He gestured helplessly. 'Frankly, I believe he's sinking fast. If he's any sense left, he'll sell up, recoup what he can before his losses become common knowledge and the business loses even the value of its goodwill.'

'Has he come to you for advice?'

'He did, some months ago, and that's what I told him then.'

'And since? Perhaps he had a scheme to collect the insurance money?'

'If he did, I know nothing about it. Look, I retired more than a year ago. I'd invested well, had a little capital left to me by my father, and Mr Trotter was kind enough to leave me a bequest for loyal service. I had hoped that my leaving would jolt young Dan into action. Make him realize that he had to take his role more seriously, but it doesn't seem to have done. It's a shame seeing all his father worked for failing on his watch, but it's not my responsibility and, frankly, it's no longer my concern.'

'So the three boys who set the fire had no business naming you as the one who paid them to do it, or who lent them the can to carry their fuel?' Mickey asked. He noted that the tea tray had remained untouched; he doubted he'd be getting a cup now. Well, he could wait until he got back to Scotland Yard.

Kimberlin first looked aghast and then he laughed. 'All I can think is they must have heard my name somewhere and be leading you a merry dance,' he said. 'What would I hope to gain? Why would I do something so monumentally stupid?'

'Well, a fire was set and a man died,' Mickey said. 'So if you have been, as you put it, monumentally stupid, you can be sure I'll find out about it eventually.'

'I think you'd better leave,' Kimberlin said coldly.

'For now, I will,' Mickey told him. 'I've no doubt I'll be seeing you again.'

# THIRTY-FOUR

When Mickey arrived back at Scotland Yard, Tibbs was waiting for him. The warrant still had not been approved and Mickey, a glance at his watch telling him it was just after one o'clock, was champing at the bit.

They took the opportunity to get some lunch and a mug of decent tea, and Mickey told Tibbs what had transpired in his meeting with Kimberlin.

'It's too much of a coincidence that he's not our man,' Tibbs said. 'And if he's indirectly responsible for the setting of the fire, then he's indirectly responsible for the death of Peters and of Betty Moran.'

'I think the courts will regard that as a bit of a stretch,' Mickey told him. 'But we'll get him on something, I've no doubt.'

A constable brought Mickey a report and set it on his desk.

'Responses to the Ethan Samuels enquiries?' Tibbs said, reading upside down.

'It looks like it, yes.' But that too proved to be a frustration. 'There is no record of either a Samuels or a Hayes boarding any kind of boat from Lowestoft at the time we think he was there. That's not to say he didn't or he wasn't, of course, just that there's no record. Enquiries will be made up and down the coast, but I don't hold out much hope on that front.'

'And the rest? The men who carried the letters to Helen Church?'

'It seems one of them has a record for petty theft, but no one knows where he might be, or if they do they're not telling. The other has been traced; local police spoke to him at a place called Meg's Cross in Derbyshire. That's one of the stopping places young Elizabeth Hanson named. However, he carried the letter only on the latter part of his journey, claims to have maybe been handed it at a horse fair, though he can't recall which one, nor can he recall who might have given it to him.

And as this happened two years ago, I suppose that's all possible.' He sighed. 'It was always a long shot and there's a great reluctance to trust the police, so I expected little else, in truth. I'd best telephone Henry and give him the news.'

His call to Henry was, however, to put Mickey in a much better frame of mind.

'We've set a date for the wedding,' Henry told him. 'And I want you to be my best man. Malina will send invitations in the next day or so. It's to be a small affair.'

'But a very happy one,' Mickey said. 'I'll tell Belle to set the sixteenth of October aside on the calendar.'

He was interrupted at that point by Tibbs informing him that the warrant had been approved. Perhaps the day was looking up after all, Mickey thought.

# THIRTY-FIVE

This time Mickey did not trouble with knocking on the door. He had constables front and back in case of an attempted escape, and a burly sergeant who made short work of the door.

'Upstairs,' Tibbs shouted, and Mickey hurtled after him, one of the constables in tow.

He caught sight of Dan running up the stairs towards the attic, and then his view was blocked by the unwieldy figure of Tibbs racing after, his booted feet thunderous on the stairs.

Where does he hope to go? Mickey wondered.

They chased him along the upper corridor, between attic rooms that would have housed servants in the house's heyday. Dan Trotter disappeared into the final room and slammed the door. Mickey heard the click as he turned the key in the lock.

Damn, Mickey thought.

Tibbs was throwing himself at the door to little effect. He might be fast but there was little weight to him. Mickey pulled him aside and shouldered the door out of its frame with an ease that took him by surprise and sent him stumbling.

'He's gone out the window,' Tibbs yelled, and a second later he had followed.

'What the hell? Come back here, you young fool.'

No way was Mickey going to follow. Dan Trotter had made his way along the narrow ledge beneath the dormer windows, old wood creaking beneath his feet. It would not have taken Mickey's weight. He had then leapt on to the flat roof of the next building and, as Mickey watched, Tibbs prepared to follow.

Mickey hardly dared to look as his sergeant gathered himself ready to make the jump, pulling his gangly limbs in and then pushing off, legs and arms splayed like a cat that suddenly realizes it has misjudged the distance. To Mickey's astonishment and profound relief, he landed and rolled, coming to his feet in a move that was almost graceful. Then he was off again, chasing Dan across that roof and on to the next.

'Get downstairs,' Mickey instructed the constable. 'He's got to come back down sooner or later. I want him caught.'

The constable thundered back down and Mickey heard the shouted instructions as men who knew the area better than he did moved to intercept the fugitive.

'Careful, Tibbs, careful,' Mickey said softly as his sergeant made yet another leap from one roof to the next in pursuit of a man who, from the look of things, had done this many times before. Dan Trotter was still ahead but Tibbs was gaining on him. Mickey was torn between wanting to watch, as though his bearing witness to the chase would keep Tibbs safe, and the need to go down and make his own pursuit at ground level. Reluctantly he headed back along the hallway and down the stairs and out of the back gate. The constables were keeping pace, looking up to check the position of Tibbs and his quarry and then running on. A little breathless, Mickey caught up the back marker.

'Can you guess where he's going?'

'Well, he's going to run out of road. He's going to have to come down in a minute. But I'm blessed if I know how.'

Mickey stepped back into the road, trying to keep Tibbs in sight, attempting to understand what Dan Trotter was playing at. As the constable had said, he was about to run out of options. Was there a fire escape on the side of that final building in the row? If so, then it was up to the constables ahead to block his way.

It seemed, however, that Tibbs was not prepared to wait that long or leave anything to chance. As Mickey watched, he was astonished to see his sergeant throw himself forwards and rugby-tackle his quarry. It wasn't the most elegant of moves, Mickey owned that, but it was damned effective. Tibbs and Dan dropped heavily on to the flat roof of the two-storey mill that was the final building in the row, and Mickey could hear Dan shouting and yelping as Tibbs held him tight. Mickey began to run again.

By the time he had reached the building and gained entry, hot on the heels of the first constable, run up yet more stairs and got out on to the roof, Dan Trotter was in custody.

Tibbs, dusty and sweating, was still trying to regain his breath, but he was grinning broadly, and Mickey could never recall his young sergeant looking as exultant.

'Right, young Tibbs,' Mickey said, slapping him on the back. 'We'll get this fellow into a cell and find you a clean shirt and then I think we'll bring our Mr Kimberlin in to answer some questions, shall we?'

Tibbs' grin got even broader.

# THIRTY-SIX

A brushed and tidied Sergeant Tibbs accompanied Mickey to collect Kimberlin and bring him, protesting, for interview at Scotland Yard. He left him waiting with a constable on a first-floor corridor while he had Dan Trotter brought up from his cell, and had the constable walk him by Kimberlin on the way to his interview. Mickey, trailing behind, watched as the two men met.

Dan, he noted, seemed genuinely surprised to see the older man there.

'Mr Kimberlin, what brings you here? I seem to have landed in a spot of bother. I hope the same can't be said for you.'

Kimberlin stared at him. 'I should not even be here,' he said. 'Some foolish accusation—'

'Oh,' Dan said, 'I shouldn't worry too much about it. You'll only be here about the fire. A poor show, by the way. What made you think those three boys could do the job? But I don't suppose much will come of it. I, on the other hand, seem to have committed a murder. Or maybe two. You know, Mr Kimberlin, I can hardly remember.'

Mickey signalled for the constable to continue on and Dan was led away. 'Mr Kimberlin,' Mickey said, 'I'll be with you shortly, though it might not be a bad idea for you to simply give the constable a statement.'

'He's insane,' Kimberlin growled.

Mickey nodded. 'Quite possibly, Mr Kimberlin, but we'll know more when we've had a chance to speak with the young man. Meanwhile, a statement from you perhaps? Save us all some time and trouble? I'm sure your motives stemmed from wanting to help a friend in trouble. I'm sure you yourself didn't stand to gain.'

Mickey left Kimberlin with that thought and went on to join Tibbs in the interview room. He was pretty certain Kimberlin would have gained something from his agreement to help Dan Trotter, just as Mickey was sure he had earned more from his employer than might be accounted for in wages. But proving those things was another matter. Proving his involvement in a fire that was set in order to defraud . . . well, that was a different thing altogether.

'I wish for legal counsel,' Kimberlin shouted after Mickey.

'All in good time,' Mickey said.

Tibbs was watching through the half-open door when Mickey arrived, studying the man they were about to interview regarding a double murder. He was sitting quietly, humming to himself, a constable standing behind him and one closer to the door.

'He doesn't look capable, does he?' Tibbs said softly.

'Killers often don't,' Mickey agreed.

Dan Trotter looked up as they came into the room. He smiled broadly. 'Good morning, gentlemen,' he said. 'How may I help you? Would you perhaps like some coffee? I can get Mrs Mead to make us a pot.'

# THIRTY-SEVEN

'And that was all we got from him,' Mickey told Henry when he called later to continue their interrupted conversation. 'Of course, he might just be acting, or he might really be barking mad. Either way, he'll be locked up, and that's the main concern.'

'You've got evidence he committed both murders?'

'We have the petrol can – found it hidden behind some junk in the attic – but we also have the weapon used to kill poor Betty Moran. A hefty poker from his father's study. He'd given it a quick wipe but made no attempt to do a proper clean-up. Just put it back where it came from, which I suppose might support his claim to insanity in some eyes. Or it might demonstrate his cleverness. Either way, there was still enough blood and brain and a couple of hairs that match Betty's for there to be no doubt this was what killed her. And there's only one lot of fingerprints, and those belong to Dan Trotter.'

'So, you'll get a conviction or a term in Broadmoor,' Henry said.

'There's a part of me that wants to see his neck stretched,' Mickey said, 'and another that wonders if he even understands what he did. I'm no judge of these things, and fortunately I have only to present my evidence in court, not decide the fate of men like Dan Trotter.'

'And what of the arsonists?'

'Well, no doubt the boys will serve a short term in clink. Kimberlin is insisting that his petrol can was stolen or maybe borrowed by Mr Trotter, but that he can't recall the last time he saw it anyway as he no longer owns a car. If he had contact with the boys and they identify him, that will make his life more interesting for a while, but as it's the word of three little toerags against an upstanding member of the community, the outcome is for the judge to guess, not for me to predict. And how is the lovely Malina?'

'Well, relieved to be home. Making her wedding dress. She and Cynthia shopped for fabric yesterday, and today the house seems to be filled with fine silk thread. Mickey, that stuff is like spiders' webs. It floats through the air and attaches to anyone and anything.'

'You sound happy,' Mickey said.

'I think I am,' Henry said. He sounded, Mickey thought, rather surprised by the idea.

# EPILOGUE

The letter from Dr Fielding arrived on Friday the sixteenth of October, the morning of the wedding. Henry read it with interest but then set it aside. His reply would have to wait.

*I did not think to be writing to you again regarding the Samuels affair, but it has taken a strange turn.*

*Dar Samuels confided in me that he would be leaving Hanson's employ at Michaelmas and that he would not be giving notice of that fact; and indeed, at Michaelmas the family left, sometime in the night so far as anyone can tell, and they've not been heard of since.*

*Hanson, as you can imagine, was in a fine fury but, as his son and daughter pointed out to him, the Samuels family had been paid off for the season and were not under any obligation to stay. I have to assume that they had it all well planned, and that well ahead of time.*

*Elizabeth tells me that there was no living with the man for days after.*

*The day after they left, Helen Church was delivered of her second child, another boy. She registered the birth and named him for her grandfather, Simeon, though she had not yet been churched or the child christened when the next part of my story occurred. Ten days after the birth, her mother came to call and found her daughter and both children gone. She left a letter for her parents which put yet another cat among the pigeons, and which Mrs Church threw on the fire before anyone else could see. It's my guess that she told her mother she was going to be with Ethan Samuels and that she had known all along where he might be.*

*You can imagine the uproar this has caused. Someone recalled seeing a flatbed lorry pulled up on the road outside the village, perhaps on the night she went, but as they were not even certain of the day, it might have nothing to do with the matter. Helen could have taken her children through the back gate and across the field to where the path meets the road and have been picked up there. Anyway, she is gone and no one knows where.*

*So you see, Henry, I did not have to buy the train ticket, after all.*

*If I hear more, then I will be sure to tell you.*

*I remain, etc*

*Fielding.*

Good for you, Helen, Henry thought. I hope you find happiness, wherever you fetch up.

The wedding was a simple affair, the guests people they both loved, the bride, to Henry's eyes, incredibly beautiful in the gown she had made and the veil she had borrowed that Cynthia had worn on her own wedding day. It was Nottingham lace, held in place by a circlet cleverly constructed of a pearl necklace of Cynthia's and flowers from the garden.

The reception was held at his sister's house. Kem and Tibbs had brought close family and others had made their own way. Untroubled, and as usual having catered as though she had to feed an entire regiment, Cynthia had welcomed them all.

Belle had been matron of honour and Melissa the bridesmaid.

It seemed somehow appropriate that Mickey and Tibbs took photographs with the cameras more usually used for recording crime scenes.

Miles away, and only a few hours before, another reunion had taken place in a steep valley, in a place Dar Samuels still could not even pronounce. When he had written it down, he'd had to spell the difficult words letter by letter.

Ethan had been summoned by a friend and told to wait beside the crossroads. 'What's going on?' he asked.

'You'll see. You'll soon see.'

A little after ten, a flatbed lorry rumbled around the bend in the road, its engine complaining after all the hills and miles.

Ethan recognized the driver at first, not a man he knew well but one who travelled regularly through the Welsh valleys, delivering supplies and taking produce to the markets. Beside him sat a young woman, and Ethan's mind could not at first process what it was he was seeing. A small child bounced beside her on the seat and pointed excitedly through the window.

'Helen?' No, his mind must be deceiving him.

In the back of the truck were four others, and now they were shouting out his name. His mother waved, his sister squealed with excitement, and his brother and father just grinned at one another. But it was Helen who held his attention.

Dar hopped out of the truck and helped her down. She moved painfully and slowly, and he was afraid suddenly that she was ill. Dar lifted the child down after her. He clung to Helen's skirts and stared, suddenly solemn and uncertain, at Ethan. He realized suddenly that she carried a baby in her arms.

'Helen? Oh my God, Helen.' His arms were around her and then he was drawing back, suddenly afraid he might crush the tiny child she held. 'They're both yours? My God, you're more beautiful than ever. I can't believe any of this.'

She put a hand on Sam's shoulder. 'This is Sam,' she said. 'Ethan, when you left, I was—'

'I know. I was told.'

'And this is Simeon,' she said, and he could hear the uncertainty in her voice. Would he turn her away because she'd had another man's child?

Of course he would not.

'Can I hold him?' Ethan asked. He saw Dar and his mother exchange a smile as he took the baby from Helen's arms. The baby yawned, opened his eyes and blinked at Ethan.

'He's tiny,' he said. 'Oh, Lord, woman, you should be resting.'

He put his free arm around Helen's shoulders and led the slow procession of wife, children, parents and siblings back into the village and home.